Trace and eliminate

'James Deely is dead. Somebody killed him. Anybody know who?' Acting Detective Chief Inspector David Stark asks the question somewhat sardonically of his detectives assembled at the briefing. An up and coming solicitor lies dead on a mortuary slab. The ensuing silence heralds the start of an arduous and protracted murder hunt, whilst a ruthless and savage killer remains at large. Within days, a second fatal assault occurs: a man is callously murdered in a car park late at night and Stark's investigation lays bare a sinister sequence of events – a roller coaster ride of hate and despair, fuelled by revenge.

The two victims are linked by a common past, which now returns to haunt the present; so are six of their college friends, two of them women. Old rivalries and new liaisons emerge as DCI Stark stages a most original eavesdrop on a solemn occasion, and the police net closes in on its unexpected quarry.

Trace and eliminate combines the virtues of an insider's knowledge with the dramatic power of a true storyteller.

Keith Wright's first novel, *One oblique one*, was shortlisted for the 1991 John Creasey Award of the Crime Writers' Association.

Also by Keith Wright

One oblique one (1991)

TRACE AND ELIMINATE

Keith Wright

Constable · London

First published in Great Britain 1992
by Constable & Company Ltd
3 The Lanchesters, 162 Fulham Palace Road
London W6 9ER
Copyright © 1992 by Keith Wright
The right of Keith Wright to be identified
as the author of this work
has been asserted by him in accordance
with the Copyright, Designs and Patents Act 1988
ISBN 0 09 471240 9
Set in Linotron 10pt Palatino
and printed in Great Britain by
Redwood Press, Melksham, Wiltshire

A CIP record for this book
is available from the British Library

For my sons, Christopher and Andrew,
from a proud father

'But bacon's not the only thing,
that's cured by hanging from a string.'

Hugh Kingsmill

James was smiling as he leaned from the car window to wave to his wife. Sarah stood in the porch, clutching their little girl's hand, and waved back. 'Bye James. See you later.'

He wound up the window and watched them troop back into the warmth of the house. Then he turned the ignition over, straining to hear the engine battling with the cold before it throbbed into life.

Sarah's goodbye, although distant, had alerted the hidden figure into a state of taut expectation, nerves tingling, mouth dry, stomach churning, hate as a companion. There was no going back now. As soon as the car was away from the house, it would be time to strike.

The route was a familiar one to James, one he took every weekday morning from home to office. Despite the bitter chill and depressingly overcast sky of that January morning, inside the car it was cosy now that he had adjusted the heating. He turned on the audio system and his tape of Pavarotti burst into life. Although it was eight o'clock the roads were still empty. He put his foot on the accelerator and let the music flood over him, his deep, slightly off-key voice endeavouring to match the great singer's. Life was going well. James considered himself one of the 'new breed' of solicitors; at Johnson & Brown he was definitely the blue-eyed boy, and at twenty-five the future was looking distinctly rosy.

He slowed down as a solitary cyclist pushed his bike across the road, and as he did so, he caught sight of his reflection in a darkened window: the sleek blue outline of the Volvo, and his handsome face smiling with a toothy grin at himself. He smoothed his slightly long, jet-black hair with his hand before moving off again.

1

His house must be worth a small fortune already, he was thinking, especially since he had had the garden landscaped. Yes, it was all going to look sumptuous ... Skeletal branches of trees etched themselves against the lightening sky as the car now passed through open country. His thoughts wandered as the music heightened his feeling of pleasure. And Katy ... Dear little Katy ... She was turning out to be a beauty just like her mother, even though she was only three.

He slowed down as he approached the deserted junction and glanced quickly to his right, the blinking of the indicator on the dashboard verifying in his subconscious his intention to turn left.

Without warning, his head slammed against the window of the car with the force of the blow to his neck. The large carving knife slid relatively easily through his carotid artery, severing his trachea and oesophagus, and chipping the glass of the window as it emerged on the other side. The killer held the force of the blow and twisted the knife savagely, then withdrew it in preparation for a second, but quickly saw that another would be unnecessary. James slumped in his seat and feebly raised a hand towards his throat. As he struggled to breathe, a rasping, gurgling noise emanated from him. His head began to jerk spasmodically. Blood spurted from his neck as the artery, fuelled by adrenalin, pumped out rhythmically. The spray of the first burst hit the roof. The second burst was slightly less as the killer opened the rear nearside door and fled, only a second before the car, still rolling, slewed into a telegraph pole. In the impact, James's head flopped like a rag doll's, spurts of blood spattering the upholstery. His harsh gasping became shallower, the jets of blood weaker. Pavarotti's final, tremulous diminuendo top C faded. The music stopped.

For several minutes the car remained undiscovered, the cassette player, having moved on to the next track, delivering a strident melody.

Then, from down the long country road, came a high-pitched, intermittent squeaking as a young newspaper-boy cycled towards the car, which was partly obstructing his path. Curious, he drew up alongside and looked through the driver's window.

The face of James Deely, grotesquely frozen in death, looked out at him: a vision of terror that would haunt him for ever. Instinctively he screamed, the futility of his cry lost in the empty road.

1

'It's easy to make a man confess the lies he tells
himself; it's far harder to make him confess the
truth.'

Geoffrey Household

Nottingham Police Station covered a large and diverse area:
streets of shops which eventually led into suburbia and on into
the council estates and blocks of flats. Because of the mixture,
anything and everything was dealt with by the police officers
who served the residents of Nottingham. Times were hard for the
British Police. The crime rate, as always, was soaring, the biggest
crime being the apathy of most of the general public regarding the
surreptitious degeneration of police powers by faceless poli-
ticians who did not have to live with the results. Everything
appeared set against them: constraints on how they dealt with
rapists and molesters; 'four-star' prisons; and pathetic sentences
by the courts. Most shrugged their shoulders and carried on as
best they could; others thought, 'Why bother? No bleeder else
does, so why should I?' Despite these adverse times, the humour
and steadfastness that had seen democracy and policing through
hard times remained intact . . . just!

Acting Detective Chief Inspector David Stark was currently
second in command at Nottingham Police Station CID. It was
only a temporary promotion; he was deputizing for Detective
Chief Inspector Rawson who was away on yet another course at
'the dream factory' – Bramshill Police Training College for
middle-rank and senior police officers. Stark had embraced his
temporary post with vigour: it was another feather in his cap and
he intended to take full advantage of the opportunity. He knew
he could do the job and now that the chance to prove it had

presented itself, it would not be wasted. His only regret was that his new role was little more than that of an administrator-cum-organizer, with little opportunity to deal with the criminals themselves.

Jack Reynolds, well known to local officers, had given him an excuse to get involved at ground level again. Jack, in contrast to the immaculately dressed Stark, was a slovenly, obnoxious character. At fifty-seven he had achieved little, other than to wreak havoc in the lives of innocent families whose only crime was to have a son who had attracted the perverted imagination of this thrice-convicted child molester.

Stark, with his wavy brown hair and hazel eyes, was one of those fortunate men who seem to grow more handsome as they mature. He was forty now, a family man, and, something of a rarity in the police force, not divorced, but happily married to Carol, although he wasn't averse to an occasional flirtation every now and then, and he certainly was popular with women. His own teenage children, Christopher and Laura, were close to his thoughts as he studied the greasy-haired, unshaven, smelly individual across the interview-room table. He empathized with Reynolds' victim, a victim in every sense of the word, a ten-year-old boy who had run out to play with the assurance that he would be home before dark. Stark imagined the knotted stomachs of the parents, glancing at the clock, the father driving around, searching, then – worse – finding his son a curled-up, naked ball. His wanting to help, his frustration that it was too late, his sheer anger. The grief of turning his son over, holding him in his arms and seeing that face. The face that had changed: no more innocence, no more trust, no more totality of giving. That face, that look.

'Where were you Dad?'

Jack Reynolds rubbed his ill-fitting sleeve across his nose and sneered across the dimly lit table at the two detectives, exposing his yellow teeth. Stark had chosen DC Carter to deal with the enquiry because of his wealth of experience. Charlie was close to retirement but was as keen as ever, particularly with the likes of Jack Reynolds. He, like Stark, had seen that smug-bastard look scores of times. It was early days yet.

Stark struggled with the temptation to lean over the table and hit Reynolds. He owed it to the boy to be professional and, yes, to

5

be Jack's friend, seemingly to condone and understand what he'd done, not because he did but because he was determined to get this bastard some heavy time locked away. It was too late for the boy, but there were other boys, boys who needed to be protected from the likes of Jack Reynolds. Bollocks to Jack Reynolds, bollocks to the naïve parole board who had been conned again. It was not going to happen to him; he was going to do the conning; he wasn't a small boy of ten, he was somebody interested in the rights of the victim. Let the other countless agencies sort out the offender. Stark's inner strength was intense: this man will admit his sordid crime, and he will do it as if he is talking about the weather.

The windowless room was filled with smoke. What with Charlie and his cigars and Jack on his roll-ups, Stark was somewhat reluctant to light his long-stemmed pipe. Charlie rested his arms on the table, close to the twin-tape machine that recorded every sound on two tapes simultaneously. Charlie brushed his hands through his greying hair and clasped them behind his neck. He leaned back and sighed, displaying his rotund figure. He grinned, tight-lipped. The interview had started twenty-five minutes ago. It was Charlie's turn to speak.

'Come off it, Jack, what do you think we are, eh? Bloody idiots?'

Jack smiled, his laugh developing into a coughing fit, the resultant saliva drops spraying the tabletop. His brow furrowed as he gave Charlie a sideways glance.

'Do you really want me to answer that?'

Stark had been scrutinizing Jack carefully; usually this type of offender was easier. Jack, however, had seen it all before, and unlike a lot of his ilk, he displayed no feelings, no emotion about his crimes – they were pure debauched lust, vile in the extreme. It would be hard to reach him. Stark smiled disarmingly before speaking.

'Jack, how many times have you been in this situation?'

'You should know, you've got me record haven't you?'

Stark decided to use a bit of mirror speech to see where that took him.

'Yes, we've got your record.'

'So if you can read, it'll tell you it's been getting on for three years since I've been arrested.'

6

Stark continued the tautology. 'Three years is a long time.'

'Too bloody right it is, and now you start accusing me of something like this again.'

'We're accusing you?'

'That's what it looks like to me. Are you denying it?'

'Are *you* denying it, Jack?'

'Of course I bleeding am! I'm innocent, how many more times?'

'Are yours the actions of an innocent man, then?'

Jack shifted his position on the seat, extinguished his cigarette and put both hands in his pockets.

'Don't come that, everybody's different, you know that.'

Stark decided to develop the rapport with 'funnel' questions – open-ended, leading to more precise ones.

'How do you think an innocent man reacts to such questioning then?'

'He tells you he hasn't done it, like I have, God knows how many times.'

'And how does he convince us he hasn't done it?'

Jack moved his hands again and folded them across his chest.

'Just stick to proper questions. I've told you I haven't done it and that's it!'

Stark continued, undeterred.

'That is a proper question, Jack. How does he convince us he hasn't done it? Come on, tell us.'

Stark raised his head slightly to give emphasis and invite a reply. Jack looked away from Stark's inquisitive expression and shook his head.

'Don't treat me like a five-year-old, for Christ's sake. He gives an alibi, tells you what the crack is, what he's been doing.'

'OK, Mister Innocent Man, tell us what you've been doing. Around about six o'clock last night will start us off.'

Jack's head lolled back and he stared at the ceiling before dropping forward and directing his speech to the tin ashtray on the table. He sighed. It's hard work for a man to portray himself as unaffected when his mind is screaming out with guilt. He shrugged his shoulders, continuing the increasingly difficult charade despite his inner turmoil.

'I went to the Chinky about half-past five, the one on Highbury Vale. I just bought a bag of chips; they cost sixty pence. I walked back home and scoffed them as I went. I got in and watched that

Aussie soap – *Neighbours*, is it? I stopped in, what's the harm in that?'

'There's no harm in that, Jack. Which way did you go to the Chinky?'

'Over the train lines – you're not going to do me for that surely?' Jack inwardly cursed himself; he had said too much already!

Stark was fully aware that a police interviewer has always got a problem: he must not do anything that is oppressive to the prisoner, or that could be deemed to be so by a judge. Stark considered that the Law seemed to imply that when a man is guilty, you simply ask him if he's done it, whereupon he says, 'Yes, you're too good for me copper, I admit it!' We all know it doesn't work like that. Can anyone tell me how on God's earth any criminal is going to admit to something that is going to get him incarcerated unless he feels under some obligation or pressure to do so? With this in mind, Stark decided it was time for more direct questions.

'Doesn't that take you on to the kiddies' playground?'

'Here we go. That's it, I'm not answering any more questions!'

'It's a simple question, Jack. Does it or does it not take you on to the kiddies' playground?'

Jack toyed with his baccy tin.

'You know damn well it does. I ain't touched no kids; I've got out of that habit. You make a couple of mistakes and you're branded for life. I've changed, I've learnt my lesson. I've done my time. You lot make me sick!'

Stark's voice was calm, but resolute.

'Everybody makes mistakes, Jack, and yours at the moment is mistaking the CID for a parole board! We're not going away, Jack. The truth will not go away. And the sooner you realize that, the sooner that big weight round your neck will go, because the truth is eating away inside you, mate, like a cancer, and they ain't yet discovered a cure!'

Not everyone can be a traffic patrolman. The candidate needs to have an aptitude for it. He must be an expert driver, have a comprehensive knowledge of traffic law – which can be the most complex there is – and be able to keep his head when everybody else is losing theirs, sometimes literally. A fatal road traffic accident is the worst a traffic officer will deal with, and it is some time before he or she will be entrusted to do so. However, once qualified, they cope with the most horrific and bloody scenarios, which must be sorted out and photographed, with speed and skid-mark equations made. They have to trace witnesses, take statements from distraught relatives, attend the hospital and submit coroner and prosecution files that are full and concise. Traffic police see all manner of grotesque scenes throughout their careers and they have to find a way to live with them. It doesn't help when you are giving the kiss of life to a small boy to have the drunken driver who has killed him sit on a nearby wall singing away to himself, without a care in the world!

Police Constable Paul Wood was a traffic man, his eyes alert, his concentration absolute as he raced through the peak-hour traffic of Nottingham city centre, the whooping of the siren more often a hindrance than a help. As soon as drivers heard the siren, instead of gradually pulling to the nearside of the road the best they could, they would instantly apply their brakes, creating an obstruction to be negotiated. 'Get out of the fucking way, you silly old fart!' Paul cursed as the umpteenth well-intentioned driver stopped in the middle of the road. Paul raced through the city streets, at times in excess of sixty miles an hour, his eyes darting at hazards, prioritizing the more dangerous, deciding the level of risk and acting accordingly: life and death decisions made in split seconds.

It was with relief that he hit the country roads leading towards Papplewick and the scene of the reported accident. As he approached the junction he saw an elderly gentleman waving both arms in the air to attract his attention, like someone waving down a 747 at Heathrow Airport. He was relieved to see that an ambulance was already there, but the relative inactivity of the ambulance men had daunting implications. Paul quickly assimilated the situation and parked his car in the most suitable spot to warn oncoming vehicles. He had to make do with a 'Police Accident' sign on the other side. It's the first job of a traffic patrol officer to ensure that there will be no further danger to the public or himself.

Despite the seriousness of the situation, as often happens

bizarre or surreal images appeared in Paul's mind. Fleetingly he thought of the old joke:

'How can the police be such good drivers, when I'm forever seeing signs saying "Police Accident"?'

Paul walked quickly over to the two middle-aged ambulance drivers.

'Morning.'

'Morning.' In unison. The grey-haired paramedic hinted at the scene to behold. 'Not a lot for us on this one.'

Paul walked up to the blue Volvo and looked through the window of the driver's door. The sight briefly took him aback. He noticed the seat-belt holding the body in place as he turned off the engine. The man was dead. He checked that there was no one else in the car and, as the rear nearside door was open, made a search of the surrounding area to make sure there were no casualties who had been thrown clear. He then opened the front passenger door to have another look at the body. The vast amount of blood in the car was obvious, but there were no easily recognizable injuries to his face or body. Paul saw the gaping wound in the man's neck. He was puzzled. The old man tapped Paul on the shoulder.

'Do you need me now or can I go home, officer?'

'Did you see the accident?'

'No, but I think our paper-boy might have. He was the one as told us like. He ran and knocked on our door.'

Paul took his details and told him he would be up to see him later. He took brief notes about the paper-boy's shop. Two other cars had stopped out of either curiosity or public-spiritedness, but none of the occupants had witnessed anything. There had simply been no one about. The traffic officer returned to the Volvo and leaned inside the car to see what the dead man could possibly have snagged his neck on.

There is a problem with categorizing telephone calls from members of the public. A road traffic accident is reported and despatched as such by the Control Room, and even though it's staring the officer in the face that it isn't one, it can take a hell of a lot of proving once the initial suggestion has been made.

Paul was starting to get the feeling that this was no ordinary RTA. He looked at the front of the vehicle. The damage caused was so slight that it would never be a 'fatal'. Paul scratched the back of his head. He was beginning to suspect that this was no ordinary call. This looked like murder!

'Bloody hell. Why me?' he muttered to himself.

He returned to the patrol car and displaced the black radio phone. Time to call for the cavalry. The few sentences he was about to utter over the radio would send shock waves throughout the force, to almost every department which somewhere along the way would be involved.

Stark equated the interviewer's role as a more advanced version of the salesman's, but with more specialized knowledge. The bland police interview room, sparsely furnished, with a tape machine screwed to the table was, however, somewhat different from the glamorous showrooms of the car salesman. When people go to their local garage to buy a car, they speak to one of the sales people – a pleasant man trying to sell them something in order to do his job. Have you ever bought something you didn't set out to buy, or didn't really want? Stark was selling something to Jack Reynolds – approximately seven years in prison! The interview with Jack had been going well and, just as the car salesman does, Stark recognized Jack's first 'buy sign'.

'I'm not going to get bail, so why should I admit to something I haven't done?'

Jack wanted bail. That he obviously knew he'd committed the offence, and was aware that the detectives knew he had done it, was irrelevant: the game was for him to admit the truth. They all knew that. Jack felt an overwhelming urge to confess, even though he knew it wasn't in his best interests to do so, but he wanted something in exchange. His urges were so strong that he couldn't think long-term, he wanted out now. He blocked out the stupidity of an admission, exploring the possibility of bail. Stark knew that this kind of remark had to be dealt with carefully. Sure he wanted an admission, but he wanted one that would stick in court.

'Jack, we can't bargain over whether you get bail or not, you know that, mate. The custody officer makes that decision when we furnish him with the full details and overall picture. It's not beyond the realms of possibility that you could get bail – stranger things have happened! I can only tell you that if and when you are

11

charged, I shall be applying to the court for you to be remanded in custody until the hearing.'

Stark's voice grew stronger for emphasis and he wagged a finger to give weight to his comment.

'But don't forget, Jack, that it is the court that makes the decision, not us!'

Trap any animal in a corner and it will search for the tiniest bolt-hole, even if it seems impossible.

Jack had been staring at the table for some minutes.

Stark spoke, now wanting to change the subject: it was time to weigh up the pros and cons for Jack.

'Jack, I've already told you the score on bail, but let me say this to you.' Stark's voice was louder and more dramatic for the first part of the speech, softening at the end: 'Nobody is saying you've gone out into the streets of Bulwell searching for a young boy to screw and then, when you've finished with him, attack him, even worse, kill him. That hasn't happened, you know that, Jack. As it's turned out, you didn't hurt the boy at all. Which is going to stand you in good stead. What I'm saying is that you – like me, like anybody – have needs. My needs involve women; yours, Jack, be they good or bad, happen to involve young men. The lad – I don't know, he might just have happened to show an interest in you, and you succumbed. We all do that, mate, and when it's done we sometimes feel guilty, but it's done, and that simply cannot change. So you've made a mistake – big deal, nobody's going to hang you for it! I'm not here to judge you Jack. You like young lads, I like women, so what? Now, you've no animosity towards that young lad, I know that; yours was an act of love, not of hate. But if you don't accept your part in it mate, that kid has got to go to court and give evidence. What's the judge going to make of that? Let the kid forget it, Jack, he's young enough to. Is the court going to punish you more heavily, if you are found guilty, because you don't give a shit about the feelings of a young kid? Eh, come on, think about it, what do you reckon? I know what I think! You don't want that to happen, Jack, I know you don't.'

There was a prolonged silence. Jack's fists were clenched, his knuckles straining the skin white. He raised his voice.

'No!' He shook his head. 'No!' He dropped his head back, eyes closed tight. Stark encouraged him.

'You don't want that kid in the box, Jack. I respect that, mate. You don't want him in that box, do you?'

Jack was once more staring at the table. He gave a heavy sigh and shook his head. The silence was unbearable, the onus to speak on Jack.

'No I don't, what do you think I am? These things just happen, you know.'

There was a sob in his voice, tears were welling up. Stark reached over and grasped Jack's arm.

'I know they do, Jack. Eh, come on, we're still all here, the room hasn't caved in, life goes on, mate.'

'What fucking life? You don't know what it's like, do you? I've got no fucking life.'

'Whereabouts did you do it, Jack?' Stark was careful not to ask too direct a question, which might prompt a sudden denial and change of tack.

Jack sighed, his eyes shut again. It was over; he'd done his best, but he was beaten.

'On the train lines. I thought he wanted to at first. His skin was so soft . . . He didn't struggle when I first kissed him, and then I had to carry on. Why did he have to struggle?'

Jack went through the whole terrible, sordid affair. Once he had started Stark and Charlie needed to say little. Charlie had shown his experience; when things were going well with your partner speaking, keep your mouth shut! It was towards the end of the interview that Stark saw the enquiry light flash on the far wall. Initially he ignored it, but then he saw it repeated twice more. Stark stood up and spoke.

'The time is now 9.26 a.m. and I am leaving the interview room.' Once outside he saw the suave young face of Ashley Stevens.

'I'm sorry to disturb you sir, but there's been a possible murder, at Papplewick.'

'Bloody hell, I'm in the middle of a bleeding interview! All right Ash, we've squared him up any way. Charlie will have to finish it off.'

'Has he coughed it then, sir?'

'Course he has, and I hope the little piss-ant rots in jail through-out fucking eternity!'

13

Stark returned to the interview and quoted the time for the benefit of the tapes.

'Charlie, you're going to have to finish it off, mate, there's a suspicious death been reported.'

'Where at?'

'Papplewick. I'll see you about it later on.'

Jack didn't want to speak but felt it was only fair.

'Excuse me.'

'Yes.' Stark diverted his gaze to the pathetic specimen.

'I think it's only right to tell you. I've got gonorrhoea.'

'You what?'

'I've got gonorrhoea. Sorry.' Jack added a nervous laugh to his revelation.

Stark had heard him; he wished he hadn't. He was incensed. The charade of the professional interviewer now over, he couldn't stop his anger. He screamed in temper, despite the tapes: the admissions were safe.

'Sorry! Sorry! You evil little shit! I hope it fucking kills you!'

Stark's eyes were wide, his nostrils flared; he knew he had better get out of that room quickly or they'd be carrying Jack Reynolds out, after he had finished with him!

He stormed out and stopped in the passageway of the cell block. He leaned against the wall and closed his eyes. Tight-lipped, he shook his head.

'You bastard!' he whispered to himself.

'Are you okay, sir?' It was the well-dressed Ashley, looking concerned.

'Yeah, I'm fine.' Stark put his hands to his face and rubbed his eyes with his fingertips. As he brought his hands down, his face looked tired and drawn. 'Come on, let's go and have a look at this murder or whatever it is. Does Superintendent Wagstaff know about it?'

'Yes, he's at headquarters. He said he'd see you there.'

Stark gave a poignant smile.

'That's big of him. You know, Ash, I'm in danger of being seriously pissed off today!'

14

2

'It's such a secret place – the land of
tears.'

Antoine de Saint-Exupéry

Stark tapped his fingers irritably on the steering-wheel of his
white Vauxhall Calibra. The queue of traffic spanned a good 200
yards in front of him as the road curved to the left, out of sight.
Ashley sat in the front passenger seat, his black hair quiffed back,
his solid gold watch and bracelet an obvious indication of the
private income he was party to.

Ashley's father had started out as a miner, but had taken early
redundancy and gambled with an investment. He had begun
with a modest video shop, hoping that it would give him an
interest and sufficient money to live on. Within five years he had
twenty similar shops in the Midlands and was virtually a million-
aire. His only son, however, refused to join his business and
remained a detective, albeit a financially secure one. It was an odd
quirk that at twenty-eight, Ashley had a better house and car than
the Detective Chief Superintendent.

Ash pulled the seat-belt away from his expensive Italian suit
and twisted in the seat as he strained to look through the rear
window. He could see the red CID Ford several places back. He
smiled at the ruddy face, seemingly hewn out of stone, of Detective Sergeant John 'Nobby' Clarke, who was leaning out of the
open driver's door window. Nobby indicated his intention by
agitatedly pointing forwards in thrusting motions out of the car
window. He looked annoyed, and was shouting something
incomprehensible.

Ashley, however, got the message.

'I think Nobby wants us to make progress sir,' he commented
dryly.

Stark turned round and saw Nobby gesticulating. He wound

15

down the window and gave him the thumbs up. Stark's foot became heavy on the accelerator, the rev counter straying into the red. He pulled out on to the wrong side of the road and turned his lights on, then pressed his horn and accelerated. A glimpse in the mirror saw Nobby follow suit. The sudden increase in speed jolted Ashley and he clung to the dashboard. A few seconds later several cars appeared, heading straight for them, but they moved over just in time and motioned their discontent with various movements of the fingers.

'Piss off!' Stark reciprocated, making similar gestures.

After a hair-raising drive the two cars arrived at the scene of the reported 'accident'. By this time there were three traffic patrol vehicles present. The young patrolman had done everything: Scenes of Crime officers had just attended, their plain white vans evident, and a uniformed inspector was strutting around, barking orders to his underlings. Stark hated this initial stage, everyone running round like headless chickens! He knew the importance of haste, since any suspects could still be in the vicinity, but he was not prepared to sacrifice evidence by poking around too early, before Scenes of Crime had finished. Stark approached the uniformed inspector.

'Morning, Bob. What are we looking at, then?'

The 'ten years of service' inspector was flushed in the face, scarcely hiding the relief he felt on seeing the Acting Detective Chief Inspector. He used his long black stick with its glistening silver top to point at the car.

'It looks a bit suspicious to say the least, Dave. Obviously you'll see for yourself, but if I know anything about anything, the bloke's been stabbed through the neck.'

Stark sighed. 'Wonderful. What've you done so far?'

The inspector swallowed. 'Well, we've preserved the scene. As you can see Scenes of Crime are here, and now you are. I've started a couple of my lads doing some house-to-house up the road. That's about it really.'

Stark was blunt. 'So basically you've waited until we got here.'

Bob smiled nervously. 'Well, yes, I mean, what else is there? There are no witnesses at all and hence no descriptions of poss- ible offenders.'

Nobby had been party to the conversation, hands in pockets, head bowed. He had little time for the new-style 'college inspectors'. Nobby was in his mid-thirties, an ex-paratrooper used to dealing with hardened men; he couldn't stand the 'hairy-fairy' way the inspector conducted his business. Nobby was a belligerent detective. He didn't understand modern management techniques, but he had a habit of getting things done. He spoke to Stark.

'Do you want me to do the biz then, sir?'

Stark replied. 'Please, Nobby. You've heard the set-up, haven't you?'

Nobby turned smartly and returned to the red Ford Escort. He spoke assertively into his radio, his voice deep and gruff.

'Juliet Quebec two nine to NH.'

The reply from Nottingham Headquarters Control Room was swift; a female voice: 'Juliet Quebec two nine, go ahead NH over.'

'Yes. We are at the scene of a suspicious one oblique one, Juliet Quebec zero two is with me. Still no update on any descriptions, no witnesses are evident as yet. Compliments of ADCI Stark, request Mounted Section, Dog Patrol, and gain authority for police helicopter to search surrounding fields and woodland. Set up a snatchplan immediately, over.'

Nobby knew his snatchplan request meant that all surrounding major road junctions would be covered by uniform and traffic mobiles within minutes, the lack of description or witnesses heralding the use of 'coppers' intuition' by those involved in the operation.

'Ten four, NH out.' The young lady had a lot to organize.

Stark peered through the open driver's door at the inanimate, terror-stricken face. His drollery was never far away.

'Well I think we can safely say he's dead!'

Despite his glib comment, he was disturbed by the irony of the dead man's wrist-watch, the second hand still ticking, fruitlessly marking time for its owner. Logical but somehow unexpected. Sometimes these small quirks of death could be the most alarming.

Stark walked around the Volvo, dismissing the oddity to the back of his mind, careful not to collide with the Scenes of Crime officers putting on their disposable white overalls. He looked through the window, focusing on the severe neck wound, glancing at the minimal damage to the front of the car. His mind was racing and he struggled to concentrate. It was a mistake to try to

17

think every thought in a second; he applied his concentration to the matter in hand. The uniformed inspector hovered behind him. Stark had an excellent detective's mind, almost like a computer at times, but he still hung on to his grass roots upbringing, continuing the myth. He liked people around him to warm to him, to feel not threatened but disarmed. It gave him a distinct advantage. It was this trait in his character that forced him to make the distinct observation:

'It's a suspicious death all right; somebody's bleeding throated him!'

Within half an hour, the circus was in full swing. All heads arched backwards as the police helicopter roared deafeningly overhead and away into the surrounding countryside, momentarily killing all conversation.

Detective Superintendent Wagstaff had arrived, the archetypal British major with neat handlebar moustache and dated suits. He had been known to be a kindly man but occasionally he would turn, and if anyone had let him down, by the following Monday they would be parading the local high street with a 'big hat on': the great threat held over all CID officers who dared to make a mistake more than once, or got caught out doing something 'naughty', as Wagstaff put it.

Stark had apprised him fully. The dog man had tried a couple of tracks but was complaining that it was 'bloody impossible!' with the amount of police who had been milling around the scene. Three mounted officers had been sent out into the fields to follow up any potential sightings from the helicopter.

Scenes of Crime had taken their photographs, and the dark-suited undertakers had 'bagged the stiff' with a deftness born of experience. This allowed the forensic experts full access: blood samples were swabbed, fingerprints taken from inside and outside the car, fibres and human hair removed from the upholstery with strips of Cellophane, and soil and debris removed from the floor. Every item was meticulously logged: time taken, where from, by whom, description of item, exhibit number allocated, and the packaging recorded and labelled. Eventually the Exhibits officer was allowed to search the vehicle, take out all items and similarly record them. The car could be taken apart later at the Forensic bay. The Exhibits officer recorded the following items:

One red and blue woollen blanket – taken from rear floor of car.
Seven miscellaneous cassette tapes – taken from centre console of car.
One opened bag of Fox's glacier mints – taken from driver's door pocket.
One Volvo owner's manual – taken from glove compartment.
Eleven 'Johnson & Brown' visiting cards entitled 'James Deely' – taken from glove compartment.
Two 'Bic' Biro pens – taken from glove compartment.
One windscreen scraper – taken from glove compartment.
One de-icer spray – taken from glove compartment.
Two photographs, one of woman, holding small girl; one of red-brick house, ranch-style, with SOLITUDE written on back – taken from glove compartment.
One ornate teardrop clasp earring – taken from underneath front passenger seat.
One car jack and tool bag – taken from boot of car.

Other CID officers – Stark's officers – had arrived at the scene. Detective Policewoman Stephanie Dawson; 'moaning' Jim McIntyre, his pock-marked face as miserable as sin; ginger-haired Steve Aston in an elasticated cotton bomber jacket that creased his ill-fitting brown suit; and the new 'Aide to CID', Grant Donaldson, one of a growing number of 'ethnic officers'. He was of West Indian origin, a rather ungainly young man, smartly dressed in a navy-blue Cromby overcoat.

Stark was aware that he had to act fast and try to make best use of those present. He sent Ashley and Steph to trace the newspaper-boy. Nobby was to return and start setting up the Incident Room. The others would be better employed going back with him for now. Stark did not want to start a disjointed enquiry, with everyone racing off at tangents. The paper-boy was the most important. All other enquiries would be prioritized and an 'action' – a logged record of each enquiry – written out with the result on a pro-forma. The detectives turned towards their respective vehicles; as they did, the radio in Nobby's car resounded.

'Juliet Quebec zero two, from NH. Quebec zero two, over.' There was a sense of urgency in the female Control Room operator's voice. Nobby turned towards Stark, who was in heavy discussion with Wagstaff. 'Sir! They're shouting you on the VHF.' Stark walked quickly over and picked up the black receiver through the open window, its curled wire stretched taut as he leaned against the roof of the car.

'Quebec zero two, go ahead.'

'Sir, the helicopter has a sighting: a white male, approximately twenty years, walking close to a copse, three miles south-west of your location.'

Stark quickly despatched the Mounted Section as the distant whirring of the helicopter carried hope of an early conclusion.

As soon as he heard the message, the mounted officer, clad in black riding gear, cracked his crop against the muscular posterior of Garth, the thumping of his heart increasing with the accelerating hoofbeats. Terence Sheridan had won many prizes for show-jumping and was the most experienced horseman in the Nottinghamshire Constabulary stables. The motion of his body was graceful, at one with the galloping horse as he jumped the field boundary walls and moved with great speed, negotiating obstacles with great ease. Before long Terry could see the woodland ahead. He slowed Garth to a trot as he approached the glade. He could see the figure of a man within the shade of the trees. He began to wonder if he should wait for backup. An officer on a horse is obviously less vulnerable to a knife attack, as long as he keeps his distance. His decision was cut short as Mary Jameson arrived on her horse. Terry signalled the location of the man, who appeared to be lying flat. He whispered to his colleague.

'I think he's seen us.'

The two walked their horses up to the edge of the wood. Steam billowed from the beasts' nostrils, matched to a lesser extent by their riders. A male voice shouted out the question from the trees. 'What d'you want?'

Terry replied. '*Police!* We want a word with you, mate. Come out here!'

The repeater radio crackled confirmation that the copse had been sealed off from the far roadside by traffic officers, who had drawn their truncheons and fanned out. Whoever was in there wasn't escaping. A young man of around twenty, with long hair, appeared. Despite the cold weather he wore only his shirt. He held a pair of faded denim jeans in his hand.

'Leave it out, mate! I've got a woman in here. What's the crack?'

Terry shouted beyond the youth, relief at the man's claim mixing with the stress to produce a slight tremble in his voice.

'Come out then, love.'

A woman of about thirty-five appeared. Bare feet slightly grey with loose soil, she negotiated the bracken and fallen twigs carefully, clutching a pile of clothes in front of her naked breasts. A short white skirt, still unzipped, hung loosely on her hips. Two lovers who had been in the wrong place at the wrong time. Terry stated the obvious. 'You must be bloody freezing, you soft boggers.'

Mary Jameson's eyes widened as the youth brazenly put his jeans back on. As the denim reached his nether regions, his semi-erect penis flopped into display before he tucked it away. She was not unimpressed and moved in her saddle as the youth cheekily winked at her.

Terry reported back to Stark. He finished off the radio message rhetorically: '. . . it's more a case of shafting in the copse than shafting the corpse!'

A smile tickled Stark's face, and he retorted, 'Just make sure you take down anything they say!'

Several cries of 'knickers' came over the air waves.

Stark's grin dissipated into a frown at the thought of visiting the dead man's wife.

The owners of the newspaper shop on the corner of Victoria Street in Hucknall had widened their horizons in recent times. In an attempt to stave off competition from the new, multibranch giants, they had started selling a variety of foodstuffs to supplement their moribund trade, attempting to hold on to the 'corner-shop' image of personal, friendly service. There was an array of handwritten ads displayed in the window, all seeking responses to various requests, from 'Part-time gardener seeks employment' to 'Second-hand pram for sale – bedding not included'.

Close to the shop doorway, at the corner of the building, an elderly man sat cross-legged on the wooden slatted bench. He wore a cloth cap, a grey decaying sports jacket and a red piece of cloth tied loosely around his neck in the style of a cravat. His left hand rested on the gnarled handle of a walking-stick, which he affectionately referred to as his 'bike'. At eighty-two years of age,

George had lived a hard life; his dingy skin and calloused hands bore witness to thirty-three years down the pit. He passed many an hour sitting on 'his' bench and over the years had attracted attention from schoolchildren who passed by. Children and the very old share an affinity in their thinking, an honesty of expression born of innocence or the acceptance of forthcoming demise. No self-image to portray, only forthright observation of life.

George had quickly sensed young Jason's terror as he had run into the shop, recklessly abandoning his beloved cycle in the gutter. He had been alarmed by the helpless expression of the paper-boy's face. It was obviously no trivial matter, but much as he wanted to enquire, his instincts told him to bide his time.

As the white Ford Escort pulled up in front of him, George pretended to toy with a piece of rubbish on the pavement with his stick. His peripheral vision took in the shapely, stockinged leg of Stephanie Dawson as it preceded the statuesque blonde out of the car. Her beige raincoat, tied tightly at the middle, accentuated her slim waist. Stephanie caught sight of the elderly gent whilst Ashley increased his step to catch up with her. She remembered the man from her days on the beat, and smiled warmly in recognition. George tapped the peak of his cap and nodded in reply. It was serious. They were detectives. His trembling hand fished in his jacket pocket for nicotine relief from the nub end he had saved for later. He lit it and struggled to his feet, pivoting on his stick, successful at the second attempt. His bow-legs shuffled into reluctant movement, his back slightly more hunched than usual, and he retched into a coughing bout as he struggled towards the solitude of his nearby flat. He realized that whatever had happened was too great for a curious old man to interfere with. He could only hope Jason would tell him in his own good time.

Steph could hear the sound of crying as the chiming of the shop bell faded and the door slowly closed behind the two detectives. The shop was small and drab and had a smell of stale tobacco about it. The crying was coming from beyond the counter. The doorway to the adjoining living-room was filled by the portly newsagent, a balding middle-aged man with black-rimmed glasses. He wore a dark-red, round-necked pullover that highlighted small flecks of dandruff on his shoulders. He spoke with a slight Cornish twang.

'Morning.'

Steph returned the greeting.

'Good morning. We're from the local CID. I understand you have a young paper-boy who works here who may have seen an incident earlier – '

The newsagent interrupted her.

'He's in the back. You'd better come through.'

The three walked into the undersized living-room. There were two large, somewhat bedraggled settees, cardboard boxes spilled over with various brands of cigarettes, cluttering the dusty old carpet. A small boy with ginger hair and freckles and wearing school uniform was hunched at the far end of one of the settees. His head was buried in the crook of his elbow, which rested on the arm of the furniture. He had cried enough; now he was aware of strangers present in the room and embarrassment encroached upon his terror. He glanced briefly at the newcomers. Steph sat down next to him. She put her hand on his knee and the smell of her perfume and the warmth of her gesture comforted him. He struggled to catch his breath; he gulped and took longer, more deliberate inhalations. Stephanie was sympathetic as she patted his leg.

'Eh, come on, it's all right, there's nothing to be scared of, darling. Try and calm down, there's a good lad.'

The boy gulped again. He took his head away from his arm and stared ahead vacantly; he did not acknowledge the others. Steph continued.

'It's Jason, isn't it?'

The boy continued to stare, his eyes red, his bottom lip trembling uncontrollably.

'Listen Jason, we're detectives. There's nothing to worry about at all, we're going to help. Where's your mum and dad?'

Jason whimpered. 'They're both at work, don't tell me mam about it, will you?'

Stephanie would do the talking. The two men looked on anxiously.

'Why don't you want us to tell your mum?'

'She'll kill me.'

'No she won't – don't be daft. You've not done anything wrong, my love. You've done everything right. We've come to thank you for doing so well.'

23

'She won't think that, you don't know her.'

'Jason.'

'What?'

The shop doorbell rang and the newsagent rose in response, somewhat pleased that the charged atmosphere was broken by the arrival of a customer. Ashley asked the man to close the living-room door, afraid that more distractions would impair the boy's concentration. This the man did. Stephanie continued.

'Are you feeling a bit better now, my love?'

'A bit, yeah.' Jason wiped his hand across his nose, transferring the mucus to his hand and on to the settee arm.

'Is your mum at work?'

'Yes, but don't tell her, please,' he whimpered, his voice trembling.

'Whereabouts does she work, Jason?'

The boy reluctantly told Steph that she worked at the local hosiery factory. Ashley did not need any prompting. He left the room and went in search of her. Steph continued talking to the boy, aware that he might have information needing an urgent response. Somewhere there was a murderer walking loose, and Jason might hold the key to his whereabouts. Eventually Steph broached the subject.

'Did you see anybody near the car, Jason?'

'No, I didn't. Is the man all right? I didn't know what to do, I've never seen a car crash before.'

'Did you see the car go into the telegraph pole, then?'

'No, it was already there when I got there. He's dead, isn't he?'

Steph lied. 'I don't know yet. They've taken him away to hospital. It doesn't look too good, though. Did you see anybody at all?'

'Don't lie! I've seen him, he's dead.' He sobbed through the rest of the reply. 'I didn't see anything, honest.'

Stephanie talked Jason through the entire scenario. She had to force him to relive every part of the trauma, every sense he used, every sight, sound, smell. Everything he did, everything he touched. It was apparent that the boy had seen little up to the discovery of the body, and afterwards he had been oblivious of everything: he had been far too upset. His only worthwhile recollection was that of a car starting up in the direction of Selby's Farm a couple of minutes prior to his discovery. Steph was just in the process of complimenting him on how brave he'd been when the living-room door burst open. It was Jason's mother. A little woman, heavily made up and with dyed blonde hair, she looked what she was – a hag. She marched up to her child and tugged at his arm, viciously dragging him to his feet, ignoring Steph completely.

'Come on, get up, you little bastard! How many times have I told you? You don't talk to these. Wait till I get you home, you little twat!'

Steph stood up quickly. 'There's no need for that! The lad's done nothing wrong. He's upset.'

The woman directed her venom at Steph. 'There's no wonder he's fucking upset, with you interrogating him, is there? He'll get over it. Dragging me out of work. This is costing me money you know!' She glared at her offspring. 'Well, it's coming out of your pocket money, you know that, don't you?'

Jason began to cry again as his mother forcibly ushered him out. The detectives looked on helplessly. Pure ignorance has a habit of stunning you into speechlessness. Steph wanted to follow the woman, to take the child away from her. She wished she had said something, but what do you say to such people? Ashley stared at Steph.

'I tried to calm her down in the car, but she wasn't having any.'

Steph shook her head. 'What a cow. What chance has that poor little sod got? Come on, let's get out of here.'

The detectives bade their farewells to the newsagent, who was obviously embarrassed for them. Little was said in the car back to the police station. Throughout the morning comments Steph should have made to the hag flooded through her mind. It was too late now.

Stark had felt it appropriate to collect Detective Constable Steve Aston from the station and take him to James Deely's house to break the news to what family Deely had had. The identity of the dead man had been traced through the Police National Computer printout of the owner of the car, the business cards in the glove compartment and the driving licence and credit cards in the dead man's wallet, retrieved at the mortuary. A surreptitious telephone call to Johnson & Brown Solicitors had revealed that James

Deely had not yet arrived for work, and was late for an appointment. Every check had been undertaken to ensure that the dead man was James Deely. On extremely rare occasions it has been known for grieving widows to be most surprised, to say the least, to see their 'dead' husbands return home from work after benevolently lending their car to a friend, who, unbeknownst to them, had wrapped it round a lamppost.

Steve Aston was a junior CID officer with only a year's experience as a detective. He was not the stereotypical DC, but a seemingly timid man, and a vegetarian. He wore bland suits and ties and had a sickly look about him that contrasted with his fringed ginger hair. Nevertheless, he was, whether by luck or judgement, a successful 'thief-taker': even with the most hardened of criminals, his polite nature would disarm them and give him the edge. Now he stood at the door of Deely's home, next to the solid, taller figure of David Stark. 'Solitude' – a bizarre name for a house.

The door was answered by a little girl with auburn hair, who peered at them suspiciously as she swung on the door handle.

'My mum says if you're selling something you can get lost.'

Deely's wife, Sarah, dressed in a navy-blue frock, appeared at the door and attempted to rescue the situation.

'I'm sorry about that. What can I do for you?' She smiled warmly.

Stark produced his warrant card. 'We're from the CID, love. Can we come in and have a word with you please?'

'Yes, of course. Come in. Don't let my husband know, though. He's a solicitor. Entertaining the police – there never were such times.'

Stark glanced at Steve as Sarah shepherded them into the elegant living-room. The room had class: the furniture looked expensive, and everywhere was spotlessly clean. Stark sat in an armchair, not wanting to sit next to Steve on the settee and appear too obtrusive. Sarah sat in a chair close to Stark, her slim figure leaning slightly forward as she brushed her luxuriant auburn hair back from her face.

'It's not very often we have the police here. I hope there's nothing wrong. I bet everybody says that; people are always looking for the black side. Well I suppose you know that more than anybody. Would you like a cup of tea?'

26

Stark was the spokesman. 'Perhaps in a minute . . .'

The little girl ran at Stark, clutching a toy train. She landed full force into his stomach, forcing him to expel air rapidly. Sarah interjected.

'Katy, now stop that. Go into the playroom, there's a good girl.'

'Oh mummy!'

'Go on, do as you're told. We want to talk. We can't do that with you whizzing around the place. Off you go.'

Katy left reluctantiy. Sarah closed the lounge door behind her. She sensed something was wrong; her heart started thumping, her mind was befuddled with stress. She fought off the paranoia and attempted to remain calm.

'Do you know, she's like that all day, she never stops. She's forever playing with boy's toys. Give her a doll and she doesn't want to know. Hark at me. I'm sorry, I don't suppose you're interested. Did you say that you would like a cup of tea?'

This was not going to be easy. Stark sat on the edge of the armchair, hands clasped, resting on his knees. 'Perhaps in a minute, Mrs Deely – '

'Oh please, you don't have to be so formal, call me Sarah. Mrs Deely – it's not very often that I get called that nowadays. Now what is it I can do for you?'

Stark sighed. 'Listen Sarah, I'm afraid I have some bad news for you. I don't really know how to tell you this.'

Sarah became agitated; her smile tight-lipped, she swallowed hard. She got up sharply. 'I think we will have a cup of tea. Do you take milk and sugar?'

She didn't wait for an answer but went into the spacious, wood-panelled kitchen and began filling the kettle. Stark had no option but to follow her there. He stood in the doorway, a dull ache filling his belly. 'Look Mrs Deely, there's a reason we are – '

'I've told you, call me Sarah.' Her voice had irritation in it as she plugged in the kettle. Stark took her arm, stopping her activity. He looked at her hard.

'Sarah, look at me, love.'

Sarah stared down at the worktop. 'This is silly – I'm very busy you know. I'm just making a drink, there's nothing wrong with that, is there? You aren't going to arrest me for that, are you?'

Stark's face remained solemn. 'Sarah, it's James. Something's happened. It's bad news, love.'

Sarah wrenched her arm free and turned to a cupboard. She began taking out cups and saucers.

'Would you prefer mugs, I know most men do. You don't have to stand on ceremony here you know.'

'Sarah, listen to me. It's James, he's been involved in something terrible. It's very bad news, I'm afraid.'

Tears began to well in Sarah's eyes, the strain evident.

'My husband hasn't been involved in anything, I'll have you know, so don't start making accusations you can't back up. I have been more than civil with you – '

It was Stark's turn to interrupt. 'Sarah, your husband has been killed. I'm sorry, my love, I really am. Come and sit down.' He put his arm around her shoulder. She shrugged him off, responding aggressively.

'If this is some kind of juvenile joke, then I'm not laughing. My husband has not been killed – I've never heard of anything so ridiculous. I only saw him a couple of hours ago, for Christ's sake. So if you're going to be silly you can leave now, thank you very much. I have some shopping to do.' Sarah rested her hands on her hips. Stark's heart sank.

'Sarah, it's the truth I'm afraid.' He produced the ornate teardrop earring found in the car. It was clearly visible from within the plastic bag. 'Do you recognize this, Sarah?'

She turned and rested her hands on the sink top. The earring had been lost only the week before. She screwed her eyelids shut, forcing a tear to trickle down her cheek. Stark placed his hand on her shoulder. He spoke gently in her ear.

'Sarah, I'm so sorry, but it is true. James has been killed.'

Sarah was abrupt. 'Oh yes, well who's identified him then? Tell me that.'

Stark was truthful. 'Nobody has yet, but it's his car, his identity documents, his business cards in the car. He hasn't arrived at work, and he matches the description his workmates gave. Don't hold out too much hope Sarah, that's all.'

Sarah went to the far kitchen wall and dialled a number on the phone hanging there. 'Kath? It's Sarah. Can you nip round and have Katy for an hour? I've got to go out, only it is fairly important. No. Nothing to worry about. Thanks.'

She walked past Stark and got hold of her coat. 'Come on then, let's go and see who this man is. Let me go and do the "identification", because I'll tell you what, mister, you are in deep trouble. James is not without connections, and when he hears about this . . .' At this point Kath, her neighbour, a middle-aged lady, arrived at the back door and let herself in. Sarah shouted to her, 'Thanks, Kath,' then turned and went to open the front door. She placed her hand on the Yale lock and her head rested on her hand. She froze. Stark could hear nothing, but suddenly a loud wail rose from within her. Sobs racked her body. 'I can't do it. Tell me it's not true. Please.' Her pent-up emotions erupted and she fell into the arms of Stark, who held her against his shoulder, frustratingly helpless. No words were sufficient to relieve the enormity of her grief.

Kath ran over. 'Come on love, whatever's happened? Come and sit down.' The two helped Sarah into the living-room. Stark noticed Katy in the doorway of the playroom, sullen, wide-eyed, a finger in her mouth.

Twenty minutes passed; Steve Aston made a pot of tea. The two men looked on awkwardly as Kath held the distraught Sarah and rocked her on the settee. Kath was crying too. Sarah instinctively held on to Katy, who was frightened. A terrible scene. 'Don't cry, Mummy,' Katy pleaded.

Stark surreptitiously radioed for a policewoman to attend and there was a brief debate with the uniformed inspector, who was reluctant to grant the policewoman overtime for the task as it would undoubtedly take her beyond the end of her shift. Stark was succinct. 'You aren't paying her out of your own arse pocket are you? Get her down here. Pronto!'

Once the policewoman arrived, Stark met her at the door and explained the situation. She was to comfort Sarah and, when the time was right, try to get as much information out of her about James and any motive a killer might have as was possible. Stark would arrange for a detective policewoman to come and assist as soon as he could.

As Stark left with Steve Aston, he grabbed the policewoman's arm and whispered to her, 'Just check her alibi, and make sure all the carving knives are here. Are you with me?' The policewoman nodded disdainfully. Stark qualified the apparent harshness of his comment: 'You never know, stranger things have happened.'

Steve Aston sneezed as they stepped out on to the drive. He fished out a handkerchief and blew hard at his nose. Stark screwed his face up as they reached the car. 'Bloody hell, Steve. Are you all right?'

'No, I've got a bloody cold. I can't seem to shake it off.'

'You want to get some meat down you. All this rabbit food is weakening your resistance.'

'There's more vitamin C in vegetables than meat. Anyway, I refuse to be drawn. I know you're only taking the piss, sir.'

The two men got into the CID car. Stark paused.

'What's the matter, sir?'

'I'm just wondering who's going to identify the body.'

'Sarah Deely could do it once she's calmed down a bit.'

'Yes I know, but I want to know now, plus I want the post-mortem doing as soon as possible.'

There was a silence.

Stark eventually decided to grab the bull by the horns. 'It will have to be a work colleague, but it'll have to be done in the strictest confidence.'

Steve sniffed and said honestly, 'I bloody hate mortuaries. It's the stench I hate, the smell that sticks in the back of your throat and to your clothes, and worse, the bloody happy-go-lucky morticians whistling about the place. There's got to be something wrong with them, you know.'

Stark started up the car. 'Well somebody's got to do it, haven't they, but I agree there's got to be something weird about wanting to sit in a room with a hundred bodies of a Sunday afternoon, with nobody else about.'

'Weird I tell you.' Steve concurred.

Stark then related a story he often relished telling young policemen. 'I had to go one Sunday morning you know, when I was a detective sergeant, and there's a fit young bird in there – have you seen her? She's absolutely gorgeous, and anyway it's her that answers the door, and bugger me if I don't go in there and there it is, she's got a bloody motorbike stripped down next to all the stiffs and she's doing the brakes! Well, she says it's usually quiet on a Sunday!'

'I don't believe you sir!'

'It's bloody well true. I couldn't believe it myself!'

'Jesus Christ, they're frigging mental. Mind you I suppose they have to be, don't they.'

Stark pulled out of the drive. He spoke. 'She wouldn't have it would she – Mrs Deely?'

Steve frowned. 'No, poor sod. You've just got to tell them when they go like that, you know, refuse to acknowledge it.'

'Yes.'

'What's next on the agenda then, boss?'

'We've got to get our act together. We'll have a briefing back at the nick. You never know, they might have arrested the offender by the time we get back.'

Steve was as optimistic as ever. 'Yes and pigs might fly!'

'Runway clear for take-off!'

Nobby Clarke parked the CID car in the space marked 'Police' at the front of the Queens Medical Centre, Accident and Emergency Department. He muttered to himself as he approached the electronic entrance doors. 'First he wants me to set up the Incident Room, then he says can you just nip to the QMC to do the ID of the body. Stick a brush up my arse and I'll sweep the floor at the same time, sir.'

The middle-aged woman at the reception smiled at him. 'Name and address please.'

'No, you're all right love, I'm not a patient, I'm from the CID. I'm trying to arrange an identification of a James Deely.'

'Oh right, who do you want to speak to then?'

'Well, if I can use your phone I could do with talking to the mortician.'

'Sure, I'll dial you the number.' The woman stared at the list of numbers displayed on the wall next to her before tapping out four digits. She passed him the phone. 'It's ringing.'

'Hello, mortuary.' It was the voice of a young woman, sounding rather happy.

'Hello love, I'm Detective Sergeant John Clarke. I'm in Casualty at the moment and I'm meeting a man here shortly to do an ID of James Deely. What condition is he in?'

'Well he's not very well, I mean . . .'

Nobby laughed. 'No, I didn't mean that. You know what I meant. Is he OK to do an ID with?'

'Let's see, James Deely. Oh yes, no problem. Give me ten minutes, I'll splash a bit of make-up on, he'll look like a million dollars.'

31

'I'd prefer it if you would leave him as he is. The pathologist likes the body untouched to do the post-mortem on, if that's OK.'

'It's fine by me. I'll get him to the COR room.'

'What's that?'

'That's what the relatives usually say when they see them – "Cor!" No, I'm only joking, it's the initials of the Chapel of Rest.'

'I'm glad you're happy in your work, anyway.'

'It's no good being any other, is it?'

'I suppose not. Ten minutes then.'

'See you in a bit.'

Nobby handed the phone back to the receptionist. 'I'll be outside if a bloke called Alan Johnson comes to reception.'

Nobby sat on the wooden bench beside the main door of the massive hospital complex. He stared down at the scores of fag-ends ditched by gasping patients and visitors alike. His mind chewed over his responsibilities, whether he would have time to finish off the Incident Room. Mind you, there wasn't a lot left to do, really. He had arranged a couple of extra cars from various corners of the force, he had commandeered the conference room at Nottingham Police Station and furnished it with sufficient tables and chairs. He had listed the men he needed – those available, those it was necessary to alert – and the poor sods who would have to hold the fort at section level for the everyday crime that would continue to pour in regardless.

He had just completed his scrounging session at the administration department when Stark had given him the news: 'I want you to do the ID Nobby, because that way you can stay on for the post-mortem and save me pissing about!' Nobby had managed to obtain scores of notepads, pens, whiteboard pens, everything possible, as well as a whole stack of 'action sheets' – A4, self-carbonating pro-formas which give details of the originator, who the action is given to, and the nature of the task to be undertaken. An 'action' could just as easily be described as an 'enquiry' or a 'task'. Detectives call them actions. Where a person is to be seen, it will simply say: 'T.I.E. Joe Bloggs' – 'Trace, Interview and Eliminate'. Space is left at the foot of the page for the investigating officer to record the result of his or her 'action' before returning it to the supervisor, who then, according to the result, either issues further actions or files the sheet and any written witness state-ments in the necessary lever-arch file. Nobby had just completed labeling the lever-arch files before setting off to the QMC. The files would keep the job ticking over until the computers were drafted in. Each file had a heading:

Original Witness Statements
Copy Statements
Actions to be Allocated
Actions Issued
Completed Actions
Press Releases
Miscellaneous
Overtime and Expenses

Nobby glanced at the various people arriving at the main door, wondering which of the men was Alan Johnson. After a while a serious-looking man in his mid-forties passed him. His hair was receding, and he wore a dark suit and tie. He was painfully thin and gaunt. Nobby looked through the glass doors and saw the receptionist indicating to the man that Nobby was outside. He stood up and went to meet him. They shook hands in the foyer.

'I'll just give them a ring downstairs and see if they're ready for us.' They were and Nobby led the morose gentleman through the maze of corridors towards the Chapel of Rest. Alan Johnson said very little.

The two met the green-smocked figure of Jenny Smith, the happy-go-lucky mortician to whom Nobby had spoken on the phone. She behaved more demurely for Alan Johnson. Nobby explained the procedure to Mr Johnson and they all stepped inside the small room. Only the sign outside the door made it a 'chapel of rest'. The body lay on its back, covered by a purple blanket with a cross embroidered in gold on it. The dead man's eyes were closed but, as often happens, they were not fully shut, and as they stepped into the room his unseeing eyeballs glistened a welcome. Alan Johnson let out a sigh and bravely marched towards the exposed face of the man. Nobby was quick to ask: 'Is that James Deely, your employee?'

Alan croaked a reply, 'Yes,' and they quickly ushered the dazed man out of the room. Nobby went back inside, just in time to see the mortician throw back the blanket and reveal the naked corpse.

33

'Thanks a lot, love. I'll be down in a minute, put the kettle on will you?'

'Seeing as it's you.'

'Oh, and one other thing.'

'What's that?'

'Wash your hands first, there's a good girl!'

3

'Two social workers walk past a man bleeding in
a ditch. One comments to the other, "We must
find the man who did this, he needs help!"'

Anon.

A mixture of detectives and uniformed personnel were gathered
in the Incident Room of Nottingham Police Station, seated round
a large wooden rectangle made up of eight individual tables
scattered with numerous coloured ashtrays sporting various
brewery names.

The detectives spoke between themselves, as did the uniformed officers drafted in by Nobby Clarke from the 'Force Support Group' – experts highly trained to cope in diverse situations,
from firearms sieges to searching premises to policing football
matches. The detectives sat closest to the whiteboard at the far
end of the room, smoke wafting from their cigars and cigarettes.
There was a high level of chatter as each group speculated on how
long the enquiry would run and various weird and wonderful
theories were expounded upon. Interestingly enough, the
theories were to be heard from the uniform side, whilst the words
'overtime' and 'expenses' could be overheard from the CID
group, who thought it was perhaps a little early for theories yet.
Jim McIntyre interspersed his brash, throaty comments with the
occasional passing of wind, which he synchronized with the
raising of his buttocks to emphasize the action.

'Oh Christ, Jim, do you have to do that?' Steph enquired
disdainfully.

The nattering hushed as Stark and Detective Superintendent
Wagstaff entered. Stark remained on his feet while Wagstaff
settled himself into a chair strategically placed at the front of the

room. Stark faced the expectant crowd, all at once silent. He spoke in a loud, emphatic voice.

'James Deely is dead. Somebody killed him. Anybody know who?' There was a stony silence. Stark's detectives were smiling; he was clearly on form today.

'Well, in that case, we've got a long way to go, and I demand your fullest attention. This poor victim – James Deely, a solicitor – was driving to work at about twenty-past eight this morning, happy as Larry, when somebody decided to stick a knife through his throat, killing him in the process. Now, I'm not going to send you to sleep at this briefing; I will simply lay it on the line for you, as succinctly as I can. It is pointless crowding your brains with incidentals. The post-mortem, which Detective Sergeant Clarke so kindly attended for me, reveals no great surprises. The man was stabbed through the left side of his throat. The thrust severed his carotid artery, his trachea and oesophagus, causing him to die from clinical shock, lack of oxygen and loss of blood. By working out the depth of thrust and width of the wound, we can estimate that the knife blade is eight inches long by two inches wide.'

Stark walked slowly across the front of his audience, one hand in his trouser pocket, toying with his loose change. He continued the briefing.

'From the direction of the blow, it is apparent that the killer was secreted in the well of the car, behind the front passenger seat. It is similarly obvious that the car was not forced to gain access. The policewoman at Mrs Deely's house informs me that Mr Deely had a habit of not locking his car overnight. Also, for what it is worth, Mrs Deely has said that Deely was going to visit an old friend today, a social worker called Roy Prentice. He will have to be traced and eliminated. The killer thrust the knife into Deely's neck extremely hard. One blow was apparently sufficient to kill him outright. It is felt that the blow would have been a thrust similar to a fencer's lunging forward for the kill.'

Stark illustrated his description by jabbing his pipe out in front of him, arm straight, then creasing at the elbow, and repeated the motion three times, for effect.

'Like that. This happened at the junction of Church Lane Linby and Linby Road itself. Now, as I have said, there's not a lot else you need to know, and I ain't going to bore you. Nobody has seen a thing apparently, so if the uniform lads can liaise with their

36

sergeants, they've got various actions for you to help locate any witnesses, whether it be house-to-house or vehicle question-naires. I'll have a word with the CID lads and instruct them on their actions. Now I know he's a solicitor who's caused us some pain in the past, but I think it would be a bit harsh to wish such a fate on anybody, do you know what I mean? Don't worry about overtime, it's all been squared up, and one more thing . . .'

Stark turned his back on the audience and began writing on the whiteboard in large black letters:

MURDER

INVESTIGATION

OFFENDER CAUGHT AND CHARGED

He pointed at the word 'murder' with his long-stemmed pipe.

'I am standing at the top of this pyramid. I want to get to the bottom of this pyramid. You horrible bunch of reprobates are going to get me down there. Each and every one of you must link together and allow me to travel down each step and through each hazard as easily as possible. If one of you breaks the chain or stumbles through lack of concentration, the pyramid will col-lapse. This of course will mean I will fall down on top of you with one almighty fucking bang! But of course that won't happen, because I can trust every one of you, can't I?'

Stark smiled wryly as he paused and lit his pipe, allowing time for his message to sink in. He finished the briefing simply.

'Thank you for your time, and good luck.'

A low mumbling returned to the room, interspersed with laughter; several officers stood up and stretched, looking for their sergeants.

Stark went to join the detectives sitting across the table from Nobby. As he did, Charlie Carter came in.

'Any chance of joining in the party, sir?' he asked Stark. 'I've charged our pervert, and all the reports are done, sufficient for his remand application tomorrow, anyway.'

Stark was pleased to have a man of Charlie's experience in on the team. 'Er, yes, OK. You can tie up with Nobby. Try and keep him out of the pubs, will you? Follow up any leads house-to-house throw up for starters.'

'Steph, will you carry on with Ashley and see where you get at Selby's Farm. Your paper-boy heard a car start there, didn't he?'

Steph nodded and flashed her perfect teeth at the gaffer. Grant Donaldson's mouth closed over the pearly whites when Stark instructed him to tie in with Jim McIntyre and go to Deely's workplace. Grant had already got the feeling that 'moaning' Jim did not care too much for blacks.

Steve Aston felt a bit out of it while Stark arranged an office manager, someone to collate all the incoming and outgoing actions, in this case a detective sergeant drafted in from Radford Road. Wagstaff had already told Stark that he would remain in the Incident Room and monitor the investigation from there, which was fine by Stark as it allowed him to go out into the field. Steve did not have to wait long: Stark seconded him to come and see Roy Prentice, the social worker Deely had arranged to see that day.

Ashley grimaced as he drove his nice clean Porsche 924 on to the muddy wasteland adjacent to the cottage at Selby's Farm. The farm buildings consisted of a cowshed down the path, a large barn for hay, several oversized garages, a pigsty and two or three outbuildings whose use was not easy to define for city folk, one of whom Ashley most certainly was. Past the buildings was a big old house covered in ivy, its plaster peeling. Both he and Steph approached the small wooden door to the right of the house. Despite repeated knocking, there was no reply. Steph peered through the dirty windows, and was alarmed by a deep male voice suddenly expressing concern at their presence.

'What d'you want?'

The two detectives turned sharply. Behind them stood a man in his thirties. He was wearing a scruffy green quilted gun jacket and the obligatory wellington boots. Obviously the farmer, he had unwashed black hair and an aura of pig shit that rapidly filled Steph's nostrils. Ashley explained the reason for their presence.

'We're from the CID. I wonder if we could have a word with you.' He indicated that perhaps the conversation could be held indoors.

The farmer's manner was brusque.

'Just here'll be fine I reckon. What do you want with me?'

Ashley continued. 'Well, it's not just you, it's anybody on the

38

farm, really. You see, there's been a murder, just across the field. Now there was a young lad who found the car who says that he – '

The farmer interrupted. 'Is this going to take long, 'cos I'm a busy man, you know.'

Steph sighed. Ashley struggled on. 'It shouldn't take too long. As I was saying, there was this lad who heard the noise of a car starting up from the direction of your farm. I wonder if you could enlighten us as to where it might have come from?' Ashley intentionally withheld the time of the morning he was referring to.

'I've no idea. There are cars coming and going all the time. I mean what does that show, sod all doesn't it? Now, as I say, if that's it I'll get back to work now.'

Steph had heard enough, what with the hag at the newsagents and now this idiot. 'Look, can I just explain something to you Mr . . .'

'Tennant.'

'Mr Tennant. Some poor sod has been killed this morning. You may or may not know that a murder enquiry means that every minuscule lead is followed up, and that's just what we're trying to do now. You see this maniac may well still be in the locality, and when you and your wife and kids are tucked up in bed, he may just decide to kill you, or your kids, understand? We're not here for our health, and the sooner you cooperate, the sooner we can leave you in peace. Now, that's not being unreasonable, is it?'

Tennant took offence. He was not used to being spoken to in such a manner by a woman. 'No need to be like that. And, anyway, I haven't got any kids, and if he did come round here he'd be looking down the business end of a twelve-bore, I'll have you know.'

Steph sighed heavily. Ashley took over. 'Look, is your wife here?'

'Yes, she is.' He yelled. *'Mary!'*

The front window opened and a small, insipid-looking woman poked her head out. Her voice was soft and the detectives strained to hear her. 'What is it, love?'

'These people are detectives. They want to know if there was a car starting up on the farm this morning.'

The woman looked through Steph at Ashley. 'What time this morning?'

'Any time around twenty-past eight.'

'Oh, that would be me, with the tractor. Why, what's wrong?'

'Somebody's been killed in Linby village this morning, and we're just checking out who the car belonged to.'

'It weren't no car, I don't think. It would be me, taking the pig feed out on the tractor, love.'

Ashley and Steph noted their details and ascertained that they were the only two residents on the farm. Steph was curious as to why it was called Selby's Farm. Mrs Tennant explained that it was the former owner, John Selby, who had since died. Mr Tennant did not wait to bid goodbye, and the two detectives returned to Ashley's Porsche. Ashley paused, prior to turning on the ignition.

'What's that smell?'

Steph screwed up her face. 'It smells like pig shit to me.'

Ashley looked underneath his shoe within the confines of the vehicle. 'Oh bloody hell!'

As Ashley scraped at his shoe with a stick outside the car, his face red with embarrassment, an Alsatian dog came up to him, sniffing, whilst he hopped on one leg. 'Piss off! Go on, piss off, you stinking great mutt!'

Steph struggled in vain to withhold her laughter, which she eventually stifled as Ashley drove off in a huff.

'I don't see what's funny.'

The afternoon was drawing to a close. A thin layer of smog hung limply over Nottingham city centre, heralding the encroaching dusk. In close-by Trinity Square, busy pedestrians darted from place to place, like bees returning to the hive, whilst others queued at a nearby bus-stop, entranced, weary from the day's activities, thinking of warmth and home, beating off the chilling air. A policeman strolled through the square, going nowhere in particular, his public face masking the thoughts he shared with the bus-queuers, seeing all, seeing nothing; only the unusual could trigger his alertness. There was sound all around, yet no sound, just background noises, the roaring of buses, the dull hubbub of pockets of conversation and the repetitive, intrusive shouts of the newspaper-seller on the corner. *'Heebin Po!'* could be deciphered by the initiated to mean *'Evening Post'*.

A beanpole of a man, prematurely balding and wearing a shiny suit, turned from the news vendor and hurried away to escape the anticipated blare of his next cry. Jim McIntyre and Grant Donaldson looked on from the CID car as the man disappeared down past a dry cleaners to the side stairs. There was a sign on the wall with 'Johnson & Brown Solicitors' emblazoned on it.

Grant's suspicions of Jim's attitude towards blacks had immediately been vindicated in his eyes, as Jim had broached the subject as soon as they had left the station. 'You know I've nothing against blacks, Grant. I hate prejudice. It's the bleeding Rastas I can't stand.'

Grant immediately regretted his reply. 'Surely you're generalizing when you say that. It's like somebody saying, "I've nothing against the police, it's the detectives I can't stand".'

'Oh sorry, I didn't realize you were so touchy.'

Grant was in an unenviable position; he was an 'Aide to CID', the lowest of the low in CID terms, yet to prove himself. He had to be careful. He bit his tongue. He was determined to change things, but you do that from the top – he had to get there first. He could take the shit for a few more years yet. In reality, Grant had been pleasantly surprised at the reaction he had got from colleagues: the racist myth of police officers had been just that, a myth. OK, there were the odd comments, but any large organization had that. Most of them just stemmed from ignorance, and the guilty were often most surprised and upset that the term 'nigger', for example, was offensive to him. They would apologize and it would not happen again . . . within his hearing. A black police officer can be an education to those who have worked in an all-white environment. What to them is just a phrase can be hurtful to a black person, even though in the vast majority of cases no malice is intended.

Grant was there to fight crime, and where necessary, he would use his black culture to do that with the West Indian criminal element, but he wasn't going to carry a chip on his shoulder, looking for comments, getting paranoid. That was how you got diverted, when you started fighting against your friends, not working with them.

However, he did not like Jim McIntyre.

The two men went up the spiral staircase that led into the firm of solicitors. The room was astonishingly well lit inside. At the

41

reception desk sat a young girl; she was fat, with black straggly hair and wooden earrings. She showed the men in to see Alan Johnson. As they entered, Alan was finishing a conversation with a younger man; it was apparent they were talking about James Deely. It was Alan they had seen buy the paper, now spread out on the desk. The younger man had dark-brown hair swept back with 'wet-look' gel. He had a slightly spotty complexion, and very dark eyebrows. He appeared upset, and rose to leave as the men came in. Grant spoke impulsively.

'Don't go. That's to say, if you've got a few minutes . . . We're here about James.'

Alan Johnson spoke. 'Yes, I've only just come back from identifying James at the hospital.'

Grant sympathized. 'Oh dear, not a nice thing to have to do. How d'you feel?'

'Not too bad, thanks. At least it saved Sarah the job. Mind you, I shan't forget the experience in a hurry.'

'No, I'm sure you won't. But somebody has to do it and, as you say, it's probably better in some ways that you did.'

Grant was correct in stopping the younger man. He was far more likely to know things about James than the older man, whose relations with James would have been more distanced.

The younger solicitor, Phillip Bond, sat attentively as Jim explained why they had come: to discuss what sort of a man James had been and whether they were aware of any serious problems he had encountered, either with a client or some other party. Alan suggested that Phillip do the talking and he would chip in with anything he felt relevant.

Jim started off. 'Well, the obvious question is, what sort of man was he?'

Phillip scratched his head. 'God. That's one hell of a question. He's a good friend . . . Sorry, it still hasn't sunk in yet . . . *was* a good friend. Always looking for a laugh with anybody. He was a bloody good solicitor. It's come as a shock to everybody, it really has.'

Jim failed to conceal his obvious lack of sympathy. 'Yes, I'm sure you're upset. But who did he associate with? In his spare time, I mean.'

'Quite a few people really. I would have the odd game of squash with him. There were a few people he'd met along the

42

way, as we all have, friends from school, you know the sort of thing.'

Jim was blunt. 'So who would want to murder him?'

Phillip shook his head. 'Nobody. He was so well liked. It's Sarah and Katy I feel for. How are they bearing up?'

Grant attempted to reassure him. 'As well as can be expected. It must be terrible for them. Phillip, do you know anything about his past? I know it's difficult.'

'I know he was a local lad, went to the High School, then Nottingham Polytechnic, took a law degree and ended up here. That's it as far as I know.'

Grant asked another question. 'What about problems with clients?'

'Nothing extraordinary. We all get the odd one or two who don't like the way we deal with them, but he never mentioned anything unusual.'

'Would he have mentioned it, or would he have kept it to himself?'

Phillip glanced at Alan. 'I think he would have mentioned it, to be honest.' Alan nodded in agreement.

'Do you keep any records of problem clients?'

Alan answered, the image of James Deely's dead face teasing his memory. 'No it doesn't warrant it really, does it, Phillip?'

It was Phillip's turn to shake his head. 'No.'

Jim jumped in with both feet again. 'What about women? Was he putting it about a bit, any mistresses?' Grant cringed at the indiscreet way Jim asked the necessary question.

'I think if it had been there for him, he may have done, but I can't give you names of anybody. I don't actually know of anyone in particular.'

'Is there any objection to us looking at James's personnel record, or his desk diary?' Grant asked.

Alan grimaced. 'I'm not so sure about that; I would have to seek advice.'

Jim didn't like solicitors and was uncomfortable in their presence. He had now found an excuse to relieve the discord he felt.

'Come on Grant, we'll leave it at that, then.' He turned his attention to Alan, looking through rather than at him.

'We may well have to come back to look at his personnel record and diary. I'm sure you want us to catch the killer, don't you? Or

43

will you be queueing up to represent the murderer if he's caught?' At that Jim quickly left, leaving Grant to mumble a 'Thank you for your time'. Grant had most certainly drawn the short straw.

Adjacent to the Scenes of Crime Department at Nottinghamshire Constabulary Headquarters was the Forensic bay, a high-ceilinged, garage-type of building where all motor vehicles were examined extremely thoroughly, and any potential evidence packaged correctly and preserved in its best condition before being despatched to the Home Office Forensic Science Laboratory. The white-coated Scenes of Crime officers, Phil and David, wearing their tight-fitting gloves, meticulously worked their way through James Deely's vehicle. Photographs were again taken, the insides of the car were swept and the dust and debris bagged up and sealed. The upholstery of the car was dabbed with large pieces of sticky tape, which were bagged, and the seats themselves taken out. Everything would be sent to the lab for intense scrutiny in the hope that there would be some evidence, no matter how small, to point them in the right direction. All the carpets and mats were also removed to be sent. Wagstaff had instructed that the car be completely stripped, with nothing neglected. When they had finished, the car was just a shell, covered in aluminium powder from the fingerprint examination, its value negligible. Its value in evidential terms, however, might prove priceless.

Saville Lodge Community Home was a large converted house which accommodated twelve boys between the ages of fourteen and sixteen. These boys were either in 'voluntary care' – put there by disinterested or incapable parents – or were the subject of care orders directed by the courts. Why they were there ranged from persistent criminal offences to being the victims of child abuse. There were two living-rooms; one had a pool table in it, the other a row of chairs and a television. Next to the TV room was a compact office where staff could go to write their reports or simply escape the kids.

Roy Prentice was small, with a large bushy black beard. He wore ragged jeans and a baggy, plain white T-shirt with Bob

44

Marley and African National Congress badges adorning it. Roy was well known to the police for all the wrong reasons: he was a militant. He would regularly attend gay rights and anti-poll tax marches, not in quiet protest but as an agitator, boosting up the younger element to fever pitch and then disappearing into the background. He was vehemently anti-police and was a member of a militant political group who employed him to make video-tapes of police activities at marches and demonstrations which could later be edited for propaganda material. Roy's colleague at the home was a total contrast. Derek Brook was a caring man, more concerned to instil common sense and values into those in his care than use his position to ram political issues down their throats. He spent long hours using his vast knowledge of psy-chology and human relationships to get the most out of the kids entrusted to him. It was a thankless task, but one which none the less gave him much satisfaction. The difference in the two men could be seen in their reactions to resident children in trouble with the police. Derek would question the child about the behav-iour that had led to the involvement of the police; Roy would question the child about the police's behaviour.

Roy sat in the office, reading a newspaper, his feet resting on a swivel desk chair. Derek was writing in the daily diary, reporting on the day's events. One of the residents ran into the office excitedly, a youth in baggy jeans and baseball cap. 'Coppers are here, Roy.'

Roy stood up, but Derek beat him to the door. 'It's all right, Roy, I'll go, if you like.'

Derek opened the front door and was met by Stark and Steve Aston. Derek smiled in recognition at Steve. 'Hiya, Steve, how are you doing?'

'I'm fine Derek, what about yourself?'

'Steady. What's happening?'

Steve introduced Stark and explained that they had come to see Roy Prentice. 'Oh, right.'

By this time four of the residents had appeared at the foot of the stairs, close to the door. One of them spoke to Stark.

'Who have you come for, then?'

Derek ushered the group to one side before Stark could reply.

'All right, anybody would think you've never seen a policeman

45

before. They've not come for anybody as far as I know. Now get back upstairs, out of the way. Come on.'

Derek led Stark and Steve towards the office to distant cries of 'Pigs' and 'Filth' from the youngsters. Prentice met them at the office door. Stark put out a hand.

'Hello there, I'm Detective Inspector Stark. I wonder if I could have a word with you.'

Prentice ignored the outstretched hand and looked questioningly. 'Yes.'

The boys had rejoined the detectives and were smiling, arms folded.

'Well, can we go into the office or what?'

It was Prentice's turn to fold his arms. 'You can say anything you like in front of my boys. We don't have secrets here, Inspector Bark,' Prentice leered.

Stark corrected Prentice's 'mistake'. 'Detective Inspector Stark actually. I know it's a lot to remember, but I'm sure you'll manage.' Stark had never met Prentice before, but had come across others like him in the past.

Derek barged past Roy and opened the office door. 'Come on in guys. I'll make you a cuppa in a minute.' Prentice leaned on the door-jamb. Stark invaded Prentice's private space, and they stood nose to nose. 'Excuse me, Roy.' Stark smiled as Prentice removed his arm. 'Thank you so much.'

Derek switched on the kettle in the corner of the room and the three men sat down. Stark had had enough of Prentice already. Steve tried to make conversation with Roy.

'What time are you on till tonight then, Roy?'

Roy put his feet on the desk and placed his arms behind his head. 'I don't know if I should answer that. Am I under caution?'

Stark recoiled. 'Have you got some sort of problem, Roy, you know, because if you have like, well let's get it out into the open, all right?'

'Me? Problem? Nah, I'm fine me, I've got a roof over my head, a steady job, three square meals a day, my freedom. I'm one of the lucky ones, me.'

Stark shrugged a laugh and shook his head, smiling. 'D'you know James Deely?'

'I might do, why?'

Derek passed round the coffees and there was a deathly silence in the room as Stark sipped at his cup. He was in no particular hurry; he could sense Prentice's curiosity burning away. Still silence. Stark smiled at Derek.

Prentice couldn't contain himself any longer. 'I said, why do you ask?'

Stark sipped again at his coffee. 'Sorry, Roy, what did you say?'

Prentice was visibly peeved. 'You heard. I said why do you want to know if I know James Deely?'

'Sorry, Roy, er he's erm dead, that's all, mate.'

'Yeah, all right, come on, why do you want to know?'

Stark raised his voice slightly, a pitch higher. 'I've just told you, haven't I? He's dead, and somebody mentioned that he was supposed to come and see you today, so here we are.'

Prentice rose from his seat, mouth open, his face aghast.

'You're joking. What . . . I mean . . . how? Is this straight or what?'

Stark sipped at the cup again. 'It's straight, all right. Do you know him then?'

'Don't be clever, you bloody well know I do.'

'Well I wasn't sure, was I? You didn't answer me. I got the impression you didn't want to talk to us.'

'That's out of order, man, that is.'

'I'm sorry, you didn't make the rules clear. You didn't seem interested in us, so I thought why bother about you, are you with me?'

Talking to Prentice was like pulling teeth, long and painful. All right, so perhaps he hadn't been particularly professional in the way he told him, but sod it, he was fed up with this continual one-sided courtesy. Let *him* have some crap for a change. He eventually gleaned that Prentice had wanted to see James Deely on a legal matter. One of the residents had told him he had stolen a car the night before and he wanted to ensure that James could be present when he took him to the police station. Prentice knew James from his college days and they had kept in touch through their professions. He himself had used James on a couple of occasions when he had been arrested at demonstrations, and had been acquitted both times. Prentice lived alone at Clifton, on the other side of Nottingham, and at the time of the murder had been driving to work. He drove a blue Vauxhall Cavalier. As they left, Derek confirmed that Roy had arrived at work for nine o'clock

47

and had not changed his clothes. Derek felt awkward as he saw them out of the house. Stark shook his hand and thanked him for the drink; he would see him again sometime.

It was 9 p.m. before Stark got back to Nottingham Police Station. He spoke in private with Detective Superintendent Wagstaff, in his office.

'You know, I've met some prats in my time, but that Roy Prentice is a major tool. I mean, what is up with the man? Most of the time there's no problem with social services. All right, they don't think like policemen, but they're not going to, are they? We can handle that. The main problem is just that they seem to believe everything everybody tells them – but that guy, Jesus!'

Wagstaff reclined in his black PVC chair, twirling his handlebar moustache. He appeared distant. 'You know David, I think it was 1971 when we had a similar job to this one. That was a tramp who had slept overnight in the murder victim's car and panicked when he was found out. I think we should bear that in mind now, do you agree?'

Stark nodded. 'Yes, sure.'

He observed Wagstaff, who never appeared to be looking at you when he spoke but would speak to the window, or the wall. Stark listened intently. Although Wagstaff was considered to be of the old school, he was no mug. He was a master at playing dumb, but he had an almost photographic memory, and he could quote conversations he'd had with you over a year earlier.

Stark grunted and nodded at the appropriate junctures. Wagstaff made arrangements regarding a press release, holding back certain information that only the killer would know in order to assist any subsequent interviews and to prevent contempt of court. He considered it appropriate to expand the house-to-house enquiries further into Linby village, and make a thorough but tactful search of the deceased's home for anything out of the ordinary whilst the policewoman was still there. The HOLMES – 'Home Office Large Major Enquiry System' – computer would be set up by tomorrow morning. The HOLMES computer was a godsend; its facilities were so great that no piece of information could hide in there, as it could in the antiquated card system. Before the microchip, detectives had had to rely on a massive card system to collate information and evidence: cardboard boxes crammed full of paper and cards that over time could become mislaid, and there would be so many cross-references that the system would almost collapse if the enquiry became extensive. Mistakes could be made when a person who had been interviewed several times would be lost in rooms full of cardboard boxes, all full of information. Now, however, the computer could do the filing, retrieving the smallest piece of information in seconds. If a red car became an issue in an enquiry, anybody or anything at all relating to a red car would be listed, whatever their connection to it. All connections or similarities between persons, events, circumstances, etc. would be highlighted at the touch of a button.

Wagstaff, stating the somewhat obvious, considered that the Force Support contingent should broaden their search area, if necessary assisted by the Mounted Section. Stark would ring them tomorrow. He casually mentioned to Wagstaff that he wanted a transfer to the Mounted Section, as he had noticed the heading in the internal telephone directory for that department was 'Dogs/Mounted' and he had always wanted to pick up the phone and say 'Inspector Stark – Dogs Mounted!'

Wagstaff grunted. 'Mmm, very good David, now where were we?'

Scenes of Crime and Forensic had to be kept close at hand for any interesting developments. Stark explained that he would have to leave those covering normal section duty at full stretch, and use extra resources from the Serious Crime Squad, Force Support Group and, if necessary, the Regional Crime Squad. That should leave plenty of detectives available for work on the murder enquiry, with a few extra drafted in from other divisions. Wagstaff finished by saying that they might well have to involve the media more as time went on, since it looked as though the murder was going to be a 'runner'. 'So keep them sweet, David. We'll do a press conference in the morning. Debrief the lads for me, and I'll probably see you later.'

Stark caught sight of the gangly, freckle-faced Detective Sergeant Stuart Bradshaw at the far end of the corridor as he was returning to his office.

'Finished everything, Stuart?' he shouted.

'More or less, sir. I've prepared a list of all items taken from the car, and obviously we've got to work closely with Forensic to see where the information is going to take us. I've got a copy of the list here if you want it.'

'Sure. Come into my office while I have a look at it with you.'

Stark's office was halfway down the corridor, a smallish room with just a desk, two chairs and a metal filing cabinet. On the wall was a photograph of Stark's CID Initial Course, class of 1972: a group of apprehensive young men in kipper ties and flared trousers smiling inanely.

Stark took a seat behind his desk and encouraged Stuart to draw up a chair next to him. He stared down at the list in front of him.

Thirty-six fibres recovered from rear seat of vehicle
Nine hundred millilitres (2 pints approx.) of blood recovered from within car
Thirty-one fingerprints found on inside and outside of vehicle
One ounce of debris (believed soil) removed from floor of vehicle
Forty-nine human hairs found inside the vehicle
Numerous fibres and hairs on deceased's clothing
No footprints of any worth found at scene
Twenty-seven fibres on front offside seat of vehicle

Stark passed comment on each entry, thinking aloud.

'Thirty-six fibres from rear seat.'

Stuart spoke. 'Yes, but of course they could be anybody's sir, family, friends . . .'

'True – but they could be shown to be somebody's who did not have access to the dead man's car. We must obtain a list of who has been, or was allowed to be, in the car, which I'm sure won't be particularly easy if he's been ferrying clients about. I suppose once the fibres have been analysed they can be compared with the clothing of the most obvious passengers, which should eliminate most of the fibres.'

Stuart agreed. 'Sure. Um, once the lab has examined them, then they simply get samples of clothing from the authorized passengers, if they have anything which matches that description. Then, hopefully, the fibres will match, and can be eliminated as not being the offender's.'

Stark was sceptical. 'Unless, of course, that authorized person killed him.' He smiled.

'Yes, sir, you know what I mean, though.'

'Now then, let's see, 900 milli what? Oh, two pints of blood, right, well, until it's analysed we can only treat that as the deceased's for now. Thirty-one fingerprints found on inside and outside of vehicle. Bloody hell, this is a rough copy. I do take it that you have itemized every individual hair, fibre and print, and exactly where in the car it was taken from?'

Stuart was quick to defend the obvious. 'You don't need to ask that, sir. I can get you that if you want it. I just thought this would give you a good overall picture for the time being, as easy reference.'

'Yes, sorry, Stuart, it does make it a bit easier, I'll grant you that. Now then, these fingerprints, where exactly are they?'

'All the normal places where passengers would leave them, but mainly on the windows. In my humble opinion they don't look particularly recent to me, but who knows? I hope I'm wrong.'

'Keep me updated on that one Stuart, as I want the full works done on it by the Fingerprint Department. The problem is, of course, that if the killer has no police record, and is not a member of Her Majesty's forces, we're knackered. We'll get a load of elimination prints from everybody as we go along. What else? Soil, well yes.'

Stuart contributed his comments. 'We've taken a control sample from the garden of the dead man's house to see if they can get a match.'

'I don't think that's going to take us anywhere. I don't know; we'll have to see. They could still have soil on their shoes or trousers, I suppose. "Forty-nine human hairs found inside vehicle". That's great. All we need to do is find the bloody killer and we may well be able to prove it forensically, especially these hairs and fibres on the dead man's body.'

'Yes, and Forensic will have fingernail scrapings from the PM to examine, so it's not too bad overall.'

'No. You've done a cracking job there, Stuart, well done mate.'

At that point Nobby appeared in Stark's office doorway. 'Are we ready for the debrief?'

Stark dismissed Stuart and they all met in the Incident Room. Each of the detectives said their little bit: who they had seen, what the result was. It was fairly obvious that they had not got very far; it was a bloody awkward one. As the debrief ran dry, so did Nobby. He spoke up. 'Can I make a suggestion, boss?'

'What's that, Nobby?'

'Can we adjourn to the bar? I'm bleeding gagging for a drink.'

Cries of 'Great idea, Nobby,' and 'Best thing you've said all day,' made the decision easy for Stark.

Nottingham Police Station bar was on the top floor, away from the everyday goings-on, next to the administration departments. It was not big, but had folding doors which opened on to a large room with a dance floor for the many functions that were held there. The bar was tastefully decorated. Above it were plaques of various police force badges and emblems; there was an obligatory jukebox, and an array of tables and chairs; the floor was carpeted. There were a number of pleasing prints on the walls. To Stark's surprise Wagstaff was already there. He had come straight from the Chief Superintendent, whom he'd been updating on the murder. Wagstaff immediately latched on to Stark, with Jim McIntyre hanging on. Stark would have preferred to have been with his men, but endured Wagstaff's enforced segregation. Wagstaff spoke in a loud, throaty voice, supplying the punch-line to his story.

'So the Chief said, "While ever Wagstaff's got his spoke in, the wheel won't come off"!' Jim McIntyre broke into uproarious laughter at Wagstaff's pretentious, unfunny anecdote. Stark smiled politely, rolling his tired eyes upwards in disdain.

Nobby had cornered Steph against the bar and was flirting with her in hushed tones. 'Come off it, Steph, an attractive woman like you must have scores of men after you.'

Steph played her tongue across her white teeth, the fullness of her mouth accentuated by blood-red lipstick. 'Nobby, you're so transparent, you really are.'

'Well, you can't blame me, now can you?'

'I don't know, and you a sergeant as well. You shouldn't flirt with people underneath you.'

'But that's exactly what I'm trying to achieve.'

'What's that?'

'Get you underneath me!' Their laughter floated into the rest of the crowd, who had somehow got into a fairly heavy conversation about racism, with Grant the obvious centre of attention.

'I think a black officer changes people's attitudes when he arrives at a station.'

Charlie examined the claim, putting a finger to pursed lips, before offering. 'Does he change attitudes, or does he make people wary of who's in the room before they make any suspect comments?'

'Well Rome wasn't built in a day, you know,' Grant replied, a nervous smile following his optimism.

'Yes and when in Rome . . .' Charlie continued. 'It doesn't really bother me Grant, I've not got a long time to do on this job. I'm not prejudiced, but I can see it coming, little groups within a police station, each terrified to relax enough to speak, afraid of who might be listening, who's going to report him for being racist or sexist or God knows what else.'

There was a lull. The detectives stood in a semi-circle at the bar, those next to Grant seemed to almost physically distance themselves from him as the debate resumed with Grant pointing a finger.

'You say you're not prejudiced, but what does that mean? What if you came home from work and your daughter was sitting on the settee with a black boyfriend. Would you be over the moon about it?'

Charlie winced. He'd not thought about that. He sat on a bar stool.

Ashley took over. He raised a palm. 'It's true though, Grant. Surely we should be fighting bloody criminals, not each other, for Christ's sake!'

Grant's voice raised an octave as the pitch of the argument raised with it.

'I agree. But all I'm saying is that there are too many "nigger" and "coon" comments made without thinking.'

Charlie had regained his composure, and shifted on the stool. 'But does that mean somebody's prejudiced? I don't think it does, mate. To me, being prejudiced is doing something for or against another, for some trivial reason like the colour of his skin or his culture. I don't do that and I don't know anybody here who's stupid enough to do that either. OK, I'm prejudiced. I don't like criminals – that's why I became a policeman twenty-odd years ago! That's who I dislike as a group – criminals!'

Grant shook his head. 'That's simplifying it though, Charlie. "Nigger" and "coon" are hurtful, derogatory words. I don't fucking like them!'

Charlie raised his eyeballs heavenwards and a wry smile appeared, decorating his mouth and approaching his eyes. 'Eh, come off it. I don't want to give you a hard time, Grant. I mean, we can talk about something else if you like. I personally think it's healthy to talk these things out, but you're a grown man, aren't you? What do you mean, "hurtful"? You don't burst into tears when somebody says "pig" or "filth", do you? Surely you don't carry this thing around with you, listening out for derogatory terms all the time?'

'No of course I don't, but it wears a bit thin, after so long.' Grant sipped at his pint of lager.

'But surely it's water off a duck's back by now?' Charlie mused undeterred.

'No, it isn't. It's personal.' Grant took another sip at his pint, regretting the onset of the topic.

'It *isn't* personal though, is it? They don't know you, they're just saying it – through ignorance maybe, but it's not personal, Grant, is it, mate?' Charlie wouldn't let go, he was fed up at such claims, and Grant had caught him in determined mood.

'You can't say that unless you're subjected to it, Charlie. I think a lot of this attitude comes about through fear. I mean, how many times have you heard a policeman ask for assistance to arrest a six-foot black guy? Would he ask for assistance to arrest a six-foot white man?'

Grant raised his eyebrows and threw open a broad grin.

Charlie thought hard. 'Yes, I accept that. It's probably true, but is that prejudice?'

Ashley chimed in. He didn't like being on the side lines too long. 'What makes me piss is the attitude of some of the blacks. I saw a television programme the other night, and they were talking to various ethnic groups. They spoke to some Asians, who have their own religion, obviously, but they contribute almost solely to it themselves – mosques and stuff like that. They spoke to the Chinese community, who again possibly under-standably want a little piece of their own culture to fall back on, but again they provide it through individuals contributing what they can. Then they showed some Afro-Caribbean place, and there he is, isn't he, some black guy complaining, "We've asked the council for this, that and the other and they haven't given it to us." Why should they be given everything? Why are they so special? Why don't they go and work for the bleeder like every bogger else?' Grunts of 'Yeah' and much nodding of heads put Grant under pressure, he was now responsible for the whole of his race.

Grant was getting tense now. 'That is unadulterated bullshit, Ash. You're generalizing now, and that's the origin of racism – generalization. I thought you had a bit more about you than that. What about the thousands of white people who are neither use nor ornament? I agree with you that you get out of life what you put in, but don't categorize me as that black man in the club. That's ridiculous!'

'OK, I suppose we're giving you a bit of a hard time,' Ashley went on, 'but everybody has a right to an opinion.' Ashley produced a gold lighter and lit a cigarette. He exhaled a plume of smoke before adding. 'Or do they?'

'Of course they do – '

Ashley continued. 'And I'll tell you something else, d'you think I'd be warmly received going into the Afro-Caribbean Club? And what sort of reception would I get from the racism lobby if I suddenly set up "The White European Club"?'

The conversation, as so often happened, had escalated, and emotions were creeping in. Charlie spoke more calmly. He placed his hand on Grant's shoulder.

'You know, I can never understand why blacks and the police clash so often. We have a lot in common.'

Grant looked puzzled. 'In what way, Charlie?'

'Well, we're a minority group within the community; we're stereotyped by the media. Members of the public judge us as a group and not as individuals, they have preconceived ideas about us, they abuse us, have special derogatory terms for us. Aren't there any similarities there?'

'No, it's too simple to say that, Charlie. Blacks have a different culture. We have special requirements, we have rights, too.'

'So you do want people to treat you differently, when it suits you?' Charlie smiled, which turned into an exaggerated frown.

'Charlie, this discussion would take days to get to a decent conclusion,' was all he could manage. Grant was alone in his opinion and was struggling to articulate his argument properly. After all, he was the Aide and, anyway, he didn't want to fall out with the guys. He always felt peeved after such talks, but felt that it was better to get the subject out in the open, to try to build bridges rather than burn them.

'I'm sorry, I don't mean to bombard you, Grant. You know I run off at the mouth sometimes, but I'm just trying to find some answers.'

There were no answers.

Stark glanced at his watch; he'd had a long day. He left the bar early and drove home; he was tired and his body ached. Once home, he clambered into bed and curled up to his wife. Carol's sleepy voice was quick to state the obvious.

'You've been drinking, haven't you?'

4

'If a man is going to be a villain,
in Heaven's name let him remain a fool.'

William Temple

Arrangements had been made for the press conference to be held at Sherwood Lodge, the Nottinghamshire Constabulary headquarters. This majestic building stood in spacious grounds in the woodland of Burntstump Park. Stark had told Carol to videotape the local news so that the children could see their dad on television when they came home from school.

The room was crowded with journalists. Two long tables had been placed in front of a large red curtain, and four microphones, crudely taped together, were propped up in the centre. As usual the two television crews took priority in the pecking order, and the presenters directed proceedings under the watchful eye of the Force Public Relations Officer. The prepared statement would be read out for the cameras, followed by questions shouted from the rest of the mob.

Wagstaff read out the blurb, with Stark looking on. It was a short statement. Several photographers crouched low and camera flashes strobed the Detective Superintendent as he spoke.

'At approximately 8.20 a.m. yesterday, 7th January 1992, James Deely, a solicitor, of Nottingham, was found dead at the steering-wheel of his car. We are treating his death as suspicious. He was driving a blue Volvo motor car, registration number H278 KWW. His car was found at the junction of Church Lane, Linby, and Linby Road, Nottingham. We are appealing for witnesses to come forward to any police station or contact us on the Incident Room telephone number, which is 0602 if you are outside Nottingham, 6387999. I will repeat that: 0602 6387999. Thank you, gentlemen.'

Wagstaff looked up from his sheet of paper. Several shouted questions merged into an incoherent babble. The Public Relations Officer attempted to be heard above the noise.

'One at a time please, or we'll be here all day.'

One journalist was quick to shout out; others would follow suit. 'You say it's a suspicious death – I take it this is a murder investigation?'

Wagstaff replied: 'The death is being treated as suspicious.'

'Surely you know by now whether it's murder or not? Come on, sir, it helps the headliners.'

'It is a murder investigation,' Wagstaff said grimly.

'Are there any persons in custody?'

'No, but a squad of detectives is working round the clock.'

'How many detectives are working on the case?'

Wagstaff gave the stock reply. 'A team of thirty detectives is working on it, at the moment.'

'Have the government limitations on police manpower hampered the investigations?'

'No comment. Stick to the matter in hand please, gents.'

'Have you any leads at the moment?'

'There are several avenues of enquiry being investigated. We are always ready to hear from members of the public with any information; even if they consider it to be trivial, it may be of use to us.'

'How was he killed? What was the cause of death?'

'I'm sorry, no comment on that at this stage.' Stark looked over at the Public Relations Officer and gave him a knowing look. The PRO man spoke out. 'Right, that's all for now, gentlemen. We will keep you updated with any developments. Copies of the press release are here for those who want them.'

Stark and Wagstaff left through a door behind the large curtain. Wagstaff patted Stark on the back; he was feeling pleased with himself. 'I think that went rather well, don't you?'

'Oh very well, sir.'

'I must remember to ring Audrey. I'm sure she'll want to watch it on the television later.'

'I bet she will. D'you think they got your good side, sir?'

'Are you saying I've got a bad side, David?' Wagstaff laughed loudly as he led Stark out of the building. He put his arm around Stark's broad shoulders and hugged him strongly.

'We'll crack this one, David. I've got a feeling in my water.'

Stark wished he could match Wagstaff's optimism as he laboriously waded through piles of action sheets. He sat at the top of the Incident Room, as a teacher might in a classroom, his detectives spread out before him. The result of each action often meant several more having to be done, and so it went on. There was little going for the enquiry: it appeared motiveless. There were a thousand theories that could be expounded upon, but at the moment he still needed something solid, something tangible to work with. In addition to the investigation, he had been ringing round, begging detective chief inspectors to release detectives from other divisions around the force. Every detective released for the enquiry meant some poor sod had double the work at section level. It lay to Stark to organize the logistics of the operation, the mundane necessities – meals, overtime, vehicles seconded from the force pool, typists – and to keep a watching brief on the other events around his subdivision that continued to come in regardless. Everything was a bleeding battle of excuses and grudging responses: 'Oh I don't think we can manage that, sir.' 'Try and monitor the overtime; don't milk it, David.' 'Can you ring back in a bit?'

Stark glanced down at the witness statement of the Home Office pathologist who had performed the post-mortem. The statement began with the details of Professor Disney-Hargreaves, followed by the declaration that precedes every witness statement: 'This statement (consisting of twelve pages, each signed by me), is true to the best of my knowledge and belief and I make it knowing that, if it is tendered in evidence, I shall be liable to prosecution if I have wilfully stated in it anything which I know to be false or do not believe to be true.' Stark marvelled at the list of qualifications that heralded the statement: 'I am a Home Office pathologist, a consultant pathologist and a Professor of Forensic Medicine at the Queens Medical Centre, Nottingham. I am a Doctor of Medicine, a Bachelor of Surgery, a Member of the Royal College of Surgeons, a Licentiate of the Royal College of Physicians, a Fellow of the Royal College of Pathologists and I hold the Diploma in Medical Jurisprudence.'

'I bet he passed his cycling proficiency test as well!' Stark laughed to himself.

The statement continued with a detailed account of the external examination of the deceased: every mark, every blemish, every graze, bruise and scratch. After a few pages the statement disclosed the results of the internal examination, with highlighted headings for each category, even if there was no interference with that body part: Mouth, Neck Structures, Larynx and Pharynx, Thyroid Gland, Cervical Vertebrae, Chest Wall, Pleural Cavities, Bronchial Tree.

As he came to the vital organs, Professor Disney-Hargreaves included the weight of each one, measured out on the scales as in a butcher's shop. 'A pound of liver, love?' Stark continued down the page.

Lungs, Heart, Thymus Gland, Oesophagus, Abdomen, Stomach, Intestines, Liver, Spleen, Kidneys, Adrenal Glands, Pancreas, Gall Bladder, Ureters. Having been to countless post-mortems, Stark could envisage the smell as each organ was removed, picturing the scene as he read on.

Bladder, Aorta, Inferior Vena Cava. 'Inferior Vena Cava! What the bloody hell is that?' he uttered. Varying lengths of observations relating to different parts of the body were written out beneath each heading. Head, Skull, Meninges, Brain, Cerebral Arteries, Skeletal System.

Disney-Hargreaves then went on to list some fifteen exhibits he had taken, including hair (head and pubic), various swabs (penile, anal, nose, mouth), blood, liver tissue and stomach contents. The learned pathologist then did a résumé of the events that in his opinion had caused the relevant injuries or peculiarities to the individual body parts. The statement terminated with several pages of line drawings with the areas of evidential interest marked on. An idiot's guide to the endless medical terms used throughout the statement. Stark had a feeling they were for his benefit as much as anyone else's. The end of the statement was signed: P. Disney-Hargreaves, MD, FRC Path, DMJ Home Office and Consultant Pathologist & Professor of Forensic Medicine.

Stark threw the witness statement on to the desk. Grant came into the office. 'Excuse me, sir, have you seen Nobby anywhere?'

'No I haven't, Grant. Oh, I tell a lie, he was in the kitchen about ten, fifteen minutes ago. He'll be around somewhere.'

The young aide caught sight of the statement. 'What's that? The pathologist's statement? Any good?'

Stark laughed. 'Any good? You want to read it mate, when you get a chance. Unbelievable. The man's a genius.'

'Why, what does it say?'

Stark laughed into the reply. 'Well, now you ask, thinking about it, it tells me that he's been stabbed through the neck!'

Grant laughed too. 'But didn't we know that before?'

'Get on, get out, you daft sod. Asking me stupid questions – you're giving me a headache.' Grant left the office smiling; Stark's diminished as he returned his gaze to the line drawings at the end of the statement. Jim McIntyre's voice could be heard from the far end of the Incident Room, which niggled Stark as he attempted to concentrate.

'I was office manager for the Marriott murders. Bloody marvellous, you do a good job once and what thanks d'you get? Buggerall, apart from freezing your bollocks off chasing shadows halfway around Nottingham.'

Stark said his piece. 'Will you shut up bloody moaning for once? It'll do you good to get outside and do some real police work for a change. In fact, you can go out with Grant Donaldson now and follow up house-to-house while you're doing nowt.'

Grant was at the door while Jim was still reluctantly fiddling about with his coat. 'And if there aren't many to follow up, have a look at the local doss-houses and Sally Army places, regarding Mr Wagstaff's "tramp in the car" theory.' Stark then instructed Nobby, Charlie, Steph and Ashley to throw up any local prison releases of note and check them out. The remaining detectives in the room were to take three actions per pair and 'work through' them. Stark went into the toilet and discovered Jim at the next urinal. Stark thought it slightly disconcerting how men discussed the strangest of subjects almost nose to nose whilst peeing in the porcelain, staring into each other's eyes whilst being very conscious of not looking towards their neighbour's 'bits' in the process.

'Not looking too good at the moment sir, is it?'

'I beg your pardon? Oh, I see what you mean – the investigation. It'll come in time.'

61

'That's what I keep telling the missus.'

Stark smiled. There was a pause which Jim broke.

'Any chance of me working with Charlie for a change?'

'Why, what's up? What's wrong with Grant?'

'Nowt's wrong with the lad, but you have to be careful what you say all the time. He can be so sensitive.'

At this the toilet door opened and Grant shouted through.

'Are you ready yet Jim, or what?'

Jim drew in his stomach as he pulled up his fly. Stark could sense Jim looking at him.

'Just get on with it, Jim, will you. You're getting worse in your old age.' Then he shouted over his shoulder at Grant, 'Get a grip on him, will you, Grant?'

'Not in there, I'm not!'

Cedar Tree Probation Hostel was on the outskirts of Nottingham and in its time had been the subject of various protests from the local community, via the local rag. Whenever one of its residents had reoffended, there were pleas to have the place shut down.

Now middle-aged, Simon Leivers had a quick smile. He had been running the hostel for almost seven years and was devoted to the rehabilitation of his inmates: he would go to the ends of the earth to help them. But he was nobody's fool and he didn't take bullshit from any of them. There were clear rules to the place and while they were adhered to he was fine; but once they were broken, he came down hard. He was a firm believer that trust works both ways. He wouldn't let them down, but if they let him down, if they were consistently late after curfew, or worse, if they talked about or brought back any evidence that suggested they had reoffended, Simon was on the phone to the police. He had seen them all come and go over the years: the con men, the maniacs, the confused sex offenders. Some, particularly the young sex offenders, could be rehabilitated with skilful guidance and counselling; others merely used or improved on whatever they had learned in prison from other inmates. Overall, he was respected by those under his supervision and police alike.

Simon had known Charlie Carter since he first came to the hostel. He liked him and trusted him to be fair whenever he dealt with those on probation. A slight man, he stood wiping his

62

glasses as he warmly greeted Charlie and Nobby. They chatted generally, then Simon busied himself with the kettle and teacups. As he served the tea, he asked the obvious question: 'Is it a social call then, chaps, or do we have business to attend to?'

Charlie had the rapport and Nobby was quite happy for him to take the lead.

'Well Simon, it's business. I don't know if you've read the papers, but we're working on a murder enquiry.'

'Oh, the solicitor. Yes, I heard it on Radio Nottingham.'

'Yes. Well, as usual, we're doing the rounds for prospective candidates, if you know what I mean.'

'I'm with you. Let me have a guess – Gerry Sanders? Released on parole after a four-year stretch for wounding a young man in a totally unprovoked attack?'

Nobby smiled his reply. 'Got it in one, Simon, however did you guess? Is he in?'

'Should be, yes. What do you intend doing with him?'

'We just want to speak to him, probably back at the nick, unless you can alibi him for yesterday between half-seven and nineish?'

'Let's see, he was in his room, or should have been, but obviously without me being in there with him, which I wasn't, I can't say for definite.'

'Does he share?' asked Charlie.

'Yes. He's in with Pete Brown, who's in for burglary.'

'Sanders is in solely for the wounding, isn't he?'

'Yes. He's not really settled in very well, though he's been here about a month. I must admit I get the feeling he's unhappy about something; he hasn't opened up to any of us yet.'

Simon led the detectives upstairs and into the second room on the right. Gerry lay on his bed, as did Pete. The room was compact and it was as if the two occupants had drawn an imaginary line down the centre, one half the mirror image of the other. Each half consisted of a single bed, a bedside cabinet, a wardrobe and a sink with a mirrored cabinet above it. Gerry and Pete drew on their cigarettes as the party entered the smoke-filled room. The two ex-cons glanced at each other in recognition of the strangers. It wasn't necessary to speak – they were obviously CID.

Simon introduced his guests. 'These gentlemen are from the –'

'CID. We know Simon,' Gerry interrupted. He was a big man,

heavily tattooed, with a 'skinhead' haircut. His face made him appear older than thirty-two. Pete, in contrast, was only twenty and had the features of the 'boy next door'. Any mother would be pleased if her daughter brought him home, assuming she was unaware of his penchant for burglary and theft. Pete sat up.

'Now what are we supposed to have fucking done?'

Gerry tried to calm the volatile youth. 'Cool it, Pete. What can we do for you, gentlemen?' he smiled broadly.

Pete wasn't impressed. 'Fucking pigs,' he mumbled.

Nobby ignored him and spoke directly at Gerry. 'We want to speak to you, Gerry. Nothing heavy like – just about your movements so we can eliminate you for a job yesterday.'

'Here we go. Are you arresting me?'

'Well no, that's not necessary, is it?'

Nobby's bluff was warmly received. He obviously had no reasonable suspicion to arrest him. Gerry lay down on his bed and put his hands behind his head. He stared at the ceiling.

'Go on then, fire away. What time yesterday?'

Charlie chimed in. 'Around about eight o'clock.'

'I was down the boozer, the Red Lion.'

'In the morning, Gerry.'

'Oh Christ, the murder. No way, my pal.' He laughed as he sat up sharply. 'Jesus. Oh no way, I'm afraid not.'

'How do you know about the murder?'

'They do let us listen to the radio here you know, and there's a television – '

Nobby interrupted. 'All right, Gerry, where were you?'

'Exactly where I am right now, only my little peepers were closed. Am I right, Pete?'

Pete nodded at Gerry, refusing to acknowledge the detectives.

Charlie spoke. 'So it isn't you?'

'How astute of you.'

'So you don't mind giving us a written statement at the nick then?'

Gerry jumped to his feet surprisingly quickly. He patted Nobby on the back, fairly hard. 'Of course I don't. Come on then.'

Nobby returned the pat and winked at him. 'There's a good boy.'

Gerry's position was clear. He would be one of the many who would seemingly cooperate and have an alibi, but hardly a cast-iron one. They would take his statement and it would join many others of a similar nature. Gerry stood at the door, hands in pockets, as the detectives quickly searched the sparse room.

Pete stood by the window, arms folded. 'Do you mind. They're personal, those things!'

Charlie reassured him. 'No I don't mind, actually.'

'Well I fucking do!'

Simon spoke, 'Look Pete, if you've got nothing here, you won't mind. I've given them permission to search the room. It's not going to take them long, is it?'

Nobby knelt down and looked under the bed, a brewery ash-tray overflowing with cigarette-ends close to his face, its stale stench of smoke and ash courting his nostrils. He glanced over at young Pete: a rebel without a cause. He smiled to himself; he was just a boy who needed a slap. The only problem was the slap should have come ten years ago, in order to illustrate firmly the boundaries between right and wrong. Charlie opened a series of drawers. 'Do you know about the murder then, Gerry?'

'Only what I heard on the radio. Some geezer has been murdered in a car. That's about it, straight up.'

'How long have you been at the hostel?'

'About three months.'

'Enjoying it?'

'Yeah, bloody wonderful, what do you fucking think?'

'Do you want a brief at the station? We only want an elimination statement and a chat, but it's up to you.'

'No, I'm not bothered.'

'Who's your solicitor?'

'Fenwick and Trueman, in the city.' Charlie made a mental note that it wasn't Johnson & Brown, and continued his search in the grime of the drawers: hygiene was not a priority for these residents. He pulled down the covers of the bed and tentatively lifted the mattress. The urine stains on the mattress increased the stench that wafted up as he disturbed the make-up of the bed for the first in a long time. It wasn't long before they had finished: there was nothing to be found. Nobby looked at Gerry, puffing on a cigarette.

'Are you ready then, Gerry?'

'Yes, sure, but you're way off mark with this one, let me tell you.'

'You've got no worries then, have you?' Charlie smiled.

As the men left, Gerry played to residents who had crowded near the door. They cheered him out of the building. His credibility was heightened by the episode. He knew he wouldn't be charged; he was brimming with confidence.

Stark and Steve Aston gazed at Sarah Deely, at the dark rings beneath her red eyes, underlining the nightmare her life had become. She was chain-smoking and drinking Martinis like they were going out of fashion. She was a mere shell of her former self – no more 'airs and graces'. The hushed conversation included a rather plump detective policewoman, from the Family Support Unit who was close in attendance, looking after her every whim.

Stark had gained Sarah's confidence and was controlling the conversation.

'I know this is upsetting for you, but it is so important to help us find your husband's killer. Tell us who his family are, please, Sarah.' Steve scribbled down the information in his notepad as they went along.

'Well, obviously, we're his family, but he has a father who lives in Torquay – that's Arthur Deely. He lives at 21 Chesterton Villas, in Torquay itself. Um, that's about it, really. He hasn't got any brothers or sisters, and then there's my side of the family.'

'What about friends?'

'He has a lot of friends at work. I know he plays squash with a couple of them. Then there's Roy Prentice – he sees him very occasionally. He works so hard he doesn't have a lot of time to socialize. Sometimes he'll go down for the last drink at the Horse and Groom – he knows the regulars there. But with him being young, he has to do a lot of the duty solicitor work, which means he's by a telephone all night and is invariably out most of the night.'

Stark didn't comment on the fact that she was still using the present tense when talking about James. 'Is that it? Anybody else?'

Sarah stared vacantly; she had started thinking about the question, but had drifted. She shook her head. 'I still can't accept it . . . Nobody would want to do this to us.' She sipped at her drink.

'Is there anybody else who could tell us about him, Sarah?'

'No ... Um, now and then he sometimes sees his old college friends, not very often though.'

'Who are they, Sarah?'

'I doubt if they can help you. They all went to Nottingham Polytechnic together years ago.'

'Are there a lot of them who meet?'

'No, just a handful. There's Stuart, Jonathon, Caroline ... There's a few more, I think. They only meet two or three times a year, all together that is.'

'Do you know their surnames?'

'Stuart, I'm not sure about. Jonathon Stacey. Caroline, um, she got married to one of the group – they were all in the same year at college. Roy Prentice was one of them, have you seen him? Surely he told you?'

'OK, what about James's habits? What did he do on his days off?'

It was unsettling to see Sarah laugh in such circumstances. 'Days off? He used to sit at the table catching up with paperwork most of the time, can't you understand that, Mr Stark?'

'Yes, I'm afraid I do, Sarah, but he must have done other things?'

'Perhaps I am being a bit unfair. It was a bone of contention between us, that's all. He just kept saying it would be worth it in the end. What a load of crap that turned out to be.'

'So what else did he do on his days off?'

'As I've said, he would play squash, or we would go out as a family together, to the park or the castle, anywhere, for a trip out, you know.'

'Would you say he was a solitary sort of person?'

'Solitary? Why d'you ask?' She looked startled.

'Well, the name of your house – Solitude. It's rather an odd name.'

'Oh.' Sarah almost smiled. 'No, that was just a silly joke of his. He was a solicitor. This house is at a high altitude. Solitude was a combination of the two words.'

'Oh, I see ...' Stark looked disappointed. 'And what sort of upbringing did he have?'

'Very good. He never wanted for anything. Spoilt, I suppose you might say. His parents doted on him. His mother died when James was only sixteen; I don't think he ever fully got over it.'

Sarah lapsed into another vacant stare. He wondered whether she would ever get over James's death. He asked Sarah a lot of questions – he wanted to know as much about James as he possibly could. He wanted to get inside the man, and his wife was the best place to start. Eventually there was no avoiding awkward question time.

'It's a horrible thing to have to ask, Sarah, but you are probably aware I've got to ask it. Think carefully before you answer – it may be crucial to the inquiry.' He paused to give added weight to the importance of the question. 'Do you know, or did you have the slightest suspicion, that James was seeing another woman?' He scrutinized Sarah as she answered.

'It had crossed my mind occasionally. What woman doesn't think about it, when she's alone and her husband is late every night from work?'

'Was he seeing somebody?'

'I don't think so, but who ever really knows?'

'Was there anything else apart from him being late that made you think that?'

'No, nothing.'

'Sarah, were you, are you, seeing anybody else?'

Again she laughed. 'No. I'm ... *was* ... very happy!'

'Was James happy?'

'Yes. I think so. Overworked, but happy, yes.' Her voice was choked with emotion.

Stark glanced at the DPW as he asked Sarah the most awkward question of all. 'Did you have a good sex life, Sarah?'

'No, not really. But in my opinion that's only a small part of a marriage. We were both pretty exhausted by the time we got to bed, and with a kiddie running around the house there's little opportunity to do anything during the day.'

Stark thanked her for her time and complimented her on the admirable way she had coped with his questions. She couldn't be bothered to see them out. She lit another cigarette and faded back to her private thoughts, clouded by the contents of her Martini glass.

For the next couple of days, with desperation never far off, Stark and Wagstaff struggled to find a motive. Their team slogged away to get some sort of clue. Scores of enquiries were done by the detectives. Deely's diaries were examined, as was his personnel record at work. His friends and relations were seen. No lover was found, no great enemies, no motive.

It was 7.30 p.m., Wednesday, 9 January. The spate of cold weather continued. The roofs of the terraced houses glistened with frost. Stuart slammed the front door of his mother's house behind him and clambered on to his Harley Davidson. Despite his own scruffy appearance – his long black hair and 'dago' moustache failed to cover the few spots that were present around his mouth and chin – his bike was immaculate. 'If you paid as much attention to yourself as you do that bloody bike, you might get a job,' was a regular gripe his mother would throw at him. As normal, Stuart zipped up his leather bomber jacket and set off towards the Fox and Grapes public house, his bike roaring, giving him a status his personality never could. At twenty-four, Stuart was popular with his motor bike friends, and he had a cheeky grin that was not lost on women.

As he pulled out of the street, he didn't notice the Ford Granada coming round the bottom, and the car followed him as he turned left at the top of the road. The Granada tailed three cars behind the motor cycle, along the main street and out into the less densely populated area of Hucknall. Stuart was oblivious; he was looking forward to his game of pool and pint of mild. When he turned right into the pub car park, the Granada continued past, but turned around in the mouth of the next junction and parked in the entrance of a quarry, with a full view of the pub car park. The driver was prepared to wait.

5

'Prejudice: A vagrant opinion
without visible means of support.'

Ambrose Bierce

Stark sat in his office, toying with Steve Aston's notepad: 'James Deely by Sarah Deely'. He was deflated. He felt they were getting nowhere. He didn't seem able to get a grip on the enquiry. What do you do? You have a man, apparently of good character, who is killed. Nobody has seen him being killed. There appears to be no reason to kill him. Is it a maniac? A psychopath who kills for the sake of it? 'Christ, I hope not,' he muttered under his breath. His desk phone rang.

'DI Stark.'

'Hello.'

Stark smiled. It was Carol. 'Hiya sprite.' He pictured her smiling eyes, framed by the short wispy haircut that gave her the 'pixie' look.

'I'm bored,' she said in the pathetic voice that sought sympathy and attention.

'Why are you bored, spritey?' He peered through the door to ensure none of his detectives could hear him.

'I've got nothing to do. I'm on my own. There's nothing on telly, so I'm bored.'

'Well get out and see somebody then.'

'Like who?'

'I don't know – your mum, my mum, any of the family. What are your friends doing?'

'Wendy's out with Bill; it's his day off. And Rebecca's at the park with the kids.'

Stark glanced at his watch, then at the notepad. Who would want to kill James Deely?

70

'You're not listening to me, are you?'

'Yes, I am. Go to the library or something. Bloody hell, Carol, you don't need me to tell you what to do, do you?'

'When are you coming home?'

'Probably late. I can't very well come home and leave the lads to do it all.'

'Why not? You're the boss.'

'Carol, we've been through this a thousand times, for God's sake.'

'All right! I knew I shouldn't have called you. I know your precious police work is more important than me.'

Stark sighed. 'It's not that, Carol. I'm busy, I haven't got a clue where this enquiry is going and every bogger's on my back. They all want to know why it isn't detected, yet nobody's come up with any better bleeding ideas what to do.'

'Haven't you got any further with it?'

'No. I don't know whether it's some maniac, a tramp sleeping rough in the car or what. I don't know, I just get the feeling it was planned.'

'What is it you used to say when you were tutoring the aides to CID?'

He smiled. 'Go on what you know.'

'There you are then.'

'It's as simple as that, is it?'

'I don't know, but what else is there?'

'Thanks, sprite.'

'My pleasure. I thought it was *me* ringing *you* up for some sympathy!'

'I'm going to have to go, love.' Stark was again torn between the exigencies of both the job and his family.

Carol uttered the words that the wives and loved ones of detectives and policemen are forced to say the world over. 'Oh OK then, see you when I see you.' She had said that a lot lately.

'Bye.'

Stark replaced the receiver. He laughed to himself and shook his head. 'I'm bored,' he mocked Carol's voice, then sighed. 'Go on what you know.'

He looked at Steve's notepad.

Jim McIntyre scoured the area looking for somewhere to park.

There was a definite atmosphere in the car. Jim had said little to Grant on the journey down. It had started to spit with rain, and the view was limited by the haze created by the street lamps, the droplets of rain on the windscreen and the inadequate wipers.

'There's a space over there, look Jim.'

He parked the car and they both scurried over to the large Victorian building that was the Salvation Army hostel. A flea-ridden old tramp was sitting precariously on the stone steps. He greeted them in a drunken drawl that was barely coherent.

'What you fucking bastards . . .' He rolled on the steps, like a seaside puppet clown activated on the insertion of a twenty-pence piece.

The detectives ignored him and entered the dimly lit, seedy world of despair and deprivation that only a few are forced to behold. There was a large foyer, with a tiled floor. A television room was to the left, crowded with derelicts, all focusing in on the comic quiz host, who to most of the observers, in their inebriated state, may as well have been speaking Swahili. To the right was a reception booth, with a young, not-so-down-and-out man in charge of it.

Grant spoke. 'Hello mate, we're from the CID. Where's the bloke in charge?'

'I'll get him for you.' The young man sauntered down a corridor, leaving the two men feeling decidedly vulnerable in this madhouse. In the distance, shouts and swearing could be heard echoing through the rafters. A semi-brawl had started in the television room.

'Ignore it,' Jim whispered out of the corner of his mouth.

The youth returned with a small, balding, bespectacled man wearing a grey shirt with the Salvation Army motto emblazoned on it.

Grant was quick to spot it. 'I now know why the Salvation Army motto is Blood and Fire.'

The Salvation Army superintendent had a soft but reassuring voice and he exuded an air of complete calm. Grant was unsure whether this was due to unfaltering faith in the Lord, or twelve years of working in a doss-house.

'What can I do for you, gentlemen?'

Grant looked beyond him to where the brawl in the TV room was still going on.

72

The superintendent spoke without looking at the disturbance behind him. 'Oh, don't worry about them, they'll be the best of friends in a minute.'

Grant was bemused, but carried on regardless. 'We're working on a murder investigation, and one of our routine enquiries is to check all doss – ' He stopped himself. 'All night shelters, to see if any of the occupants were out at the relevant time.'

'Well, what's the relevant time, my dear boy?' the man smiled.

'Between half-seven and nine on Monday morning, 7 January.' The superintendent took the men into the reception booth and began thumbing through a jotter. He perused the entries for the relevant date and time.

'Let me see . . . There were only two missing from the whole hostel.'

'How many do you have at the hostel?' Grant asked.

'Well, it's peak time now, because it's winter, you see. We have 112 with us at present.'

'How can you be so precise?'

'They are all logged in and out, and we do a physical check on the hour every hour.'

'How do you check them?'

'Well, each resident has his own cubicle, and we have a look in it. You see, if they don't sleep here for three nights, then their cubicle is designated to someone else.' Grant was appalled that all this was happening in a supposedly civilized society, right under peoples' noses, yet no one seemed to care or even to be aware of the situation. Jim was more interested in the facts.

'Who are the two who weren't here then?'

'Jock Pulton and Barry Weir.'

'Are they here now?'

The superintendent glanced through the glass at the TV room; the fighting had ceased. 'Jock was in the TV room about half an hour ago, but I think he's gone up to his cubicle now. He's in 209. I'll take you up.'

'What about Barry Weir?'

'He's not been back since Monday night, but that's not unusual for Barry.'

Grant scribbled down the details of the two men from the jotter: both were in their late fifties. The superintendent led them up the stone staircase, the relentless wails and hacking of phlegm becoming increasingly close with each step. He led them to the landing of the second floor. The lighting seemed barely adequate, but the heat was almost overwhelming and unfortunately seemed to emphasize the smell of sick and urine coming from the vagrants' cubicles. It was a lengthy corridor, the cubicles coloured blue with small numbers stuck on the doors. Grant counted down the numbers as they walked past each one. Eventually they reached 209 at the far end. The superintendent stood aside. 'This is it, gents.'

Grant was unsure whether to knock or not, but decided he would. There was no reply. He knocked again. No reply. Jim pushed at the door, and it swung open gently. A giant of a man was lying on the metal-framed bed, which was matted with grease and grime. Apart from an off-white shirt and multicoloured tank top, he was naked. They were embarrassed to discover the man had an erection. The cubicle might have been better described as a cell. Beside the bed, there was a bureau and a locker, and that was it. There was just enough room for the two detectives to stand in the small space between the locker and the bed. Grant reluctantly pushed the man's shoulder.

Jim spoke. 'Come out, Grant.' He roughly shook the man. *'Come on Jock. Let's have you awake. Come on pal.'*

Jock eventually opened his bulbous, bloodshot eyes, and queried the presence of the two intruders in a broad, almost incomprehensible Glaswegian accent.

'What dyee fackin' want?'

He rose from the bed and struggled into his drab trousers, which stank of excrement. As he pulled them on he fell back on to the bed and sat there, his face blank. He blew through his lips, making a neighing noise. As Jock attempted to fight off his befuddled state, the intoxicants flooding into his brain, causing him to close his eyes, head bowed forward. He shook his head from side to side sharply, his jowls flopping loosely as he did so. Suddenly he stopped his waking routine, sat bolt upright and stared at Jim.

'Who the hell are you?'

'We're from the CID. Are you all right to talk?' As Jim said it, he realized that whatever time of day they spoke to him, his condition would not be much different.

74

'Oh, it's the rozzers, is it? Shit! What in Christ's name have I been doing now, lad?'

Grant sat down next to him on the bed.

'We just want to know where you were on Monday morning, Jock, that's all.'

Jock didn't acknowledge Grant, addressing Jim.

'All I'll say to you is this, lad. If that chickaboo doesna take his fat black arse off my bed we're fighting, dyee understand me now?' Jock stared at Jim. Jim looked at Grant. Unbelievably, this derelict was speaking to an intelligent, honest, useful member of society like he was a dog turd. Grant reverted to the front he had had to display many times. He smiled. He stood up and retired to the door. He could rip the tramp apart with little effort, but he decided to place the murder before his pride. Jim was on his own; it was pointless for Grant to attempt to indulge in any further conversation with the inebriate. Jim sat next to Jock, and then moved away slightly, unable to bear Jock's halitosis.

'About half-seven in the morning, Jock, last Monday. What about it?'

'You're a Scotsman, are you not?'

'I'm a Jock, yes.'

'Where dyee hail from?'

'Edinburgh originally.'

'It's a fine city is Edinburgh.'

'It sure is, Jock. What about Monday then, my pal?'

'Oh Christ man, ma head hurts.'

'I can see that, but try and remember.'

'To be honest with you, lad, I canna remember.'

'You're gonna have to try, so you are.' Grant noticed that Jim had enhanced his previously almost indiscernible Scottish lilt for Jock's benefit. Jock scratched his mess of hair.

'All I can remember is walking doon Mansfield Road, aboot two in the morning, and Christ I remember waking up in some bloody coal shed, whatever it was, in Sneinton. I think that was Monday, sure enough.'

In the car on the way back to the station, Jim seemed in better spirits. Grant, however, felt somewhat peeved that Jock's display of racism had to be witnessed by Jim of all people: he would never have the sense to commend Grant for his professionalism. And then not only was the enquiry seemingly going nowhere, but there was now Barry Weir to see as well as God knew how many other tramps who had been roaming the streets that night and morning.

The noise in the Fox and Grapes was incredible. Heavy rock blared out from the jukebox, the customers had to shout to be heard, and there were loud cries and cheers from the group watching the pool match in the alcove at the end of the room. Most pubs have a layer of smoke hanging in the air; this pub had a layer of air hanging in the smoke. The smoke was mixed, mainly cigarette, but the piquant smell of cannabis joints was all too evident. It was a 'spit and sawdust' pub which a couple of years earlier had been ready for closure before it became a regular for the bikers. Since then it had had the best takings of the region. The pool table and dartboard were the focal points. Apart from these there was little else in the pub other than wooden tables and chairs. The police were aware of accusations from various quarters that cannabis was being smoked in the place, but it was apparent that that was the full extent of the drug abuse. The smoking of cannabis is only a cautionable offence, and, anyway, there was never any trouble with the bikers. Out of all the cult groups they were the best behaved. They were surprisingly mature and in some matters were often a help to the police.

Stuart Millichip had been beaten at pool but sat close to the table and watched his mates' progress. He was puffing on a particularly strong joint. The mixture of his pints of mild and the dope had warmed his mind into a relaxed state: he was at one with himself, and every muscle in his body tingled as he sprawled on the wooden chair. He was beyond intelligent conversation; he would laugh into his pint when he heard others around him laugh, the reason behind the amusement unknown to him. He had got to the state where the ale seemed to brim in his throat and he decided it was time to leave. There would be no 'lock-ins' for him tonight; he had had his quota. All he had to do was guide his machine towards home and collapse on the settee, or his bed if he could make it.

As he staggered to his feet he grunted his farewells and his wave to the crowd was prolonged and exaggerated. The freshness of the cold night air brought a shiver and some relief to his smoke-filled lungs as he began to walk across the car park towards his Harley Davidson. He did not see the Ford Granada now pulling into the far entrance. Stuart's mind was cloudy; he felt a little sick, and swallowed hard to combat it. He paid scant attention to the blurred headlights in front of him. The Granada slowed momentarily. Within seconds its rev counter was in red. The great noise made by the powerful engine stopped Stuart in his tracks and he attempted to focus on the cause of the din. The driver observed him candidly, pausing to take in the moment, contempt coursing through taut veins, malevolence tightening into concentration. No mistakes. Stuart's puzzled expression appeared strangely comical as his befuddled state struggled to ingest the situation. A smile tickled his lips. 'Who's pissing about?'

The driver revved hard and the engine strained to unleash the power. The car covered the thirty yards. Stuart had no time even to take his hands out of his pockets as the vehicle hit him with almighty force. Stuart was thrown into the air, his legs going backwards, pivoting at the waist. He slid up the bonnet and struck his head on the windscreen surround, landing face first on to the tarmac, breaking his neck instantly. He was not dead.

The Granada screeched to a halt at the far end of the car park. The driver wound down the window to reveal a hooded head, simultaneously reversing so that the car was sideways on to Stuart, who lay motionless on the ground, hands still in pockets. Waves of pain seared into his brain, his every fibre squealed in agonizing torment. His eyes flickered sporadically, the only sign of movement in the moribund figure, and a low moan emanated from his lips which turned into a gurgle as vomit raced up his throat and into his mouth. The driver could not be sure that he was dead.

Stuart felt no pain this time as the front tyre crashed into his face, squashing his head as it travelled over, leaving a faint indentation of tyre tread on his cheek. His brain had been compressed and pulped. There was no doubt any more. His left eye had popped out and rested on his cheek. The slaughter was complete.

The screeching of tyres had drawn the attention of a young couple who had just left the pub. They witnessed the latter part of the macabre incident. The Ford Granada left the car park on the far side, its registration plates covered in black cloth and the driver wearing a black hood. The couple were frozen in horror. Then the man ran towards the corpse, hesitantly, stopping some yards away. He grimaced and turned, running as fast as he could back towards the pub. There was a telephone kiosk in the foyer. He shouted to his girlfriend. *'Don't go near him!'*

He fought his way through the crowd, people reacting harshly to being skittled out of the way. He was breathless as he tapped out the three digits.

'Which service do you require, Police, Fire or Ambulance?' The female voice was calm and aloof.

'Ambulance . . . Police! Both the fuckers, you silly cow!' he gasped.

'Thank you. Putting you through.'

6

'A fellow who is always declaring he is no
fool, usually has his suspicions.'

Wilson Mizner

A thousand thoughts clouded David Stark's mind as he approached the turning into the Fox and Grapes' car park. He had
been passed the call only minutes ago. There was no way he
could deal with two murders at once, surely it would have to be
another DI. He turned the corner and parked his car on the road,
both entrances to the car park having been cordoned off. Despite
popular myth, there were no blue lights flashing at the scene;
those were used to get vehicles somewhere, or warn drivers of a
hazard in a road, not to flatten the battery once they had arrived.
The entire scene was lit by floodlights drafted in by the Traffic
Department. Policemen were milling around and all heads
turned as they almost visibly threw the problem at the approaching Detective Inspector Stark. He spoke with a traffic sergeant; his
inspector was elsewhere, dealing with another 'fatal'. Stuart's
body had been removed by the ambulance to the Queens Medical
Centre, where he had been declared 'Dead on Arrival'. A considerable number of Stuart's friends were gathered close to the
entrance of the pub, sitting on a wall. Stark spoke to the grey-
haired traffic sergeant.

'Please tell me it's an accident.'

'Sorry, boss, it appears to be a deliberate act. According to a
couple over there, the car reversed back to finish the job.'

Stark rubbed his chin and stared at the sticky, congealed lump
of blood and God knew what else that revealed where Stuart's
head had been.

'Have you got everybody's details?'

'Oh yes, everybody,' the traffic sergeant said in his experienced way. 'Even the voyeurs who've arrived late for the show.'

'Which couple witnessed the . . .' He had to say it: '. . . murder.'

The sergeant pointed out the pair and Stark approached them. The girl with long blonde hair and leather jacket was crying. The guy seemed older than her, probably mid-thirties, with black hair and a heavy stubble. He seemed close to tears himself. Stark took the couple back inside the pub, out of the cold. They sat in a corner of the now deserted bar. Stark lit up his pipe.

'It's all right love, there was nothing you could have done. We have to make sure we find out exactly what happened. You take your time and try to be brave.' The girl sobbed into her lover's denim jacket. The man spoke.

'I've never seen anything like it, I tell you. Jesus, man, the poor sod.' He shook his head.

'What exactly did you see?'

'The guy, Stuart, was just lying there and the car just like ran over his head, man. I tell you.'

'Did you see how Stuart happened to be lying on the floor?'

'No, but he was groaning. The driver of that car knew exactly what he was doing, he waited, he watched and then he killed Stuart, right in front of us, for Christ's sake!'

'You say "he", did you see him?'

'No, he had a black hood over his face.'

'What about the number of the car?'

'The plates were covered with a cloth. That's what I'm saying – it was intentional.'

'What sort of car was it?'

'A Ford Granada, new style. I'm not sure what colour, though.'

The girl pulled away from her boyfriend and sobbed in anger and grief. 'Tell him Steve, you fucking tell him what Stuart was saying.'

'Tell me what?' Stark was puzzled.

'It's probably nothing.'

'Well, let me be the judge of that one.'

'Stuart was only talking about that solicitor tonight, you know, the one that got killed. You see, Stuart knew him very well; they were mates, they went to college together!'

Stark, Wagstaff and Nobby Clarke sat in the Detective Superintendent's office sipping mugs of coffee. Wagstaff spoke.

'Well, we have two murders in a matter of a couple of days that have a common link. We know Stuart Millichip and James Deely used to hang around in the same gang of friends at college. The question is, do we treat them as separate, or tie them in from the start?'

Stark offered his opinion. 'Well I don't think we can treat them as completely separate, I mean it's a bit coincidental, don't you think? When you consider that we usually only have five or six non-domestic murders a year in the whole of Notts, now we have two associates killed within a couple of days. Very coincidental. I mean, it's not just that they went to the same college – they were in the same year, the same tutorial group and in the same group of friends at the same time. Although you would never know that by looking at them.'

Wagstaff toyed with his handlebar moustache. 'Very true, David. I think the best thing to do is compromise.'

'In what respect?'

'We'll have two separate teams, but also have a third team which investigates any connections or constants between the two persons or murders.'

Stark nodded. 'Sounds good. Can my men be the third team? I know their individual capabilities, whereas I don't those that have been drafted in.'

'I don't see why not.'

Nobby spoke. 'Who decides what is a connection between the two?'

Wagstaff reassured him. 'I will, and in my absence the Incident Room DI will. We can create personal profiles of both victims.'

There was a lull before Stark uttered, 'Is that everything done for tonight?'

'Yes I think so,' Wagstaff replied. 'The post-mortem will be around 11 a.m. tomorrow, and we've got a team of five detectives under the supervision of the Incident Room DI starting us off overnight. The investigation proper will start in the morning. I don't think tonight will yield too much; it's three o'clock now, for heaven's sake. The snatchplan hasn't brought us anything, and Traffic are doing a sweep of the surrounding area for the car. The Incident Room have got strict instructions to contact us at home if anything startling happens. I suggest we try to grab some sleep, and start back at eight o'clock tomorrow morning.'

'You mean today, sir,' Stark smiled.

Dave's mind was awash with waves of sound which faded into the voice of a Radio One DJ. As he lay in bed, eyes closed, his mind whirled, drifting from sleep into the waking drone of the radio. He rolled over and peeped from beneath the covers at the digital read-out – 7.02 a.m. He closed his eyes again and buried his head into the soft, accommodating pillow, languishing in the warmth of the quilt . . . 7.02 a.m. 'Bloody hell!' He sat up, grimacing, squinting. He turned on the light, making his eyes water. He felt hot and sticky, his tiredness had not been chased away and his head throbbed as he staggered out of bed and put on his robe. He collapsed on to the toilet and closed his eyes; he just couldn't wake up. He clumsily went downstairs, slipping on the second to last step, the momentum causing him to burst into the living-room.

'My God, the creature from the lost lagoon,' Carol smiled.

'Why didn't you wake me up?' the creature asked.

'You've got plenty of time. What's the matter with you?'

Christopher and Laura sat transfixed at the television as it pumped out more soporific trivia. David lurched into the kitchen in a trance, facial muscles in a state of collapse. He slapped two strands of bacon out of the sizzling pan between slices of bread and returned upstairs, holding his breakfast loosely in his hands; the thought of using a plate had not entered his mind. He had to get to work quickly; he couldn't be late.

Carol stood, hands on hips, at the bathroom door.

'Well I've seen it all now!'

David had placed the bacon sandwich on the lavatory cistern and had begun to shave, intermittently biting into the bread. Dave, his mouth full of bacon, barked out a garbled reply that Carol interpreted as 'Shut up, I'm late.'

He didn't have time for a full shower but quickly brushed his teeth, washed, and rinsed his head under the shower handset. He dressed hurriedly and shouted farewells as he left via the front door. Carol shouted back.

'Dave.'

He returned to the door.

'Don't I get a kiss?'

He pecked her on the lips, his now tight with irritation, and clambered into the car. He took pot luck as he reversed out of the drive, condensation on the windows hindering his all-round vision. His heart sank as he heard a dull scraping noise; he had caught the offside wheel arch on his perimeter wall. He glanced at the clock: 7.47 a.m.

'Sod it.'

He crashed the gears and sped off, spinning his tyres in temper.

Once at the police station car park, he examined the damage to the car. Dints and scratches – 'Fucking hell!'

Throughout the morning briefing Stark was sullen. He was in a bad mood, he had been a minute late and he had damaged his car – what else could happen? The night-shift detectives had passed on their actions and were instructed to explain their individual results before he would allow them to go home. The Incident Room detective inspector had been Phil Dowty, a balding, wiry man who for some inexplicable reason spoke with a cockney accent, despite never having lived outside Nottingham. He explained how he had visited Mrs Millichip and broken the news to her. He confirmed that both Deely and Millichip had not only attended the same college – Nottingham Polytechnic – but had associated closely together within the same group of friends at the time. Phil listed the college cadre of friends on the whiteboard.

> Jonathon Stacey
> Tracey Sewell
> Caroline Winner
> Mark Winner
> David Seaton
> Roy Prentice

Stark recalled the horrendous meeting he had had with Roy Prentice. As the briefing closed, Charlie shouted to Stark, 'Phone call for you, boss.'

'Cheers Charlie. Eh, did your pervert get locked up?' asked Stark, referring to Jack Reynolds.

'No, he's been bailed, would you believe, to an address out of town.'

'Yes, I would believe it.' He diverted his attention to the phone. 'DI Stark.'

'Roy Prentice here. I shall be at Saville Lodge all morning and I won't go out the house until two of your detectives get here.'

'Hold on a minute – what are you talking about?'

'What am I talking about? What am I talking about, you ask? I'm talking about my life, Inspector, that's all, and I demand protection until this nutter is caught.'

'Obviously you're talking about the murderer of Stuart Millichip.'

'There's no wonder you're a police inspector, is there? Well? What about it?'

'What about what?'

'Protection. It could be any one of us next! This murderer is obviously something to do with the college, with our gang. He's got it in for us. I'm here to tell you.'

'Look, there are more people involved than just yourself. I'll get somebody to come round to see you. Don't worry about security. They'll make the appropriate arrangements for all of you in due course.'

'In due course? Let me tell you, I'm no fool, Inspector, and I think I'm entitled to a bit more than that.'

'You are entitled to the same treatment that everybody else in your position will get, and that's all you're getting. Now good day to you.'

Stark slammed down the phone. 'What a twat. First to complain about the police, and first to want our help. Well fuck him, he can wait!' He spotted Grant walking in the far door. 'Hey! Grant. Did you trace Barry Weir?'

Grant strolled over towards Stark, and sat down next to Ashley. 'Yes. We've not spoken to him, though.'

'Why not?'

'Well, the day before the murder he was a resident in the cells at Central Police Station – overnight and well into the afternoon the following day. He'd been arrested for being drunk and incapable and for criminal damage.'

'Have we double-checked?'

'Of course we have, sir. I've spoken to the officer who dealt with him and checked the custody record personally.'

'Great stuff.' The phone at his side rang.

'DI Stark.'

'Yes, your attitude is typical of the entire police force! I have rights and I'm going to ensure that I get them. My basic right is that my life can be protected by the police when it's in imminent danger!'

'Look, Roy, I've told you that somebody is coming to see you when they can, and you telephoning me every verse end is merely delaying me sorting out who is going to see who. Goodbye.' He replaced the receiver harshly, before leaning back in his chair, raising his clenched fists and roaring loudly. Ashley looked puzzled. 'Are you all right, sir?'

'Never been better. I'm late for work, I prang the car, and Roy Prentice gives me GBH to the ear, but apart from that everything in the garden is rosy. Thank you so much for asking.'

Grant covered the scoop of the phone as he whispered: 'Mr Stark, phone call for you. It's Roy Prentice.'

'Inform him that I have a brilliant solution to all his problems. Tell him to go upstairs, check if the windows are closed and if they're not, to throw his pathetic little body out of one of the fuckers, preferably on to something extremely hard!'

'I'm sorry Mr Prentice, but DI Stark has gone out. Can I take a message . . . ?'

Stark covered his face with his hands in despair before peeping through his fingers at the list of six names on the whiteboard. What had he got into?

Wagstaff looked silly. His portly build and heavy moustache did not go well with the paper overalls he sported within the confines of Nottingham City Hospital mortuary. He sat in a small annexed room with two Scenes of Crime officers and an Exhibits officer, Detective Constable Pete Simpson. Pete had done several post-mortems as Exhibits officer. He had nineteen years' service, to most of which he attributed his now greying hair. He wore glasses and had a kindly face. They all wore ill-fitting paper suits and plastic disposable shoe covers – it was like an Andy Pandy convention.

Eventually the call came to go through the clear plastic doors into the operating room. It was a fairly large room, big enough to accommodate five slabs and a viewing gallery. Stuart's naked body was on the first slab, no doubt the one used the most. In front of the slab was a wooden table and a large, twelve-inch knife. This would be used to dissect all the organs once they were out of the body and on the 'chopping board'. Underneath the table was a sink and flexible tap for rinsing away excess blood and offal whenever necessary. Behind the first table, on the far wall, was a blackboard with body parts printed on the left and blank spaces to be filled in with the weight of heart, brain, spleen, etc.

Professor Disney-Hargreaves entered the room, somewhat theatrically, dressed in a green cotton V-necked T-shirt, green trousers, ankle-length rubber boots, a white full-length plastic apron and surgical gloves. He was a cheerful man of around fifty, with short, straight brown hair and gold-rimmed spectacles. He was ex-public school and spoke with a plum in his mouth. Disney-Hargreaves always commentated on the proceedings, consulting regularly with the senior officer in the case at points of interest. He wasted no time now, and made a large cut to the chest in a V-shape, exposing the sternum and ribcage. The mortician then proceeded to use a surgical hacksaw to take out a piece of the sternum, pull open the ribcage and reveal the organs beneath, swimming in their ocean of blood. Disney-Hargreaves took out the heart and lungs as a whole, slapped them on to the scales, then began to dissect them on the wooden table. He would repeat this with every organ. Wagstaff had never liked post-mortems and had suppressed his nerves by lighting up a cigar as the heart and lungs were juggled into the scales. Pete passed comment in hushed tones. 'You can't smoke in here, boss.'

'Can't I? What do you think I'm doing now, then?' He winked at Pete. 'The Prof doesn't mind. I'm not hurting anybody and anyway, it helps ease the stench. You get on with your writing.'

The mortician assisted the pathologist with the more strenuous activities, like sawing off the top of the skull with a trepan to get the brain out, and folding the face down, away from the skull. Occasionally the Scenes of Crime man would photograph various parts of the dismantled body, with Disney-Hargreaves thrusting a ruler against the part for scale. As the pathologist examined the area of Stuart's throat, he became rather interested: the back of it was very decayed and swollen, extending down the oesophagus. It was the first sign, and it would have to be verified, but it was worth commenting on.

'Mr Wagstaff. Your man could well have acquired immune deficiency syndrome.'

'What does that mean? Oh AIDS. Oh. Bloody hell!'

PC Cox had worked for some seventeen years in the Traffic Department, and was well respected throughout by his peers and supervisors alike. There wasn't much, if anything, that Dick Cox hadn't dealt with in his time and because of his experience and know-how he was an accident investigation man. He was brought in to deal with any major Road Traffic Accidents and Fatals. It was suggested that they be called Major Accident Investigation Men, but of course the initials were perhaps rather too appropriate! Dick telephoned Dave Stark's extension.

'DI Stark.'

'Hello sir. It's Dick Cox here. How are you?'

'Hello Dick, I'm fine. How's Jackie?'

'Still nagging, but otherwise fine, thanks. What about Carol?'

'Similar, you know.'

'Yes, I do. Listen, I've got you the minimum speed the vehicle was travelling at the time the deceased was hit, you know, your murder – Millichip, is it?'

'Wonderful. What was it?'

'Thirty-seven miles an hour.'

'What are your views on that then, Dick?'

'Nothing really. A collision at twenty miles an hour can kill. The car park of the Fox and Grapes is absolutely huge, but even so, to get up to that speed you would have to be giving it some heavy throttle. In a Granada, you wouldn't have much trouble.'

'Fair enough. Anything else, mate?'

'I would say that the car was accelerating at the time of the impact with the deceased, which substantiates the murder allegation.'

'How have you got that, Dick?' Stark scribbled on a note pad as he spoke to his old friend.

'Well, I know we haven't got the offending car, but by looking

87

at the initial impact injuries to his legs, and measuring the height of a Granada bumber – which obviously is the first point of impact – we reckon the bumper was at its usual height. If the car had been braking, the bumper would have been lower to the ground.'

Stark smiled. He didn't have to query Dick but, the AIM men fascinated him. 'Lovely work, Dick. Well done, mate. I don't think there's much forensic on the body from the car.'

'Well, Scenes of Crime will tell you that because of the way he was hit and fell, there's very little, in fact nothing, sir, to be precise. As he's been hit, his legs have been taken from under him, he's slid on to the bonnet and unfortunately his head has hit the windscreen surround, which is one of the hardest parts of a car. Something has to give and it's usually the skull rather than the car!'

Stark became grim, as he contemplated Stuart's head exploding. 'Right, what about car tread?'

'Difficult to say. I would have thought Michelin, but get it verified through Forensic. It will only help you when you've found the car anyway.'

'Yes, possibly. But if it's an unusual make or whatever, it might help us to get the car back.' Stark leaned back in his chair, placing both feet on his desk. He crossed his legs.

'True.'

'Right, thanks very much for your help. Will you do me the relevant statement and shit?'

'It's already done, sir. I'll get it over to you today.'

Stark could tell Dick was smiling by the tone of his voice. 'Great. Will you leave it at the Incident Room if I'm out?'

'Sure. OK then.' Dick replied.

'I'm really impressed with the way you can tell me the speed. How does that work, Dick?'

'Well, we had skid marks left by the offending vehicle, so we did two test marks for comparison at a given speed and then put those figures into the formula.'

'So basically, you would, say, drive a similar car at thirty miles an hour and apply brakes, leaving a skid mark, which would be comparable in length to the one left by the offender?'

'In essence, sir, yes. There is another pedestrian test which I think is less reliable, although they tell me it isn't, but, dependent on whether it is an adult or a child, if you know the point of impact and where the body finishes, it should tell you the speed of the vehicle.'

'That sounds a bit strange.' Stark toyed with the telephone cord and stared at the ceiling as he concentrated on the PC's superior knowledge of the subject.

'It does work. I mean, cleverer people than you and I say it does, mathematicians and scientists, so who are we to argue? But as you know, for a court of law I have to be precise. Where I've got skid marks, I like to use this way. Plus the fact that it bamboozles the barristers for a change.

'It amazes me how you can be so precise. What sort of formula is it, for Christ's sake?'

'Well, if you're asking me, Dave, the basis of it is D squared equals U squared minus 2 a s. Then, transposed for a value of "a", A equals U squared minus V squared over 2 x 5. That should give you the acceleration rate – '

Stark was smiling. 'All right, I get the picture. You lost me at the first minus sign.'

Dick laughed. 'Oh no, you asked me sir! Then by making V squared which equals U squared plus 2 a s. Therefore becoming U equals the square root of V squared plus 2 a s. Now that gives you the speed in metres per second of the actual braking speed of the offending vehicle, so from there – '

'Dick, stop it, stop it, mate, I get the picture. I'd be here all day trying to understand you. I'm very impressed. I'll be in touch. Love to Jackie.'

'See you, sir. All the best.'

Stark muttered to himself. 'The only equation I understand is two ton of car at thirty-seven miles an hour, equals death – '

7

'A cynic is a man who, when he smells flowers, looks around for a coffin.'

H. L. Mencken

Jim drove as Charlie sat almost regally in the passenger seat of the rusting CID car. 'Two old stagers in an old stage,' Charlie had said. Jim appeared to be in fairly high spirits, commenting on a variety of scantily clad young ladies braving the cold in the name of fashion. He spoke again, testing Charlie.

'What do you make of Grant Donaldson, then, Charlie?'

'Bloody hell! Are you obsessed with the lad or what, Jim?'

'No, but you know I've been put with him a lot on this enquiry, and I keep having to bite my tongue.'

Charlie laughed. 'Yes, I know what you mean. Times they are a-changing.'

Jim gave Charlie a sideways look and licked his lips like a python flicking its tongue, sampling the undercurrents. 'There are rumours going round that he's keeping written notes about all racist comments, or what he interprets as such.'

Charlie's petulant sigh was greeted by a glint in Jim's eye.

'You're joking. Mind you, nothing would surprise me nowadays. Surely not Grant, though? So he's going to make the world better for himself and screw everyone else then?'

'Looks like it, Charlie. Course, I'm not saying it's true. I've just heard it, that's all, from a lad that used to work with him.'

Charlie had to check himself. He'd known Jim for years, knew what a troublemaker he was. He'd almost allowed himself to be carried away by gossip. Charlie was only too aware of the DC subculture that can make a man's life hell should they take a dislike to him or distrust him. He had seen a detective sergeant hounded out by his detectives turning against him and hunting in packs, never mind an aide to CID! He spoke.

'Just hold on a minute, Jim. Grant's a good lad; he'll make a good detective, I reckon, given time. All right, his written reports aren't masterpieces, but I'll let you into a little secret, shall I? Neither were mine when I first went on CID, or probably yours either for that matter!'

'I'm not saying he isn't any good. All I'm saying is that I don't trust these bloody spooks. They're troublemakers, paranoid, they should concentrate on their work instead of sagging under the weight of the chips on their shoulders. They want to make the rules up as they go along. You wait and see, there'll be civil war in this country, blacks against whites, and guess who's going to have to sort it out? That's right. Us. There's no wonder they call us pigs, that's what we are – piggies in the middle, every bastard time!'

'Bloody hell, Jim. Take a deep breath, for God's sake. I know what you're trying to say: we're going too far the other way now, but you can't generalize. That's half the problem nowadays – "the pigs this, the niggers that" – who are these people? Every bogger's different, Jim.'

Jim grunted. 'Huh, you're going soft in your old age.'

Charlie smiled and pointed ahead. 'Here it is, Jim, that semi on the left with the green door.'

They pulled into the kerb. As they strolled over to the house, Charlie noticed ultraviolet light coming from an upstairs window. Eventually the door opened. A vision with long blonde hair cascading over her shoulders stood before them, draped in a towel and little else. She was tanned, very tall and athletic-looking.

'Mrs Caroline Winner?'

She looked surprised to see the two ageing, corpulent gentlemen grinning inanely at her on the doorstep. Her voice was deep and sensuous: 'What can I do for you, gentlemen?'

Charlie's mind flashed: I know what you could do for me, madam! 'Good morning,' he said. 'We're from the CID. I wonder if we could have a word with you? It is rather important.'

'Oh well, as you can see I've just come out of the solarium, so you'll have to excuse me for a moment whilst I make myself decent.' Caroline ushered the detectives inside and sat them

91

down in a sparsely furnished room of pastel shades while she ran upstairs.

There was a stony silence between the two men, then Charlie mouthed some words to Jim, pointing at a large bookcase. He got up and whispered to Jim, giggling like a schoolkid.

'The book, you soft prat, near the top corner – *One Hundred Sexual Positions*.'

'Where?' Jim whispered, his face alight and excited.

'There, look.' Charlie stretched towards the book. It was awkwardly placed, high up above a table, and his fingers stroked at the spine in an attempt to grip it.

Caroline breezed into the room, now fully dressed in a tight-fitting woollen dress. 'Sorry about that. What can I do for you gentlemen?'

Charlie turned around to face her, book in hand, eyes wide, a look of abject fear on his face. 'I . . . I was just admiring your literary collection.' He offered a nervous laugh. Jim was loving every minute. Caroline took the book from Charlie and read the title aloud: '*The Origin of Species* – Charles Darwin, I used to have that at school.' Charlie was thankful that he had managed to grab a book off the lower shelf instantaneously, as soon as he heard her voice behind him, but Jim looked cheated. She replaced the book, her hand lingering close to the sex manual. She tapped the book a couple of times with her long nails, her lips pursed as she turned to address the strangers. 'Yes, it is an interesting collection, isn't it? Tea?'

Jim spoke. 'Never let it be said that we would ever refuse such an offer. One sugar each, please.'

'Milk?'

'Yes please.'

When she had gone Jim emphasized his exaggerated laughter by covering his mouth.

'Shut up, you sod, you're like a big soft kid!' Charlie whispered forcefully.

Caroline returned. 'The kettle's boiled, it won't be a minute. I'm afraid Mark's out at the moment; he won't be back until late tonight. He's got housewives' aerobics at the leisure centre. We like to try and keep fit.'

Jim spoke. 'Oh you're fit all right. Nobody could argue with that, my love.' He forced a smile with his nicotine-stained teeth.

92

The comment flew past Caroline simply because never in her wildest nightmares had she contemplated romantic innuendos from a pock-marked, middle-aged DC. 'I'll pour the tea.'

Charlie was first to speak. 'Have you read in the papers about James Deely and Stuart Millichip?'

'Who?'

Charlie began to repeat himself. 'James Deely and Stuart – '

'Oh, from college. Sorry I wasn't thinking. No, I've not heard from them. Let me see, it must be over three months ago now. Why, what's happened?'

'Surely you've seen the papers or the news on the telly?' Jim said.

'No, we never do. It's too depressing. Our lives are too full to bother about such things. What have they done?'

Charlie broke the news. 'They've not done anything, but I'm afraid I have some bad news for you; prepare yourself for a shock. They've been attacked and killed.'

Caroline rested her forehead on her hand, almost closing her fluttering eyelids. 'Oh my God, those poor, poor men – and their wives, well, Stuart wasn't married, but you know what I mean. Officer, do you mind fetching me a glass of water?'

'You have some tea there, Caroline,' offered Jim.

'Of course I have, silly me.' She took hold of her cup momentarily before spilling some of the contents on to the table. She covered her eyes and spoke to herself. 'For God's sake, Caroline, pull yourself together. I really am sorry, gentlemen. I'm usually fine in a crisis, but both of them? Were they together or . . . ?'

Charlie felt that Caroline was being somewhat melodramatic about the news, to say the least. He was curious as to why.

'Well, without being rude, surely it's hardly a crisis, if you don't see them very often?'

'Perhaps you misunderstood me, Inspector . . .' Charlie passed over the mistake in his rank. '. . . but James used to ring at least once a month, though, as I say, it must be three months now. You see we were fairly close, but not *too* close, you understand – I am a married woman. We more or less grew up together, we were the gang – "The Magnificent Eight", we called ourselves, ready to take on all comers.'

Caroline stared into space. She had an annoying habit of inter-mittently shaking her hair back over her head, then stroking it with her hand. Again she exaggerated herself as she snapped back to the present: 'Sorry, I was just thinking about the good times, halcyon days I think you might call them . . . Were they together, then, you know, when they were killed?'

Charlie glanced over to Jim. 'No, they were separate killings. James was stabbed, and Stuart was run over by a car.'

'I can't believe it. Why ever has all this happened, do you think?'

Charlie continued to do most of the talking. 'Well, we were kind of hoping that you could tell us that.'

'Why me? I mean . . .'

'Well, obviously we view it as rather a coincidence that two relatively close college friends are murdered within a couple of days, and being one of the "Magnificent Eight", you may be able to help us.'

'Are you sure that Stuart was murdered? I mean, people are getting killed every day on the roads.'

Jim nodded. 'We are sure, Caroline, believe me. What can you tell us about either of the two men?'

'I take it you'll be talking to all the other members of the gang, then? Surely it can't be connected with us? It's years since we were at college.'

'We will be talking to everyone, rest assured on that one, my love. What were Stuart and James like?'

'Um. I knew James fairly well, Stuart not so well. James was a charming, clever man, everyone loved him. Every so often we have a bit of a reunion, you know, no spouses allowed, apart from mine of course.' She laughed, and became slightly distant as she spoke. 'I must admit, and the others will probably tell you, I had a little soft spot for James, but that was all a long time ago, and I think you'll find that Tracey – Tracey Sewell – had the hots for him at one time too. In fact, I'm not sure they didn't have a little bit of a fling with each other at one time, if you know what I mean. But it's all so long ago now. She still dresses the same as she did then, though. Have you met her?'

They shook their heads.

'Very tight skirts, heavy make-up, attractive still – in her own way, of course. But it doesn't do for us all to be the same, does it?'

Jim spoke. 'I take it you don't get on too well with her, then?'

'Oh yes. No, don't get me wrong. *She* slags *me* off when I'm not around, there's nothing malicious or anything. She's got really tense of late, though, certainly in the last couple of years or so.' Caroline whispered needlessly. 'I think she's got problems at home. He's a very bland sort of person, her husband I mean, a bit dull I should say.'

'What about Stuart, what was he like? Did you have a crush on him?'

'Crikey no. He was a year younger than us, but he was always there, a nice lad really, quite a sportsman you know at college. The girls used to like him, but there was always something a little different about him. He was a very quiet and shy boy really . . . I can't put my finger on it, to be honest with you. He's really gone downhill now, you know. Occasionally I bump into him in town. He speaks, but I've heard he's on drugs and he's always in a group, a right set of jobbos they are, too. Give me the willies, they do.'

Charlie glanced down at his list of names. 'What about David Seaton?'

'What about him? He's quite a nice, respectable bloke, an intellect certainly, perhaps even a little eccentric for a young man, but he wouldn't hurt a fly. I always used to feel a little bit sorry for David. I don't think he had the best of childhoods; his father was a bully. Sometimes he would confide with me and Trace. Are we all under suspicion then? Is that why you're asking me all these questions?'

'Well perhaps suspicion is a bit of a strong word. You are the only people who can give us detailed background about their college days, that's all.'

'Here, you don't think there's going to be another one killed, do you? It might be me.'

Jim smiled his yellow smile. 'I doubt it very much, Caroline. Don't start worrying about that, my love.'

'Oh well, I hope you're right, because if someone murders me after you said it was all right I shall come and haunt you, so there. What else do you want to know?'

'What about Roy Prentice?'

'Now then, you can definitely lock *him* up. Don't say anything to anybody, but I don't like him at all. He's a pain in the you-know-what. He's always moaning about your lot, the government, everybody apart from himself, of course. Strange, he was a

95

good friend of James, and they weren't really alike at all. Odd that, isn't it? You'll have to judge for yourself when you meet these people. You did say you were going to see everybody, didn't you?'

'Yes we did. I suppose it's pointless asking you about Mark because you'll only be biased, being his wife.'

'No. I won't be biased. Mark doesn't like lingering on the past. He comes with me to the get-togethers we have. I think he's a bit jealous of James; still, he won't have to be now, will he? But when you look at Mark you'll see why all the wrinkly housewives fancy him; he's a cracker.' She whispered again. 'A bit thick, but a cracker all the same. Go and see him at the leisure centre.'

'Who else is there?' Charlie asked aloud.

'Jonathon . . . Jonathon Stacey. He's a medical student, soon to take his finals. He's a dish as well. We get on very well together. Tracey always thought we should have been the ones who got married, not Mark and I.' She laughed. 'If you're looking for your killer amongst that lot, you can forget it straight away. Everyone will be upset about the news. I'm surprised nobody's rung me about it.'

'You won't be the only one we ask, Caroline, but can you tell us where you were between eight and nine o'clock in the morning last Monday?'

'In bed.'

'That was quick.'

'Well, I'm a computer programmer and I can work flexi-hours, so I don't have to be at work on a Monday until around half-ten. I can have a lie-in. Mark was at the leisure centre.'

'You can't say that, Caroline. All you can say is that you know he wasn't at home.'

'Well, I don't even know that, to be honest. I was zonked out until ten and was nearly late, believe it or not.'

'Can anybody alibi you for that time?'

'No.'

'What about last night, around eleven?'

'Now I do have an alibi for then.'

'Who?'

'Mark. He had just come in. He stops for an orange juice at the club sometimes, but he got in at around ten-thirty and we sat up watching sport on the telly until about half-twelve.'

'It sounds as if you don't have much of a family life.'

'It suits us. We're both very independent people. I mean, I haven't seen Mark all day today.'

'Have you got a Ford Granada motor vehicle, or do you have access to one?'

'No. Oh, I tell a lie, Mark's sister has one, but we haven't seen her all week, so I don't know if that helps at all?'

Charlie took a witness statement from her, committing her to paper regarding general background and her movements. He also took down her details on a PDF – a Personal Description Form. The two men left, slightly bewildered and intrigued by her behaviour.

Detective Policewoman Stephanie Dawson and Detective Sergeant John 'Nobby' Clarke were made for each other really. OK, so Nobby was an ex-para, a hard man, but Steph knew just how to handle him. She enjoyed his endless attempts to bed her and led him on just enough to keep the game alive. No way would she ever give in to him. It wasn't good practice to sleep with your detective sergeant; it would cause all kinds of problems. And anyway, Steph enjoyed his friendship; she didn't want to jeopardize that. Steph was wearing a well-tailored, clinging dress, which was blood red; her blonde hair stroked her back with every movement. When she leaned forward, Nobby could see her bare breasts almost down to the nipples, the outlines of which were also apparent through the material.

Nobby spoke. 'You know you handle that gear stick very sensually, Stephanie.'

She began to massage the top of the stick as she sped along, purely for Nobby's benefit, and put on a Southern American voice in reply. 'Why thank you all for saying so, sir.'

Nobby reciprocated with a similar accent. 'They're a mighty fine pair of legs you're displaying, little lady.'

Steph giggled, and stroked his knee. 'You really are so kind, saying all those things to a little old country girl who ain't never bin with a real man before.'

'Pleasure's all mine, miss.'

Steph threw a glance at Nobby. 'Has anybody ever told you you're mental, Detective Sergeant Clarke?'

'No, Detective Policewoman Dawson, they haven't. Anyway, you started it. How come you never let me finish it, though?'

'Because it wouldn't do. I've told you a hundred times, Nobby, we can't go to bed because we work together. Never mix business with pleasure.' She shook her head.

'Well, we could be sleeping partners?'

'You never give in, do you?'

'There's absolutely no reason why anybody should know. I'd carry on as usual. I'd still shout at you if you were naughty.'

'I like to do a bit of shouting myself, but it's not while I'm at work, it's usually when there's something hot and stiff being rammed between my legs.' She smiled incorrigibly at Nobby.

'You're a dirty bleeder.'

'It's not a crime to like a bit of cock, is it? Or is it only men who're allowed to enjoy sex?'

'Of course not. You know I like it when you talk dirty anyway.' There was something about a beautiful and articulate woman talking dirty that did strange things to Nobby. 'One day,' he thought to himself. 'One day . . .'

Tracey Sewell was just how Caroline Winner had described her: a very tight, short dress, which made her slim body look younger than her twenty-five years, and heavy make-up that made her face look considerably older. Her bobbed brown hair was like the rest of her at this moment – in a mess. She never had time to make herself look really attractive. In contrast, her husband Gary, now standing in the middle of the living-room, looked a real non-entity: the sort of man who wore woolly pullovers to parties, sipped half-pints and bought Cliff Richard CDs. But his appearance belied his real personality: he was someone without pretensions, someone who always had time for other people, and when he had your confidence, he had an excellent sense of humour. Tracey leaned on his strength of character whenever there were problems. Despite her outwardly abrasive traits, she lacked the inner strength that only Gary could give her. They were both so different, their strengths and weaknesses cancelled each other out. Recently it had been a testing time for them both, but they were struggling on stubbornly. They loved each other dearly, despite the strain they were so obviously under. They had been arguing heatedly for some time.

Tracey had her back to Gary and was staring blankly out of the rear patio doors. She turned quickly, swivelling at the hip, arm outstretched, striking Gary fully in the face. The force of the blow rocked his head to one side. He clenched his teeth and slowly turned his head to face her. 'You bitch, what is the fucking matter with you?'

Tracey's anger was self-evident. She fought the tears that had welled up in her eyes. 'Don't you ever throw Sally in my face again, you bastard. What do you know about it all? Sod all, and you never will know just what it's like, will you?'

Gary shook his head, tight-lipped. He spoke. 'So we've come to this. This is the extent of our relationship, is it? People come through worse, but there are no half measures with you, are there? You've gone fucking crazy.'

Gary caught her hand, in mid-swipe, close to the wrist, and bent it back, causing just enough pain for her to squeal. 'Stop it, Gary. You're hurting me!'

The sudden ringing of the doorbell startled them.

'Sssh. Ignore it,' Tracey ordered as she bent at the waist and peered round the living-room door, along the hall, towards the front door. She could see the outline of a man and a woman fairly clearly behind the frosted double-glazing. The man knocked this time, loudly. They could hear the two strangers laughing, a close laughter that indicated an intimacy between the two. Tracey's heart thumped so much she felt certain the intruders would hear it. Gary whispered, 'This is silly. Go and see what they want.'

The silence was interrupted by the crackling of a police radio.

Tracey jumped. Gary whispered again: 'Bloody hell, it's the police. I'm going to let them in.'

'What the hell do they want? Leave it!'

Gary ignored the comment. He strolled down the hall and opened the door. 'Hello, what can I do for you?'

Nobby showed Gary his warrant card. 'CID. Nothing to worry about. I wonder if we can have a word with you. Is your wife in?'

Gary shrugged his shoulders. 'Sure. You'd better come in.'

Tracey disappeared into the kitchen to make cups of tea for everyone. Once she returned, Nobby explained the reason for their visit. Tracey spoke freely about her college days and seemed to reminisce with a certain conviction; it was as if they had only finished yesterday. Gary interrupted her. 'Tell them about James and the row with Jonathon.' Tracey gave Gary a nasty glance before continuing.

'There isn't a deal to tell, really. Of course, as Gary says, James and Jonathon Stacey didn't get on at all. It was all so petty.' Tracey, who was sitting on the plain black settee, had bronzed, muscular legs that rippled as she crossed them.

Nobby seemed interested in her comment. 'Why didn't they get on, Tracey?'

'It was nothing really; we were only kids and fifty quid was a lot of money in those days.'

Steph looked puzzled. 'I'm not with you.'

Tracey sighed. 'If you don't hear it off me, the others will tell you about it. Jonathon accused James of stealing fifty quid from his jacket pocket when we were at college one day.'

Gary again butted in. 'Tell them about the fight. That's relevant.'

Tracey tutted. 'Will you stop sticking your oar in. I'm quite capable of telling them, thank you very much.' She was terse and obviously annoyed.

'All right. Keep your hair on.' Gary walked over to the patio doors and leaned against the frame, his back to his guests. Tracey continued to explain gossip and scandal which should have been lost in time. Tracey obviously hadn't forgotten a thing; it was as clear as a bell to her.

'There was an almighty row, which ended in Jonathon getting a bit of a good hiding from James. Jonathon never broached the subject again in James's presence, but he often made comments about him when he wasn't there – "No wonder he defends criminals; it takes one to know one!" You know, things like that, silly really.'

'How long ago was it that he made comments like that?' Nobby asked.

Tracey reached over for the ashtray, which she placed on the settee arm, and lit up a cigarette, her hands noticeably shaking as she endeavoured to match flame with tobacco. She took a deep inhalation of smoke and then blew it out in a long sigh. She leaned forward in her seat, resting her elbows on her knees.

'Sorry, what did you say? I was miles away then.' She laughed politely, slightly embarrassed that she had missed the question.

Nobby smiled. 'I said who – no, sorry, you've got me at it now.

Where am I? Oh yes. When did Jon last make such a derogatory comment about James?'

'Oh the last time we met, a couple of months ago. You see, if he saw me in town he would give me a lift home, the same with Caroline too.'

'What did he say? Can you remember?' Nobby immediately regretted tagging 'Can you remember?' on the end, because invariably when you ask that, they can't. This occasion was no different. 'Do you know, I'm afraid I can't. It was something about James, nothing serious, just a bit "sarky", you know.'

'Was it a quip about James as a college student or about him now?'

'I'm sorry, Sergeant. I don't honestly know.'

There was a slight pause and Steph noticed Nobby's gaze being drawn towards the black shadowy cavern at the top of Tracey's legs, revealed by her very short 'pilot' skirt. The local girls called them pilot skirts, because they went all the way up to their 'cockpit'. Gary came and sat next to Tracey on the settee and looked at Nobby, who met his stare with an affable expression, similar to a ten-year-old shoplifter caught for the first time.

'Caroline seems to think that you had a bit of a soft spot for him, James, that is,' Steph said, giving Nobby a sideways glance.

Tracey laughed. 'It's all a long time ago now. He did cut a dashing figure, though, and yes, I did find him attractive.' She took hold of Gary's arm and smiled warmly at him. 'Don't worry darling, you're still the only man in my life.'

Gary squeezed her hand rather too hard. 'I believe you; thousands wouldn't.'

Nobby continued. 'What about Stuart Millichip. What can you tell me about him?'

'I liked Stuart. Shame he didn't get on. He was no dummy, mind you. He just dropped out. Perhaps he had the right idea, who knows?'

There was a pause. Tracey continued, still staring at the carpet, as if reliving the experience. 'You're better talking to David Seaton than me; they were good friends. Now he *is* a weirdo.'

'David Seaton?'

'Yes. He gives me the creeps. I mean, he was never the most popular member of the gang, but he looks really scruffy now, for a teacher I mean. I reckon he's gone a bit funny.'

101

'What do you mean, funny?'

'You know, *funny*. Um, eccentric then, if you like. I don't think hygiene is high on his list of priorities.'

Nobby asked rather a difficult question of Tracey. 'What type of girl were you at college?'

'Oh God. Um. All right I think. Bloody hell. I enjoyed being with the gang, it gave me security. I enjoyed the night times particularly. If I could ever drag them into a disco, I would do. I loved to dance, still do as a matter of fact.'

'Can you think of any reason why anybody would want to kill Stuart or James?'

Tracey shook her head and pursed her lips. 'No. It's all a bit of a mystery, to be honest with you. I hope you'll sort us out with some kind of protection, just in case.'

'Yes, you'll all get fitted with police alarms and panic buttons to give you added security.'

The phone rang. Gary answered it in the hall and returned. 'It's for you Tracey.'

'Excuse me.' She stood up and went into the hall. Nobby and Steph could hear Tracey and Gary's muffled voices. 'Who is it?'

'Work. Some kids have got into the compound again and damaged the cars.' Gary explained.

'Oh, fancy ringing me at home for that.'

Gary mocked Tracey's boss, who was apparently not dissimilar to Buggs Bunny. 'Anything that happens in the compound is your responsibility, Tracey.'

'You're a sarcastic bastard,' she whispered as she took the phone. 'David, hi. Problems I understand . . .'

Whilst Tracey was on the phone, Gary spoke candidly. 'I'm sorry if Tracey seems a little sharp, but we've got quite a bit on our plate. You see, we've had a recent death in the family.'

Nobby made the right noises. 'Oh dear, I'm sorry to hear that.'

'It's some weeks ago, but these things take time. We're both under a lot of strain.'

Steph as ever was to the point. 'Who is it that's died, if you don't mind me asking?'

'No, I don't mind at all. Our little baby, Sally. She wasn't even two yet. A cot death. Change the subject, for God's sake. Don't mention it to her; she'll go up the wall if she knows I've said something. We're trying to get our lives together now.'

102

Nobby and Steph were somewhat relieved when they left the strange vibes of the Sewell household. As they walked down the drive, Nobby surreptitiously pinched Steph's backside, forcing a stifled scream out of her. 'I'll get you for that – sergeant or no sergeant!'

She got into the car and refused to let Nobby in for some time. Once inside, Nobby asked Steph her views.

'What did you make of the Sewells, then?'

She shrugged. 'I just think there's a bit of veiled domestic strife there, that's all. So they're a bit strange. It's not a hanging offence is it? I think you might be a bit distraught if your child had just died, which is exactly what you will be if you pinch my bum in public again.'

'Is it all right to do it in private then?'

Subdivisional Control Rooms are the nerve-centres of everyday police work. The Control Room operators can be police officers or trained civilians. They have a thankless job generally, and because a dozen things are often happening at once and everybody wants it done now, their enthusiasm for the job can often wane. They have to deal with the police radio and the internal and external telephones; they have to prioritize and hand out incoming jobs of various types; they operate two computer terminals for name and vehicle checks; and they enter scores of any kind of updated information on the terminals. Faxes and teleprinters are sent and received, messages compiled and monitored, and so the list goes on. If things go wrong in there, it can ruin a job before it has even started. Misinterpretation, apathy and disinterest are all danger signs that a person has been in the Control Room too long. Unfortunately, officers who, for whatever reason, cannot be trusted to work the streets, are often kept inside out of harm's way, and as there are really very few desk jobs, they often end up in the Control Room. Of course, not all are like this. Some soak up the pressure and are willing to help; only some are disinterested, cynical and feel that everything is too much trouble. It is because of this that the good operators get put upon and used twice as much.

Bill Saint was a cynic. He had been in the Control Room for twelve years; he only had another four to go before his back or

103

knee – he hadn't yet decided which – would go and then so would he, with twenty-six years' service, a big fat medical pension and no more hassle. The Chief Constable would have no objections. For the wages Bill was being paid, the Chief could have two keen probationary PCs out on the streets.

There were six lines available for use on the internal telephone system and all were ringing. The switchboard operator had gone to lunch, thereby diverting all calls through to the Control Room. The civilian operator was ensconced in the teleprinter room and the other policeman had a snooker challenge going during his 'snap time'. Bill was on his own. He had just completed a computer check for an officer and was slowly filling out the details on the log, his ears long since desensitized to the buzzing and ringing. Once he had finished, he stared at the array of lights on the external line. Nine times out of ten such a call would be delegated to a patrolman and the Control Room operator would have very little to do.

'Nottingham Police.'

It was a female voice; she sounded pleasant. 'Oh, hello. I wonder if you could help me. My name is Monica Kendall . . .' Bill started to fill in her details on the message pad. '. . . I work for Green Acres Rest Home and I have an elderly lady here who is obsessed with the thought that she can help you with your murder investigation.'

'What murder investigation? Oh yes. I'm with you. I'll put you through to the Incident Room . . .'

'No, don't bother doing that. All I want is to get it out of her mind, so that she has at least told the police about it. I don't for one moment think that it's of any use whatsoever, but once she's told someone in uniform that should appease her.'

Bill lit up a cigarette and raised his eyes towards the wall clock. It would soon be two o'clock – off duty and next door for a quick bevvy. 'Well, I haven't got any men to send round, so the best thing for you to do is to pop in to the station. Is she mobile?'

'Oh yes. She most certainly is. She has all her faculties, but she keeps going on about messages in the *Evening Post* personal column, which she thinks are connected with the killings. We just want somebody to humour her, that's all. Is there anybody we should ask for?'

'No. Just come to the front desk and somebody there will sort you out if you explain the circumstances to them. OK love?'

'Yes. Thank you very much indeed. Bye.'

Bill screwed up the partly completed message form and threw it expertly into the waste-paper bin across the room. It landed dead centre. He had done it before.

David Stark sat in his office, sipping the mug of steaming coffee that Grant had just brought in for him. He was talking to Carol on the phone.

'What's sad?'

'The entries in the obituaries column in the *Evening Post*. Haven't you seen them?'

'Who are they for?' Dave leaned across and picked up that evening's edition from his side-table. He thumbed through the pages as Carol spoke.

'Stuart Millichip, from his mother. It's very touching.'

Stark found the page and read down it until he saw the message: 'Millichip, Stuart. A mother's heart is broken. Memories are all that's left. I was always proud of you, son, Your Loving Mum, Winifred.'

Dave agreed. 'Yes, it is sad, isn't it?' He began doodling on his blotting-paper as he listened to his wife.

'There aren't any messages in from his friends, I notice,' Carol observed.

'They probably don't even read the *Evening Post*, and anyway, blood's thicker than water. She is his mother, after all.'

'Have you met her yet?'

'No. She was seen on the night by another detective. The Incident Room DI is keeping her posted with events, but nothing's going to bring the lad back, is it? What's happened at home?'

'Nothing really. The usual. I think Christopher had a fight last night.'

'Why, is he bruised or something?'

'No. I saw Mrs Alladice in town and apparently her neighbour's son came in with his face all bruised and grazed and told his mam that our Christopher had done it.'

'Well, if she comes round, tell her, oh I don't know, tell her I'll give her a ring and sort it out, but I would have thought if she was going to come round she would have done so by now.'

'Yes, you're probably right; you usually are.'

'Of course.'

'I'd better get going then. Are you going to be late?'

'Probably, but it won't be too bad. Go to bed if you get tired.'

'I will, don't worry. I've long since stopped waiting up for you, Mr Stark. I just thought I'd ring to tell you about the obituaries and stuff.'

Dave raised his eyeballs towards the ceiling and they bade their farewells. As he wrestled with the telephone cord, he knocked his mug slightly. A stain began to grow on the paper, soaking into the area of the personal column, adjacent to the obituaries, and obliterating all the messages.

8

Interviewer: 'You've been accused of vulgarity.'
Brooks: 'Bullshit!'

Mel Brooks

Grant Donaldson felt far more at ease in the company of Steve Aston than he did with Jim McIntyre. Grant was driving the blue Fiesta to the home of David Seaton, in the Bulwell area of Nottingham. Grant was laughing and joking with the slightly banal Steve, who was most amused by it all but was never quick enough to think of anything funny to say in return. Grant drove past a bus shelter on the right-hand side: there were five people in the queue. He pipped his horn and waved at them. All five instinctively waved in return, before realizing that the others were waving too and perhaps the person in the blue Fiesta wasn't pipping them after all. They sheepishly pulled their hands down to their sides, flushed with embarrassment.

'Who was that?' Steve asked.

'No idea, but it works every time!' Grant thought the whole scenario was terribly funny, whooping and screeching with laughter. Steve slid down the seat, out of view.

It was with some disappointment that they discovered David Seaton was not in but at school, teaching. They spoke to the woman next door, who turned out to be the epitome of the nosy neighbour, one of those women whose voice is charged with a sense of scandal or shock even when talking of the most normal of events. She was a big woman, in her fifties, wearing a smock-type dress and with thin, straggly hair. She stood with her loose-skinned arms folded, relishing the prospect of telling the policeman everything she knew about one David Seaton.

'Oh, I'd got him weighed up – don't you worry about that – as soon as I set eyes on him.'

Grant looked puzzled. 'What d'you mean?'

'Pervert!'

'A pervert? What makes you say that?'

'Listen, young man. I've got fifty-six years on God's earth, and one thing it qualifies me for is knowing when a man is a pervert or not!'

The two men couldn't help but smile at her serious face; she obviously believed every word she was uttering.

'Have you anything that backs up your claim, Mrs . . . ?' Steve asked.

'Mrs Roberts. Oh, I can back it up all right, young man. I'm not one to make allegations without proof. Binoculars!'

Grant was inwardly laughing at the sensational way the woman delivered her lines. He repeated the supposed revelation.

'Binoculars?'

'I've seen him at the windows, upstairs, peering out, usually late at night when the courting couples are outside. Our Glenis put two fingers up at him one night – he just stepped back into the room. Didn't know he could be seen, you see. That showed him all right. She's not backwards at coming forwards, our Glenis. Proof you want is it, how about that then?'

Hardly beyond all reasonable doubt, thought Grant to himself as he winked at Steve. 'Any other strange habits, Mrs Roberts?'

'I've got a list as long as your arm. Curtains drawn morning, noon and night, mysterious bicycle rides with a knapsack on his back and sometimes he doesn't return at all. He's a strange one – I've seen his like afore.'

'What school does he work at, Mrs Roberts?'

'Alderman Sears; he's a history teacher. I don't know how he's survived there all these years. It's a rough school, you know.'

Grant nodded. 'Yes I know it is, love, I used to go there myself.'

'Oh you didn't, did you? No offence meant you understand. Did he teach you then?'

'No, I left before he arrived. Sounds a good job I did. Listen, Mrs Roberts, you've been a great help and we appreciate it. We might see you again, I don't know yet.'

'You drop by any time, you'll get a cup of tea as well. Our Glenis might be in next time. You wait till you see her, you'll be back then, you mark my words.' She waved to the men as they returned to the car.

Grant spoke to Steve. 'What do you reckon then?'

'Take it with a pinch of salt. Shall we go and see Roy Prentice?'

'Yes, let's get it over with.'

The killer sat in an armchair, staring vacantly into space. Escape from the predicament seemed elusive: determination to see it all through was the lifeline that offered vague calm in a sea of doubt, reproach and hatred. The murderer spoke through gritted teeth. 'I must keep going. I promised, and I must see it through!' The voice was hoarse and gravelly, the result of too many cigarettes smoked in anguish as the mind's eye played back the torrid images of murder destined to haunt the brain until death itself would steal them from the killer's brain. Rising from the armchair, the criminal stood at the window, staring out. An old couple walked by arm in arm, past the group of small children who were playing with a ball in the street. It wasn't over yet, but then would it ever be over? A Panda car turned round the corner, causing the killer to drop the curtain and return to relative normality, to continue the façade.

Grant sat in the comfortable armchair of the staff room of Saville Lodge Community Home. He leaned back and crossed his legs rather elegantly, sipping at his mug of tea with some aplomb and letting the excited voice of Roy Prentice wash over him. Steve was perched on the edge of his seat, a most concerned look on his face. He had been hooked, and now Prentice was playing with him before trying to land him.

'It's taken you two hours to get to see me. Where the bloody hell have you been?'

Steve stammered through an answer only to be interrupted. 'Well, we had to see other people and – '

'Fine. That's great. Ring up the *Evening Post*. Tell them to write that in my obituary: 'Sorry, but the police had to see other people'. I could have been killed. Anyway you're here now, so I can rest. Are you armed?'

Grant spoke. 'I'm not being funny, Mr Prentice, but what the hell are you talking about?'

'You're here as my protection, aren't you?'

'No, we are not. We're here investigating a murder. There will be a man from Crime Prevention coming round later to fit some alarms at your place of work and at home.'

'You what! This is typical. This is because of who I am, isn't it? Political views should mean nothing to the police. You're supposed to be impartial.'

Steve attempted a conciliatory response. 'Listen Mr Prentice, I'm sorry that you're upset. We can't offer twenty-four-hour protection – '

'You're sorry!' He laughed mockingly. 'You're sorry! That's rich that is, I've heard it all now.'

'It isn't definite that the two murders are connected. All the uniformed patrols are informed of the situation, and whenever they are available they will perform high-profile policing in the designated target areas.'

'What a load of shit!'

Steve was offended. 'No it isn't. It's far better to have a visible deterrent than a surreptitious one, I assure you.'

Prentice sighed. 'Sure. Listen, you might be able to fob off the general public with this sort of crap, but I know exactly what's happening, don't you worry about that, and I assure you that you will regret it.'

Grant remained unconcerned. 'So what is it you want us to do, then?'

'I want two armed police officers with me twenty-four hours a day. That's what I want. Do I have to spell it out to you? Do you want me to do your job for you?'

Grant enlightened him. 'There's no way we can undertake such a project, bearing in mind that policemen don't work twenty-four hours a day – they would be working shifts. And it isn't just a question of yourself. There are about half a dozen other people who would want the same protection. What if the murderer isn't caught for a year? His mission might be completed now with no more killings. It's not unusual for murder enquiries of this sort to drag out for months, even years. Believe me, we're doing the best for all involved.'

Prentice smiled sarcastically and muttered. 'Bounty bar.'

Grant nodded; he had Prentice weighed up. Steve hadn't heard the expression before. 'What do you mean, Bounty bar?'

Grant interrupted. 'Black on the outside, white on the inside, that's right, isn't it, Mr Prentice?'

'You said it, brother.'

'And what do you know about being black? Don't you consider that a racist comment?'

'I do more to help the black community than your sort ever will. How can you turn your Babylon back on your brothers? They have rights which you destroy. You make me sick. You're just another pawn black boy, a puppet of the Establishment, the State police. If you expect me to cooperate, you can bollocks! What about the proletariat? We're just forgotten, are we? Trodden over by the jackboots of fascism, of which, like it or not, you brother, are a follower.'

Grant smiled; it was pointless going into this. They were supposed to be here to conduct a murder enquiry. There was a lull. Prentice fished around in his desk drawer, carelessly leaving it open. He spoke, his attitude apparently changed.

'So, what can I do for you, officers?'

Steve was a little taken aback after Prentice's political soap-boxing. 'We want to know what you can tell us about Stuart Millichip and James Deely.'

'Well, Stuart is a bit of a mystery to me. I haven't seen him at all since college. He was a bit of a loner then, but he didn't fall out with anybody. He was pretty ineffectual. He came from a working-class background. He was OK.'

'What about James Deely?' Grant asked.

'I came across James in my professional capacity. If any of my boys were in trouble with the law, we would use James as their solicitor. Occasionally, we'd have a drink and a chat over lunch – on him, of course. He was a good man, who fought for real justice. He was genuinely interested in why the boys had gone off the rails.'

'Would you say you knew James well?'

'Fairly well. And in answer to your next question, no, I can't think of anybody who would want to kill him.'

'What about at college?'

'Oh, I'm with you. Sure, James and Jonathon Stacey weren't the best of friends. Don't ask me what it was about, because I don't know, but I hardly think it can be anything to do with this.'

'What about his love life at college?' Grant went on.

111

'Now then, how long have you got?' Prentice almost smiled. 'Let's say he enjoyed female company.'

'Anybody in your group of friends?'

'Well Tracey Sewell was one of his conquests, and although he would never admit it, I thought he had a thing with Caroline, but don't quote me on that.'

'What about Stuart? Was he involved with women?'

'No. He'd just started getting involved with motor cycles. They were his love. If he did have any flings, I didn't know about them, let's put it that way.'

Prentice had become far more affable and answered all the questions readily and with some conviction, but Grant was suspicious of what had caused the change of tack. Perhaps it had been the accusation of racism? Anyway, other than James's alleged assignations with both Tracey and Caroline, there was little he told them that they hadn't already known.

As the detectives stood to leave, Prentice was most polite.

'If there is anything else you want from me, don't hesitate to ask. I shall be in for the rest of the day – I'll only nip across the road to get a Bounty bar or something.' He was smiling, one arm across his chest, the other displaying an erect middle finger at Grant. Grant walked over and looked him straight in the face.

'The only thing I want to say to you, you pretentious, misguided, fucking idiot, is that, sure, you have rights, but so do I, and one of them is not to be spoken to like a piece of dog shit purely because I play by the rules and you fucking don't. You, as it happens, make me want to vomit. You slag the police off and then as soon as there's a threat to you, you come squirming up to us, asking for help. You haven't got a clue what we do or how we work. Your estimation of us is pure conjecture backed up with propaganda shit! So, you lock up all your doors and hide under the bed, and if you need us, give us a call.' Grant gave a clenched-fist salute. 'All right, brother!' he mocked.

After they had left, Prentice turned sharply to his desk drawer and turned off the miniature tape recorder. 'Gotcha!'

'I don't think he's available at the moment. Just let me check for you.'

The young woman reached for the telephone and Stark turned away from the reception desk of the Queens Medical Centre,

112

head bowed, hands in pockets. He tutted and shook his head. Ashley Stevens asked what the matter was.

'I'm just a bit disgruntled that every time I try to contact somebody, he isn't available, that's all.'

'A pig that's lost its voice.'

'What are you talking about, Ash?'

'You're feeling like a pig that's lost its voice.'

'You what?'

'Disgruntled. That's what a pig is that's lost its voice – disgruntled.'

Stark sighed. 'You prat.'

There was a shout from the nearby doors of the Accident and Emergency Room. It was a buxom black nursing Sister.

'Christ, I wouldn't want to tangle with her on a dark night,' Stark whispered.

She spoke with a Jamaican twang. 'Dr Stacey will be with you as soon as he can, if you can wait a few minutes. He is due to go off duty shortly.'

Stark nodded. 'Yes, OK. We'll wait out here then, thank you.'

The Sister disappeared. 'And don't call me shortly,' Stark whispered. He perused the people sitting in the waiting area: coughs and splutters; a couple of drunks, heads lolled back, their gaping mouths rasping; the walking wounded, displaying an array of cuts and crude self-made bandages.

Ashley strolled over to the drink dispenser and studied its operating instructions. As he did, he felt a nip on his backside. He turned round sharply. Deep-blue eyes gazed at him vivaciously.

Ashley's face lit up. 'Hello, fancy seeing you here.'

'Well, you did know I was a nurse, so it's hardly surprising, is it?'

He smiled. 'No, I suppose it isn't really.'

'You're a policeman, aren't you?'

'However did you guess?'

'It's obvious, even if you did tell me you were an insurance broker.'

'I didn't then?'

'Oh yes you did. Three weeks ago, at Blitz's nightclub.'

'I know, how could I forget it?'

'We all know it's like a CID convention in there. Why did you tell me porkies?'

'I don't know. I suppose it's because it saves a lot of endless questions about the job, that's all.'

'Why didn't you give me a ring?'

'I lost your number, what is it?'

'It's 367 4557.'

Ashley scribbled it down in his diary. 'I'm sorry, what's your name again?'

'Sharon. God, you weren't that drunk. In fact, I know for a fact you weren't that drunk!' A wicked smile tickled her lips. 'And if you were, I hope you're that drunk again next time we meet.'

Ashley returned the smile. 'I will definitely give you a call. I was kicking myself for losing your number, but like an idiot, I just couldn't remember your name.'

The doors opened and a doctor shouted to Ashley.

'Hello, I'm Dr Stacey. Did you want me?'

Ashley glanced over at Stark, who was observing the scene close by with a wry smile. Ash spoke. 'Yes we do.' He turned to Sharon. 'I'm going to have to go, Sharon. I'll give you a bell.'

'You make sure you do.'

Stacey wore a white waist-length cotton jacket with cheap pens sticking out of the breast pocket. He was dark-haired, dark-skinned, and beneath his trimmed moustache had a ready smile. Stark produced his identification and explained the reason for their visit. Stacey's manner was casual and he was easy to talk to.

'I've just finished. We'll go and find an annexe room, shall we?'

Jonathon strode before them down endless corridors. He was fairly tall, not quite six foot. Mid-twenties, Stark supposed. At an open door he paused. 'This'll do.' He winked at Ashley. 'Nice girl, young Sharon, isn't she?'

Ash laughed. 'Very nice.'

'Now then, I take it you want to talk about the murders. Tragic, isn't it?'

Stark took over. 'Yes, it is.'

'I saw James Deely in the mortuary, you know. I nearly fell over when they wheeled him in. I'd just nipped in for some toxicology bags, and there he was. Quite horrendous when it's a mate of yours.'

Stark asked him where he had been at the relevant times.

'When James was killed I must have been at the hospital, if I

114

remember correctly. Although, to be truthful, I was on call, so I would probably have been skiving somewhere.'

'Can anybody corroborate that, Jonathon?' Stark asked.

'Um, I don't know to be honest. Various people saw me, but whether they could put a time to it, I don't know.'

At Jonathon's dictation Ashley wrote down a list of possibles who might have seen him at the time of the murder.

'What about when Stuart Millichip was murdered?' Stark continued.

'I was in the postgraduate library.'

'Who with?'

'Nobody. I was on my own, and before you ask, no I can't remember who else was there.'

'Well, who was at the desk?'

'I think June was . . . Yes, it would have been June's turn to be on afternoons in there.'

'Is she on duty now?'

'Let's see . . . She'll be on afternoons today, yes.'

'Times must be changing. I knew a couple of junior doctors who would have been out socializing at ten-thirty every night, not studying in the library,' Stark observed.

Jonathon crossed his legs and lit up a cigarette.

'You mustn't generalize. No, I've a lot of catching up to do for that very reason, so I'm trying to discipline myself.'

Stark looked at the tobacco stick. 'It's bad for your health, you know.'

'The amount of people who come through this place and the amount of ailments they die from, smoking's just another one of them to me, another statistic. Statistics can say anything – like the government figures for drink-driving. Twenty-five per cent of all accidents involve drink, but that means that seventy-five per cent don't, so it's safer odds to drink and drive?' He smiled. 'I'm only being facetious.'

'That's very good,' Stark said. 'But to go back to the murders, have you any theories or ideas?'

'Not really. It's all very strange. I've been racking my brains trying to see a connection, other than the fact that we were all mates, particularly in view of the fact that one of us could be next. I'm trying to work out if it could be me.'

115

'Just tell us what you can remember about your college days – the things that mattered to you, that have stuck in your mind.'

'The people themselves, really. David Seaton being a bit of a loner. Stuart Millichip was quite a good mate of his. He was into motor bikes and eventually dropped out. Roy Prentice and his socialist views. James Deely and his bonking exploits. He was a bit of competition to me, old James was, and of course there were Caroline and Tracey, both attractive women. James had a bit of a play about with them, I think.'

'Did you?'

'I'd be a liar if I said no. One or two of us did at one time or another, even bloody Roy Prentice had a bit of a look at Caroline, you know. They were just kids. I was a bit older than them, but when in Rome . . .'

Stark pondered. Strange that Jonathon hadn't mentioned the rift over the stolen £50. He would put that on hold for now. They seemed to be getting nowhere. Perhaps there wasn't a connection, perhaps it was all a fluke. No way. He was almost thinking out loud as he asked Jonathon his next question.

'Why now? What has happened after all this time that could be connected with college?'

Jonathon wore a broad grin, his brow furrowed. 'Don't ask me. I'm afraid that's your problem. You do have my hearty good wishes, though, in your quest. Drop by any time if you think I could help you.' Jonathon stood and shook the hands of both men. He bade them farewell.

Stark and Ashley had a stroll round to the Postgraduate Centre while they were in the hospital complex. It was a dry night and it looked as though a frost would be setting in. Ashley asked Stark what he thought about Stacey.

'I don't know. It's difficult to say. I don't think he's all he tries to portray.'

'In what way?'

'I think he's a bit of a good-time boy, and I'm not sure I believe this bullshit about being in the library.'

'Well, we'll soon find out, but I suppose he could be right. If he has been going out too much, then he would have to try and catch up late at night.'

Stark nodded. 'Strange he didn't mention the £50 argument.

Mind you, he must know that we're looking for motives. Still, it doesn't give him one for Stuart, does it?'

The two detectives stopped at the junction. 'Now then, which one is it? I think it's that small building over there, Ashley.'

Once at the library Stark introduced himself and Ashley to June Clifford, the library attendant. June had wide-rimmed, ornate spectacles and frizzy hair. In her turquoise woollen top and old-fashioned bra (Stark surmised) her breasts looked pointed. Stark explained the reason for his visit. June was positive. 'I know for definite that Jonathon Stacey was here, because funnily enough, he and I were talking about it only last night.' She fingered her gold chain as she spoke.

'So you're definite that Jonathon was in here?'

'Yes.'

'Anybody else?'

'No, it was deserted apart from him.'

The swing doors of the police station bar burst open and Stark's men marched to the counter in quick time. Nobby muscled his way to the front, shouting over his shoulder. 'The gaffer's gone for a pee, but he's given me a tenner to get you all a drink.'

Cries of 'Fine fellow,' and 'What a star,' greeted the announcement. Nobby distributed the drinks and the men formed two circles of conversation.

Ashley looked drawn. 'I'm knackered. How about you, Grant?'

'Not too bad really. Are you going down to the place of no return tonight? That infamous nightclub?'

'Blitz's? I don't know. As I say, I'm a bit cream-crackered.'

Nobby spoke. 'Chief Inspector Turley came into the office today.'

'Oh yes, what did he want?' Charlie asked.

Nobby laughed. 'Very important job. Health and Safety at Work inspection.' He mocked Turley's mousy voice. 'Oh this telephone cable's a bit long . . . I don't like it. Oh dear me, these chairs should be pushed under the desks for extra safety . . .'

Charlie shook his head. 'Bloody hell, how ever does he cope with the pressure?'

'You know, when I was in the army – '

'Here we go,' Ash interrupted Nobby.

117

'No, hear me out. When I was in the army, you were given a job to do as a private, at which time you couldn't be a corporal, but by working hard you eventually developed the nous to become a corporal. You couldn't do the job of sergeant but, again, after so long, you learned the ways and, yes, you could do that job, you got promoted to sergeant, and so on and so forth. But in this job, you look at blokes like Turley and you think to yourself, could I do his job now? And the answer has got to be yes.'

Ashley started: 'Yes, you're – '

'No, let me finish. But the burning question is, could Turley do my job or your lads' jobs? And we all know what the answer to that is, don't we?'

Charlie was in a benevolent mood. 'Yes, very true. Not all of them are like that, though. I mean Turley is an administration chief inspector. What the hell does the man do all day?'

'Christ knows,' said Nobby. 'But I know one thing: it ain't the crap we have to deal with.'

'Has Turley ever been on CID?' Ashley enquired.

Charlie shook his head vehemently. 'No way. He did an aide years ago, but he was bleeding useless. He didn't stop on.'

Grant spoke up. 'He was moaning to DI Stark the other week that every time he walked past the office we were sat drinking tea, doing nothing.'

Ashley was incensed. 'You're joking!'

Nobby confirmed the rumour. 'He's right.'

'Christ all-bleeding-mighty, that makes me sick. What does he know about being a detective? Does he see us at midnight when we've been on since eight that morning? Where the bloody hell's he? Tucked up in bed after getting home at four o'clock! What a prat! What did Stark say to him?'

Nobby explained to the men the way Stark had used the intricacies of supervisory debate.

'He told him to fuck off!'

The men laughed. 'Good old Stark.'

Stark came into the bar with his men's laughter ringing in his ears. Nobby grunted out of the corner of his mouth. 'Here's Stark, keep shtum.'

Stark picked up his glass of lager from the bar and joined Steve Aston, who was engaged in conversation with Steph. Jim McIntyre was listening in.

'Yes, but as police officers we're never going to be made redundant, are we?'

'You never know, Steve, the way inventions and technology are going.'

Stark changed tack. 'Charlie, who would you put your money on for our murders?'

'Bloody hell, it's too early to say. But if we are having a guessing game, I'll have a tenner on David Seaton.'

Jim was sceptical. 'Nobody's spoken to him yet.'

'I know, but it's got to be a weirdo and so far he fits the bill.'

Steph commented. 'Talking of weirdos, Tracey Sewell seems a bit strange to me. There's definitely something wrong there.'

Grant chipped in. 'I hope to God it's Roy Prentice, because I want to be the bloke that nicks him if it is!' The memory prompted him to say, 'Eh, Steve, did you do a full pocketbook entry about his aggressive attitude?'

'Yes, but I don't see the point, to be honest with you.'

'As long as you have, that's all. I've met his sort before. I don't trust the pillock.'

Nobby had a guess. 'I'll put my money on Jonathon Stacey. He sounds a bit too clever for me, and he's the only one with an actual grudge against James Deely.'

Steve didn't agree. 'Do you really think that he would kill somebody for fifty quid?'

'Steve, people commit murder for a fiver, never mind fifty quid! Who knows? There may be more to it than that.'

'True, but what about Stuart Millichip? Where does he come into it?'

'I don't know. We're only guessing. I mean, if we knew for definite, we'd be out arresting him, wouldn't we?'

Jim gave his considered opinion. 'I don't think it's any of them. I think it's a fluke. More importantly, though, boss, what do *you* think?'

Stark agreed with Nobby. 'If we knew who it was, Jim, they'd be in the cells, mate. It'll come. It's early days yet.'

The speculation continued. As the night wore on, Nobby sidled round to be close to Steph. When they went round the sliding screen partition to put something on the jukebox, Nobby asked his regular question. 'Have you got your kit on today then, Steph?'

She smiled seductively. 'Have a feel.'

Nobby stroked her upper thigh; it was hard and shapely and he felt the strand of lingerie that confirmed that, yes indeed, she did have her 'kit' on. 'Steph, you're evil. You know that, don't you?'

She caressed Nobby's muscular backside. 'Have you got your undies on?'

'Steph, why don't we sneak off? We can leave separately and I'll meet you back at my place.'

She tickled him under his chiselled chin. 'I've told you, Sergeant.' She exaggeratedly mouthed the words. 'No!'

Ashley and Grant had decided that Blitz's nightclub needed a visit. Jim McIntyre had followed them and asked if he could come too. Grudgingly, they had agreed. Blitz's was renowned as one of the best nightclubs in the Midlands. Once inside, the visitor could behold the most incredible light display, and the music was fantastic. Blitz's was also known for ladies of a more mature age attending for a 'good time'. On this particular night it was local knowledge that scores of policemen, mainly detectives, would be in attendance. And everyone loves a policeman, don't they? It was a quarter to twelve and the dance floor was already crowded with women cavorting and gyrating to the beat of the music. Ashley, Grant and Jim fought their way to the bar and Ashley shouted to his colleagues, 'What do you want?'

Grant had a Coke, Jim a beer, and the three moved slightly away from the bar. They said little as each surveyed the scene. An array of women filed past them, some absolute dragons, some very nice and every once in a while, a stunner. The small talk of the three men consisted mainly of nodding at various women. After so long, Grant made a suggestion. 'Shall we have a walk around?'

'Yes, OK,' Ash agreed.

All around the room was a balcony where couples could go in search of privacy, and lechers to spy potential prey. At Blitz's it was usually unnecessary to have much plan of attack when chatting to ladies; the good thing about the place was the un-pretentious and honest way most behaved. Unlike some night-clubs, where the customers are too busy posing, Blitz's clientele were straight to the point, and if one fancied the other it was usually only a matter of time before they were leaving to have sex somewhere. From the balcony it was evident that most of the people walked round the perimeter of the dance floor for some considerable time, looking for that smile or that hint of a chance. Ashley had seen his: a group of ten women all together.

They stopped. 'What d'you reckon, Grant?'

'Let's go for it!' They both stared at Jim – he was a problem. Still, if he got a 'piss off' tablet, that was his hard luck; he would have to swallow it. The three wise men approached the individuals they had chosen. A clean sweep. They sauntered on to the dance floor; it was smoochy time. Ashley had chosen a stunner: long blonde hair, tanned complexion, slim, blue eyes, long eyelashes. As they danced, they surveyed each other's trophies. Jim's wasn't too bad, a woman of around forty, slim, brunette, quite presentable really. Grant's was a bit of a tart: late thirties, blonde, in a tight-fitting leopard-skin minidress and heavy mascara. Ashley could see the outline of a butterfly tattoo on her shoulder. He winced. Jim was dancing a bit at a distance from the woman he was with, who assured him her name was Sheila. 'How d'you get down here tonight then, love?' he asked her.

'Taxi, why? Have you got a car? I don't live far.'

Jim couldn't believe his luck. He hugged her closer towards him.

Grant had chosen his woman purposefully: she looked a slag, and who was he to be fussy? There would be no messing about. They would sleep with each other, both asking for nothing but a good time.

The woman had a high-pitched voice: 'I've seen you here before, I think.'

'Yes, you have my love.'

'I fancied you then, but it's not easy for a woman to get herself noticed.'

'Well I noticed you eventually, that's the main thing.'

The woman rhythmically ground the area of her pubic bone into Grant. He put his hand on her backside and held her on to him rubbing up and down her, exciting himself and her as well.

Ashley always chose the more attractive women. He had a whole host of women he could contact if he wanted some company, so an occasional refusal was of little consequence. The only drawback seemed to be that the more attractive woman often wanted a couple of meetings before dropping her knickers. This one seemed OK, though he could hardly hear her with the music being so loud.

'Are you a copper?'

'No. What makes you ask that?'

'You look like one, that's all.'

'I don't know if that's a compliment or not.'

'Take it as a compliment. What do you do for a living then?'

'I'm a gynaecologist.'

'Get away with you.'

'OK, I'm not, but you did ask.'

'Are you really? No, you can't be.'

'All right then, I'm not.'

'A gynaecologist! My mate's got a problem in that area. You'll have to have a word with her.'

'I never mix business with pleasure,' he smiled.

'Here hang on a minute, in that case . . .'

As the music faded into the next song, Ashley suggested to his woman that they go and have a drink and a sit-down. The attractive blonde returned to her seat and Ashley queued at the bar which by now was three deep.

Suddenly, he felt a tap on his shoulder, and he turned round sharply.

'Hello, Ashley.'

It was Sharon.

'Hello love, fancy seeing you here.'

'Yes. Are you on your own?'

'Sort of. I'm just having a chat with a young lady, though.'

'That's what they call it, is it? A chat?'

'Well you know how it is. You've got to keep your hand in, haven't you? If you pardon the expression.' Sharon laughed. Ashley returned the question, glancing at the barman, who was still ignoring him. 'Are you on your own then, Sharon?'

'Unfortunately no, but I can get rid – ' She stopped speaking quickly as her escort arrived next to her. 'Oh Ashley, can I introduce you, this is – '

Ashley beat her to it. 'Jonathon Stacey. We meet again.'

Jonathon appeared embarrassed. 'Hello, fancy seeing you here.'

'Funnily enough, we've just been through all that.'

'Oh, right.' There was a pause.

122

'I take it you're not studying tonight then, Jonathon?'

'No, er, not tonight. You know how it is – the brain can only take so much.' He turned to Sharon. 'Are you coming, Sharon?'

'Yes, OK.'

'Perhaps see you again, then,' he said to Ashley as he led Sharon off by the hand. Sharon let her other hand hang loosely over Ashley's leg and stroked up his thigh and over his bulge. She winked as they parted company. Ashley returned to his newly acquired female for the night, smiling to himself.

9

'Contraceptives should be worn on every conceivable occasion.'

Spike Milligan

The double doors of Nottingham Police Station led into a foyer that varied from shabby to scruffy, depending on who had passed through it that day. Invariably, old newspapers, scraps of paper and fag-ends littered the dingy, puke-orange carpet. At 9 a.m. it was still fairly clean and tidy. A somewhat bizarre mural decorated the left-hand wall, a notice-board festooned with crime prevention leaflets facing it to the right. The counter was protected by a glass partition which had a sliding panel in it, and to the right of this was a Perspex bubble shielding a telephone. A handwritten notice pinned to the wood instructed: WHEN COUNTER UNATTENDED PLEASE USE TELEPHONE.

Stark considered the foyer telephone a disgrace. It was a sad indictment of society's decline that members of the public were treated in this manner by the police who served them. The idea was part, no doubt, of 'value for money' policing. Why have one officer in the Control Room and one officer employed at the counter when the installation of a telephone could halve the cost? People came to the police station to get a service, at least to set eyes on a human being. They didn't come to speak into a bit of plastic to some faceless person who might as well be the cleaner!

Roy Prentice spoke into the phone.

'I wish to speak to the Inspector in person, please.'

'Good morning. Which inspector do you want to see?'

'The duty inspector. I wish to make a complaint about one of your officers and I won't be fobbed off, so be prompt about it, if you would.'

'Certainly. Take a seat. He will be with you shortly.'

'I'll stand, thank you.'

124

He paced around the foyer, rehearsing his speech. Fairly soon, Bob Stanswick, the 'college-boy inspector', as Nobby called him, appeared and ushered Roy up the stairs into his office.

It didn't take long for Roy to relate to the inspector how rude DC Grant Donaldson had been to him at the children's home, and not only that, he had tape to corroborate his accusation. Inspector Stanswick asked for the tape. Roy passed it over, hastily assuring him that it was only a copy and that the original was going to his solicitor's office first thing tomorrow. Bob Stanswick tried to appease Roy, but he was on a loser right from the word go. With some regret he filled out the little form he was obliged to forward to the Complaints and Discipline Department for their full investigation. He knew Grant Donaldson quite well and thought the accusation out of character. But when it was on tape, what else could you believe? Of all people, it had to be Roy Prentice . . . He would want to take it to the ends of the earth.

Once alone, Bob reached for the telephone and tapped out a number.

'DI Stark.'

'Hi Dave. It's Bob here. Just a word on the QT.'

'Why, what's the matter now?'

'It's Roy Prentice. He's made a complaint about Grant Donaldson.'

Bob surreptitiously explained the situation to Stark. He shouldn't have done, but he hoped Stark would have done the same for him.

Stark took hold of Grant's arm as they met in the corridor and dragged him into the nearby toilets. Grant was smiling. 'I never knew you cared, boss.'

Stark's face remained stern. 'A word in your shell-like.'

'Why, what's the matter?'

'That git Roy Prentice is the matter. He's made a complaint about you.'

'What! You've got to be joking, sir.'

'I'm afraid not, Grant. Do I look as though I am?'

'What's he saying I've done, then?'

'Well, he's said you were uncivil to him, swore at him and that your conduct was discreditable and unbecoming to a police officer.'

125

'Is that all?' Grant laughed incredulously.

'It's awkward it coming up with you being on your aide, because the gaffers upstairs will hear about it.'

'Yes, but surely they'll see it for what it is?'

'Oh yes and what's that? Lies?' asked Stark.

'To be honest with you, sir, off the record, no it isn't. But you should have heard him. I just put him straight on a few points, that's all.'

'He's got a tape of you being aggressive and swearing at him.'

Grant looked aghast, his mouth dropped open. 'What! The crafty bastard. I see it now, I see why his attitude changed after he went over to his desk. He suddenly went all polite – he must have turned the tape on then. You've seen him, you know how anti he is. If you've heard the tape, he's as nice as pie, when in reality thirty seconds earlier he was more or less calling me a nigger traitor.'

'Shame you didn't tape him.'

'Sure, that really would go down well with the public. Be careful what you say to a policeman, because he's got a tape recorder whirling round in his arse pocket.'

'All right, calm down. Have you made a full pocketbook entry about the incident, including his anti-police attitude and his sudden change?'

'You bet your life I have. I knew he was up to something, I just knew it!'

'Does Steve Aston's book corroborate yours?'

'Yes. I made sure he put something in about it, because I just had a feeling about Prentice, that's all. I've met his sort before.'

'I got a bit of something in my book before you even visited him, about his anti-police attitude towards me, so it's a start. All I can say is to forget it for now, but when you get your official notices about the complaint, contact the Federation and make sure they represent you. Don't make a federal out of it, but if it goes as far as a tribunal, I'll give evidence for you. All right?'

'Thanks, boss.'

'Thanks for what? I don't know what you're talking about. What complaint? Are you with me?' He winked.

'Yes, OK. I've got you. Thanks.'

As the two men left the toilet, Grant, without realizing, began to chew at his lip. He didn't like the sound of this one. 'Forget it.' How could he?

Weekdays weren't particularly busy for the leisure centre staff. Apart from schoolchildren and housewives, only the occasional shiftworker would patronize the facilities available courtesy of Ashfield District Council – for a small charge, of course. Mark Winner was busy in the multi-gym. He was a handsome man, and was, moreover, only too aware of the fact. Six feet tall, his well-defined, tanned, muscular body was complimented by his figure-hugging cotton vest and track-suit bottoms. In the heat of the gym, he was revelling in supporting the waist of an attractive woman who was working on her deltoids, pulling down on the bar above her head as she knelt at the machinery. It was noticeable that all the half-dozen women who were working out had their eyes focused on Mark. It wasn't his wavy black hair, capped teeth or very slightly stubbled chin that they concentrated on, oh no; it was the outline of a thick, bulging pipe of muscle that stretched at an angle down his leg. As he held the woman's waist, it was obvious that every one of those women wanted Mark Winner, and that they were trying their utmost to get him in the sack. In their imaginations, they had all already had him whilst their husbands sweated and grunted, or when they were alone with their vibrators. They fantasized about how Mark would have a clean, rhythmic stroke, a powerful, unrelenting screw that would herald a sea of multiple orgasms.

Mark was surprised and apparently puzzled to see the suited figures of Jim McIntyre and Charlie Carter gesticulating at him from behind the closed, glass double doors. It was apparent that they wanted to parley. Mark walked easily towards them, his movements like a cheetah about to break into a trot towards its prey. The women could see the men talking through the glass. As Mark led the way to a private office on the second floor, Jim furtively held in his belly. Mark looked drawn, as most extremely fit people do. He stared blankly at the two men sitting in the uncomfortable orange-coloured seats in the staff office.

As usual Charlie did most of the talking, saving Jim the bother.

'It's about the killings,' was all Charlie said for starters.

'Oh yes . . .' There was a pause before he added, 'Um. Terrible really, wasn't it?'

'You don't seem over-emotional about it, Mark,' Charlie observed.

'Oh, I am, yes. Oh Christ, I am bothered. But life goes on, doesn't it?'

'It sure does. Have you any views on the murders?'

'We are talking about James Deely and Stuart Millichip, aren't we?'

'Yes we are, Mark.'

'Oh right, 'cos I wasn't sure. I didn't even know about them until today. Caroline mentioned it briefly in passing, but I didn't go into any great detail with her. I read about it this morning, actually. There was an old newspaper in the bog. According to the paper the two are connected, aren't they?'

Jim chimed in. 'Possibly. D'you mean to tell us that you haven't read a paper or heard any news since it happened?'

'No. Believe it or not I haven't. I find the news a bit depressing, to be honest, so I don't bother listening. After all, there's sod-all we can do about it, is there? By the time it's on the news it's already happened, hasn't it?'

Charlie noticed how Mark had the habit of answering every question with a question. He took over where Jim left off. 'As you know, we've spoken to Caroline about this as well – '

'Have you? No, I didn't know you'd seen her. Should I have done?'

'Well surely she told you we'd seen her?'

'Yes she did. Sorry. You've caught me at a bad time to be honest, my mind's elsewhere today. Anyway, what can I do for you? And no, I didn't do it.' He grinned at Charlie, who politely returned the smile and asked where he had been on the two dates in question.

'I don't know, who can tell?'

'Well, were you at work, at home, out? Where were you, Mark? It's important we know.'

He laughed. 'I honestly can't tell you. I'll have a think about it, honest I will.' He was smiling again.

Jim became serious. He wasn't smiling; he grimaced annoyance. 'Well have a think about it now, all right, because it's bloody important!'

'I'm thinking, I'm thinking!'

There was an embarrassing silence, punctuated by Jim's impatience. 'Bloody hell fire, it's not that long ago.'

Mark shook his head. 'Nah, sorry, but I can't think like that under pressure. If I could I'd be a cabinet minister or something, not working at a leisure centre.'

Charlie was more patient than Jim. 'Tell us what you know about James Deely, then.'

Mark laughed. 'Look, to be honest with you, I can't help you. James Deely was a solicitor, wasn't he? That's all I know about him. I don't see any of the college lot any more.' Mark held his palms open and furrowed his brow.

'OK, you can't tell us what you don't know, but what about Stuart Millichip?'

'You don't appear to be listening to me. *I don't know these people.*'

Jim intervened. 'But you do know *of* them, because you went to school with them.'

'College. Yes, I did.'

'So tell us about them when they were at college.'

'What do you mean? What do you want to know?'

'Let's go for gold, shall we? Tell us a reason why somebody would want to kill the two of them.'

'I've no idea. Look, I know I'm being a bit of a pain to you but, seriously, I don't know a deal about them. Have you seen all the others?'

It was Charlie's turn to look puzzled. He decided to try the question for a question technique. 'All the other who?'

'All the others in our group at college.'

'Most of them, if not all, Mark. Why?'

'Well, they no doubt told you about Stuart trying it on.'

Things were getting interesting. 'What d'you mean, trying it on? In the biblical sense you mean?' Jim asked.

'Yes. He had a feel of my arse in a pub toilet when we were all steaming one night. Jonathon Stacey came in at the time he did it and made a big song and dance about it. I'm surprised he hasn't told you about that little escapade.'

'So you're saying that Stuart was queer, are you?'

'I don't know what he is now, well he's not anything now, but you know what I mean.'

'Was he a full-bore queer or did he turn both ways?' Jim asked laconically.

'I don't know. He certainly had the hots for Tracey Sewell because David Seaton told me that, one lonely night. In fact, I'm not sure, but I think he gave her one – something to do with seeing her at a party or something. Then again, though, Tracey has been seen to by a good few men, but don't tell her I said so, will you?'

'So at the time you were at college he was interested in you *and* Tracey Sewell?'

He laughed. 'You could say that, I suppose. I'm referring to David Seaton though. Have you met him? He's far more weird than everybody put together, he is.'

'I thought you didn't know what they were like now?'

'Assuming he's stayed the same, that is. Let me finish.'

Charlie became a little sombre. 'Mark, we're investigating two murders, and we have to bring things like this up.' He paused. 'I notice you have two criminal convictions. Well, I say convictions – two cautions by senior police officers.'

'Hold on a minute. That was a long time ago.'

'I appreciate that, Mark. Don't get me wrong, but I need to know about them. Now, I shall speak to the officers who dealt with them, but I want your version of events as well, my duck.'

Mark's face became tense. 'Look, I was at college at the time; the kerb-crawling was the zest of youth. I'd never been with a prostitute and it was exciting, a bit of fun. I still never got off with one – she turned out to be a policewoman!'

'Who was with you then?'

'Nobody. When I say it was fun, I mean it was exciting for me. Sometimes you need a change, don't you, and with Caroline close to me morning, noon and night, I seized the opportunity to try to score. I'm not some sort of pervert, if that's what you're thinking.'

'Don't be daft, Mark. I just find it curious. Looking at those women drooling in the gym now, you could have any woman you want, yet you chose a prostitute!'

'It was a long time ago, mate.'

'What about the other caution?'

'Oh, that was nothing. Just some tart in Nottingham near to Christmas. We'd all had a bit too much to drink and I grabbed hold of this bird and gave her a Christmas kiss. It was just a laugh, you know what it's like in town before Christmas. It's one big party. But she got a monk on and reported it to the police as indecent assault! Bloody crazy! Eh, don't mention this to Caroline, for God's sake. She doesn't know about it, and I want to keep it that way, if you don't mind!'

Jim replied. 'I'm sure we won't say anything, just as I'm sure that you'll remember where you were at the relevant times and dates and save us some bother.' He smiled knowingly at Mark.

'I really can't give an alibi, but I will think about it and try to remember, honestly.'

'Good, because it has to come from you, Mark. Nobody else.'

'That's OK. I've got nothing to worry about.'

The concrete playground of Alderman Sears Comprehensive School was barren. A sharp breeze swept the mounds of dust across it, along with scraps of sweet papers. It was almost four o'clock, and there wasn't a person in the place who wasn't aware of the time. David Seaton suddenly appeared from a corner of the playground. Carrying too many jotters somewhat precariously in his arms and fighting the wind, he shuffled towards the main block entrance. He heard the bell sound just as he staggered over the netball centre-circle markings. It was as he met the double doors that the tidal wave of holdalls, loose-fitting jackets and flailing arms showered over him. 'Walk, don't run!' he shouted to the skies, his squeaky monotone voice lost in the hubbub.

David was an oddity. Only twenty-six he looked at least ten years older. From under his mass of dark greasy hair, he would peer at you through black, thick-framed spectacles: His short torso sported polo-necked sweaters, even in the height of summer. He was a bachelor and a complete introvert, so badly lacking in communication skills that he had become a source of amusement to his pupils and of bemusement to his colleagues. 'See you, Orville!' a scruffy kid shouted as he disappeared through the doors. The kids called him that after Orville the Duck, a popular puppet whose high-pitched, squeaky voice was similar to his own. A sad figure of a man, David buried himself in reading to escape life's harsh reality.

Once he had made the sanctuary of the staff room he collapsed into the leather armchair with great relief. He let out a sigh, seemingly oblivious to the other members of staff in various

131

conversation groups around the spacious room. One of the PE teachers spotted David and shouted over to him.

'Are you going down the nightclubs tonight then, David?'

David hunched his neck into his shoulders and smiled insipidly at the man. He giggled to himself but failed to answer. Another young man joined in the banter. 'No, you don't waste time down the nightclubs, do you, David? You prefer the public toilets, don't you?'

David attempted to speak up for himself. 'Now listen, that's just not fair, you have no right . . .' At that point the headmaster, a balding man with glasses, entered. The room fell quiet.

'Goodnight everyone. I'll be in my study for a couple of hours should anyone wish to see me. David, would you hang fire for a moment? There're some policemen outside who wish to speak to you. I would think it's about your college murders. They're from the CID.'

David nodded. 'Oh right.' He gave a sycophantic smile.

'You can use the deputy head's office if you like. Do you want me to sit in with you? I know it's out of school time, but you are on our premises.'

'No, I'm fine on my own, thank you.' David's nasal way of speaking enforced the listener to strain to hear.

'So you're all right on your own, are you?'

David nodded.

Once in the office, Grant Donaldson and Steve Aston stared across the desk at David Seaton with some disbelief. This man was teaching the adults of the future. A frightening prospect. David was nervy and his hands appeared to be shaking as he toyed with the pencil in his hand.

Grant was the first to speak. 'We want to talk to you about the murders of your college friends. We did go to your house, but you were out.'

'Yes indeed,' David replied as he fidgeted with the pencil.

'I understand that you were close friends with Stuart Millichip, is that right?'

'Yes it is. You've obviously spoken with the others.'

'Yes, we have. Look, I'll be open with you right from the start, Mr Seaton – '

'David, please.' He smarmed an ingratiating smile.

'To tell the truth, your group of friends – including yourself – are as much under suspicion as anybody, if not more so.'

'I thought as much. You aren't suggesting that because Stuart and I were friends I'm some sort of mass murderer, I take it?'

Steve concurred. 'Not at all. We'd just like you to tell us what your relationship with Stuart was, David, if you don't mind, my duck.'

'We were just very good friends, we ...' David struggled to hold on to his emotions, tears welling up in his eyes. He put his hand to his mouth. 'I'm sorry, this has all been a bit of a strain for me.'

Steve was sympathetic. 'That's OK. Take your time, we're in no rush.' David smiled at him. Steve had gained the rapport and would take control of the conversation now. 'Are you all right to continue?' he asked.

David produced a white handkerchief and blew hard on it. 'Yes, I'm fine now, thank you.'

Steve continued. 'David, whatever is said within these four walls is completely confidential, and will go no further. I have to ask you a somewhat delicate question. Are you homosexual?'

'I would prefer not to answer that, but if you're asking if I loved Stuart, yes I did.'

'Were you close to James Deely?'

'No, I wasn't. I never liked him at college, and I didn't have anything to do with the man at all.'

'David, it's come to our attention that you ... well ... stare out of your window with a pair of binoculars at courting couples.'

'Don't worry, I know where that's come from, the nosy old cow. Yes, I do stare out of the window with binoculars, and no, it's not at courting couples, for heaven's sake!'

'Would you explain what you mean?'

'Astronomy is one of my pastimes, and although I wouldn't profess to be a barrister-at-law, I'm fairly confident that astronomy is a legal practice.'

'Where were you on – '

'It's true you really do ask that, is it?'

'Well, yes. We need to know your movements on those dates.'

David placed his elbows on the desk as Steve asked him where he was at the time of the murders.

'Well, the first one isn't a problem. I would be cycling to work. I set off from my house at eight o'clock on the dot every day, come hell or high water.'

'Did you set out at eight o'clock on that day?'

'Yes, so that's my alibi for that.'

Grant interrupted him. 'That isn't an alibi, is it?'

'What do you mean, it's not an alibi? Of course it is.'

'Well, have you got anybody who can say they were with you on that particular date and at that particular time, and give evidence to corroborate it?'

'No, sorry. I just thought if you asked my nosy neighbours, they could confirm I go out at that time of day every day.'

Grant broke more bad news. 'Even if your neighbours can say that, it doesn't mean you didn't commit the murder, David. You still had time to do it before getting to school.'

David was speechless.

'What time did you get to school that day?' Grant asked.

'I'm sorry, I can't say, but I'm usually here for twenty-five to.'

Steve then chipped in, asking David's whereabouts at the time Stuart had been killed.

'I'm afraid I would be at home at that time of night. You see, I don't go drinking, but I sometimes treat myself to a glass of beer and watch *Prisoner Cell Block H*. Do you watch it at all?'

Grant smiled. 'No, I don't.'

'When did you last see Stuart?' Steve asked.

'We'd been out the day before. Stuart had ridden me into Matlock. We often went out in Derbyshire. Occasionally we would camp for a night.' David put the handkerchief to his mouth and shook his head. 'I don't know, what a waste of a young man.'

Grant queried the statement. 'Surely you were at school the afternoon before?'

'No. I had a few free periods, so I took the afternoon off.'

'What time did you get back?'

'About ten o'clock at night. Stuart dropped me off at home.'

'What did you do in Matlock?'

'Walked the hills, had a couple of beers. We were very much free spirits, Stuart and I.'

'Did Stuart literally drop you off, or did he come in?'

'He came in for ... a coffee and a chat, and left about one o'clock.'

134

There was a bit of a pause.

David broke it. 'It is possible for two men to be good friends without being gay, you know!'

Having got as much as they could out of David, the two detectives left.

As they approached the CID car, Grant asked for Steve's opinion on David Seaton. 'The man's an emotional wreck, but I don't think he's got a murder in him, do you?'

'I don't know about that, but if he's not queer I'll show my bare backside in the Market Square as the clock chimes twelve!'

Generally there weren't many cars at Brickyard Cottages at twelve midnight. The long track leading to the wasteland at the far end was occasionally used by local youths to swap stolen cars, but other than that it was well known as a lover's lane. Sam Dewer wasn't sure which of the two purposes the car was being used for, so he decided to investigate. As he swung the police car round, the headlights exposed the bare backside frolicking inside. He did a full turn and caught a glimpse of some rather attractive, pendulous breasts and a lady's head, which bobbed down with a look of abject terror displayed upon it. Sam noticed another vehicle parked close by. It looked empty. But he made a note of both registration numbers and when he was out of sight, he checked them by radio and the Control Room on the Police National Computer.

The radio controller gave his reply: 'No reports on either vehicle. Not stolen. Do you require keeper details?'

'Affirmative.'

'First one, Jonathon Stacey, 12 Stafford Villas, Hucknall. Second vehicle, Caroline Winner, 16 Rawson Street, Nottingham.'

'Ten-four,' replied Sam.

He glanced back at the panic within the vehicle before resuming patrol. The names meant nothing to the patrolman, although her face did seem familiar. Perhaps it was wishful thinking. The poor woman looked as though she was going to die of embarrassment.

10

'She gave me a smile I could feel in my hip pocket.'

Raymond Chandler

Stark and Ashley were outside the secretary's office of Nottingham Polytechnic. Stark sat on a pink, back-straining chair, legs crossed, tapping his knee impatiently. Ashley stood with his hands in the pockets of his grey double-breasted suit. He seemed puzzled as he peered at the notice-board, moving his head at various angles to examine the display. 'What the bloody hell is this lot supposed to be?' he asked.

Stark rose to join him. He saw an array of drawings, strange angular lines and disturbing images conceived in adolescence and emptied from the minds of young artists. Stark stroked at his chin. 'Well, I think it's art, Ashley.'

Ashley's observation was facetious. 'Is it really? Art is it, how fascinating, how absorbing, a pessary to the anal eye of discomfiture.' His mocking arty voice underlined his sarcasm.

Stark laughed into his reply. 'You're bleeding crazy. Just behave yourself, you idiot.'

'Inspector Stark, the Principal will see you now, sir.' A middle-aged, brown-suited lady raised her voice across the echoing hall. The two detectives crossed the tiled floor and Stark knocked on the door briefly as he entered.

At one end of the spacious room stood an imposing desk, with four chairs around a rectangular glass coffee-table at the other. Rows of books lined the far wall, and there was an odd mixture of old and new furniture. The secretary brought in tea and biscuits, before retiring gracefully to her adjoining room.

The Principal, Mr Bolton, had been at the college almost nineteen years. When Stark had telephoned him, Bolton had remembered the group of individuals fairly well, but he had researched them prior to the detectives' arrival so as to refresh his memory. With his grey hair and half-spectacles, the Principal looked as though he was nearing retirement. He was slightly unkempt, gave the impression of being kindly but indecisive, and smiled broadly at the least excuse. His judgement of character was good, finely tuned after years of intermittent contact with students whom he had to assess. Stark quickly warmed to him. He enjoyed meeting a man like him. He liked the way his polite platitudes were punctuated with sharp observations and down-to-earth comments.

Mr Bolton sat down with them on the low chairs around the coffee-table. 'I didn't know how far you wanted me to go, Mr Stark. I've got everything I could possibly lay my hands on and I've spoken to their former teachers. I mean, where do you want me to start?'

Stark placed his hands together as if in prayer, putting them against his pursed lips. 'I'll tell you what you could do, could you just go through each one very briefly and describe them all in a couple or three sentences, just for starters? We can scrutinize the gumph at our leisure, but I'm interested in your observations, and those of the teachers who came into contact with them when they were here.'

'Any particular order, or as they come?'

'As they come, Mr Bolton, please.'

The Principal cleared his throat and looked at the first folder on his lap. 'Caroline Simpson, now Caroline Winner of course. Let me see, a clever, attractive girl, who competed with Tracey Oliver, now Tracey Sewell, for attention, but never seemed quite to manage it. If my memory serves me correctly, she used to like Jonathon Stacey at the time. She was studying history and art. The girl-next-door type really, always very polite and well turned out. Um, is that OK, or do you want a more detailed picture?'

'Let's keep it simple. I mean, if there's anything you feel you want to say about an individual that might help us, by all means do so.'

'Rightio. Well, that was Caroline. Rather appropriately, next on the list is her husband, Mark Winner. I always found Mark a rather bland character, not much personality. A very good sportsman, in fact an excellent sportsman, but that was his lot. Not very good at other subjects. He certainly lacked communication skills, though don't misunderstand me, he never once caused any trouble. Just a good athlete for the college. I anticipated him becoming a physical education teacher at a school, but they tell me he's not doing that at all, he's working at a leisure centre. So, that's him.

'Right, next on the list is ... Tracey Oliver, now, as I've said, Tracey Sewell. Let's see ... Tracey, I felt, was a popular member of the college, very well known, yes, perhaps a bit of an attention-seeker, quite flirty, even with some of the teachers I understand. She would occasionally become rather intense. Whether that was a touch of the old PMT, I honestly don't know. Tracey was studying English literature and sociology. She always wore black, and short skirts, very short skirts – so I'm told, you understand.'

The men laughed. Stark sipped at his tea, listening intently as Ashley made notes in a pad.

'Who's next on the list, then, Mr Bolton?' Stark enquired.

'Next is Jonathon Stacey. A not unintelligent boy this one. He's done very well for himself now. He was always a leader, always got his own way, and didn't have to shout or bawl to get it either. He was well liked and respected by all the kids. Jonathon studied the sciences. He enjoyed the company of the girls, especially Tracey Sewell. There were rumours at the time that, to use their parlance, he had "given her one".'

'You mean they had sex?' Stark asked.

'That was the rumour; I wasn't in the room with them at the time, you understand.' The men laughed again. Mr Bolton continued. 'I suppose while we are on that subject, I also heard from some of their former teachers that James Deely had had sex with Tracey and Caroline, on separate occasions, of course. It's amazing what gets back to the teachers you know. So take your pick. I'm sure you remember your college days, Inspector. It's nothing unusual.'

Stark was thoughtful and there was a slight pause, but his thoughts were of murder rather than reminiscence. 'Mmm sorry, Mr Bolton, please carry on. Who's next? Oh, Stuart Millichip – deceased.'

'Yes indeed. Such a waste. Well, Stuart actually was a year below the others, but he tended to tag along with them. He didn't really have anything to do with the lads, but Tracey and Caroline took him under their wings a little bit and he used to get along quite well with David Seaton. He was an average student who struggled to concentrate. Towards the end of his college days he started to get in with the motor-bike crowd and became a bit of a drifter.'

'What did he study, as a matter of interest?'

'Let's see, yes, sciences again. Now then, I've mentioned David Seaton already. He was a good student, somewhat quieter than the rest. He had a studious temperament. I often wondered why he put up with the ribald comments of the likes of Jonathon Stacey and James Deely.'

Stark interrupted. 'Did they give him a hard time, then?'

'A little bit, yes. He was an easy target in one sense, being studious and, dare I say, a little bit effeminate. He studied literature and the classics, which segregated him slightly also. He tried to win approval from the lads by doing crazy stunts for them.'

'What d'you mean?'

'Well, I got the impression that he wanted to prove that he was just as much a man as they were.'

'Did the teasing have a great effect on him?'

'I don't know. Who can tell? He kept going back for more if it did.'

'What about our friend Roy Prentice?'

Bolton laughed. 'Roy, well he caused us quite a few problems.'

'You do surprise me,' Stark said caustically.

'I take it you've met him, then?'

'Yes, we have, funnily enough.'

'Well Roy, as you know then, is rather politically motivated. He studied sociology and politics, and was chairman of the Students' Union at the college, hence the reference to the problems he caused us. He was very serious for one so young, cynical too.'

'Were any of the others in the Students' Union?' Ashley asked.

'No, they weren't. That didn't stop Roy trying to recruit them, though. I think he just bored them to death with it. He's no fool, mind you.'

'Right, OK then, is that it? No, we're forgetting James Deely. What sort of guy was he?'

'Nice enough young man, another one who did well for himself. He was a bit of a go-getter, quite money-oriented. He didn't get on particularly well with Jonathon Stacey, however.'

'Why was that, do you think?'

'I'm not a hundred per cent sure. Perhaps a bit of rivalry between the two, stags locking horns, that sort of thing. I must admit there seemed to be a bit more to it than that. James studied English remarkably well, I hasten to add. I'm afraid I really can't enlighten you any more than that. As I say, though, all the papers are here. You're welcome to scrutinize them.'

Stark smiled. 'OK. We'll do that. Thanks very much for your help. I don't suppose you can throw any light on the mystery at all?'

'No. I've racked my brains trying to think. Do you really believe the murders are connected with the college?'

'Personally, yes I do. I think it's all a bit too coincidental not to be. Obviously there's a whole team of officers pursuing the normal channels, as if they are two separate murders, but we're working on any connections between the two.'

'Right. Well, obviously, if there's anything else you need, don't hesitate to ask, and if there is a link, I would be intrigued to know what it is. It's all rather disconcerting. The education authority has somehow got wind of it and asked me to play down any connection, but, if there is, it's only right and proper that we help you find it.'

Stark and Ashley left shortly afterwards. The paraphrased character profiles had clarified the picture of the suspects they had already built up, and somewhere in amongst it all was a link, something that was haunting the present, something which had happened in the past and had come home to roost now.

Mavis Smith was seventy-two and fairly corpulent so it was a struggle for her to get out of the Ford Fiesta outside Nottingham Police Station. She was helped by the care assistant from the residential home. The picture of camel-coated Mavis in her large-framed spectacles being manhandled by Monica, the care assistant in combat trousers and with pierced nose, was somewhat incongruous. Once inside the police station foyer she asked to speak to a police officer, and eventually one arrived, with pen and paper.

Stark had finished collecting his mail from the Control Room and happened to walk past the rear of the foyer as Monica uttered the reason for their visit. 'This is Mavis Smith, it's about the murders in the paper.'

Stark stopped abruptly and listened intently behind the door. 'Tell the policeman what you know then, Mavis.'

Mavis cleared her throat and began her rehearsed speech. 'I've seen the murders in the *Evening Post* and I also read the personal column, before going on to the Births, Marriages and Deaths. You do that when you get to my age, you know . . .'

The policeman nodded at Monica, who was smiling somewhat sceptically. 'Yes, love, go on, I'm listening.'

'Well, I've seen these entries in the personal column . . .' She produced three cuttings. 'Don't laugh, I know you think I'm a daft old bugger, but I think they could be something to do with the murders. The first message was put in just before the first murder, and the other messages were put in the day after. See what you think.' She handed them to the officer, who started to read them. As he did, Stark felt it necessary to have a look himself and appeared in the doorway.

'Let's have a look, Steve.' The PC handed the clippings to Stark and he read them aloud in the order he was given them:

> Baby darling, I did not lie,
> others now must say goodbye.

> Baby darling, you now know,
> there are only two to go.

> Baby darling, there were three.
> now there's only one to see.

Stark paused before saying, 'Bloody hell!'

Mavis joined in. 'I know you're busy, and I don't want to waste your time, but I thought you ought to know about them.'

'Yes, you've done the right thing, my love. Thank you very much for bringing them to our attention. Have you got the dates when these were published? Well, it doesn't matter; we can get those from the *Evening Post*.'

'They fit in with the murders, that's what drew my attention to them, like,' Mavis observed with a smile.

Monica looked a trifle embarrassed about her overt scepticism,

141

now that it was revealed there appeared to be some substance to the newspaper clippings. She took Mavis by the arm. 'Well, if you don't need us for anything else, we'll get on our way then,' she said.

Stark was reading the messages to himself. He broke off. 'Yes, of course you can. This officer will just take your details, and thanks very much, this could be a great help. It really could.'

Stark ran up the stairs three at a time. As he passed the CID office, he shouted out, *'Nobby. Come in here, mate, and see what you make of this!'*

Nobby appeared in the doorway and Stark excitedly showed him the clippings. 'Maybe something,' he said after he'd read them, and gave a shrug.

'Oh piss off, Nobby – it's our murderer. It's got to be. Oh all right then, I *hope* it is. Get two of the lads to go down to the *Evening Post* and find out who put this lot in. It may just be as simple as that!'

When Nobby returned they studied the clippings, and Nobby commented, 'Hold on a minute, there are eleven words to each message. I wonder if that tells us something?'

Stark said his piece. 'I know what that last message tells us. There's going to be another murder!'

Steve Aston wiped the copper slab, which was about eight inches long, and used the petrol-based cleanser to get the printer's ink off. The Fingerprint Room was small, with a high table and some filing drawers underneath. In the corner was a sink, with a huge tub of Swarfega close by. Fingerprint ink is difficult to get off sweaty hands. In the other corner was a revolving seat with a metal frame in front of it into which a card giving details of the prisoner could be slotted for the photograph. The camera was opposite the seat, on a permanent base with a white arc lamp fitted above it. Caroline Winner smiled at Steve as she stretched to pull her jacket over her shoulders. Her large nipples were protruding and the embarrassed Steve couldn't divert his stare. She took hold of his hand. 'Do you know, I've never had my fingerprints taken before, but if I ever have them taken again I want it to be by you.' She smiled. Steve smiled nervously.

'Thanks. Do you wish to witness their subsequent destruction?'

'Will you be there?'

'I don't know.'

'In that case, no.'

Steve thrust the completed green fingerprint form in front of her. 'Just sign here please, and you can go.'

Steve watched as she leaned over the table, throwing her hair back so that she could see what she was signing. He showed her to the door and them promptly ran up the stairs. As he entered the CID office he appeared flummoxed.

'Christ all-bleeding-mighty!'

Ashley looked over at Steve, somewhat puzzled. 'Steady on, Steve. That's not like you to blaspheme. There never were such times.'

'Get knotted, Ash! It's that Caroline Winner.'

'What about her?' Grant Donaldson joined in.

'I've just taken her fingerprints. God she's fit, isn't she? Anyway, I'm not kidding, as I'm taking them, she starts rubbing her left breast against my arm.'

Grant and Ashley both interrupted him. 'More like the other way round.'

'No seriously, it was really firm. She's a right hot arse, she is. She kept smiling at me – you know, one of those smiles.'

Ashley defined it further. 'One of those smiles that say get your kit off, you mean?'

'Yes, one of those.'

Grant brought some decorum to the room. 'Can I ask why you were taking her fingerprints?'

'She was one of those who said she hadn't been in James Deely's car recently. I think they're going to get blood off them as well, to compare with the DNA on the hairs in his car.'

'Oh right, I'm with you. I suppose it's pointless taking them off those who say they were in the car because it doesn't prove murder, it simply proves they were in the car.'

Ashley pointed his pen at Grant. 'You know Grant, there's hope for you yet!'

'Who else is down there?' Grant asked Steve, ignoring Ashley's joke.

'David Seaton, Mark Winner and Gerry Sanders from the Probation hostel. They're doing them a batch at a time.'

Ashley stated the obvious. 'They might not need all that if

Steph is triumphant at the *Evening Post* and finds out who put those messages in the paper!'

Stephanie Dawson and Jim McIntyre drew up alongside the grandiose *Evening Post* building. Jim parked immediately outside on double yellow lines.

'You can't leave it here, Jim. We'll get a ticket!'

'Bollocks to a ticket, we are the Queen's men, on Queen's business. We'll be all right.'

The two strolled over and eventually spoke to a very attractive, businesslike young lady with swept-up blonde hair and glasses. It was not every day that the CID called on a murder investigation. Although she was not a journalist she could smell a story, and she attempted to glean as much information as she possibly could.

'So let me get this right,' she said, pushing a few strands of blonde hair back into place, 'we have a serial killer on our hands, and he's sending messages to the *Nottingham Evening Post*.'

Jim corrected her. '*Could be*, I said. Nothing definite has been found out. That's the reason we're here – to discover who arranged for the personal column entries to be put in.'

'D'you mind if I take notes about all this? It's terribly exciting.'

Steph was getting a bit peeved by her enthusiasm. 'Are you a journalist or a clerk or what, love?'

'I'm a clerk, why d'you ask?'

'Because we're here investigating a couple of murders with the prospect of there being some more and so I want you, and you personally, to take me to the Editor's office now.'

'I can't do that. Why, what have I done?'

'Listen, you do exactly as I say, young lady. Where is the Editor's office?'

'It's on the top floor.'

'Come on, then. You'll understand why when we get there.'

Steph spoke briefly with the Editor's secretary and the three of them were shown in. Jim was hanging on to Steph's coat-tails. Whenever she got something in her head like this there was no stopping her. She had cursed herself for not going to the top straight away. The Editor, one Peter Thrower, appeared not a little surprised by the intrusion, but he eyed them deferentially over his half-spectacles and gestured welcomingly.

'Come in, make yourselves at home, why don't you?'

Steph apologized as they entered the light, airy office. 'I'm sorry for the intrusion, but it's very important, and I hope you'll understand why I've had to do it this way. You see, we're police officers . . .' Jim closed the door behind them.

'I take it this can't wait. What's the matter?'

'We're investigating the murders of James Deely and Stuart Millichip. You obviously know about them, you've been covering them every night on the front page.'

Peter removed his spectacles. 'Yes . . .'

'Well, we think that the murderer has been putting messages in your personal column. It's not definite yet, of course.'

'I see, That's rather a turn-up for the books. I suppose you'd like to look through the system, then?'

'Yes we do, if you don't mind. The most important thing is that we don't want anybody knowing about this until we've completed our enquiries. Only those people in this office know about it, other than the detectives working on the case. I would like an undertaking from you that you'll hold the story off, and that this lady will keep her mouth shut, until we let you know.'

The Editor scratched his distinguished grey head. 'Wow! This is one hell of a scoop!'

Steph continued. 'You've a ready-made story that's not going anywhere, and we'll give you everything we can at the end of the day. You know the problems that could arise if the paper obstructs the course of justice. You could be held in contempt of court at any subsequent trial of the offenders, not that you'd put yourself in such jeopardy, I'm sure.'

Peter leaned over to shake her hand. 'OK, you've got a deal. But we'll review it every fortnight with your detective superintendent.'

Steph and Jim left Peter's office and sauntered through the main office searching for the young clerk with the glasses.

The lady clerk eventually got the relevant documents relating to the personal column messages. Three envelopes, all plain white, with a typed message on them and the exact money enclosed.

'Who sent them?' Steph asked impatiently.

'I've no idea, I'm afraid.'

Jim spoke up. 'What d'you mean, you've no idea?'

'Well, these were pushed through the letter-box, with the right money in cash. That's all we require, especially with the personal column.'

Steph was despondent. 'That's fair enough, I suppose, if not a little disappointing. We'll take everything you've got for now for forensic examination, please, if we may. And remember, keep shtum.'

'Of course.'

The detectives turned to leave. Steph stopped in her tracks.

'D'you have a cleaning lady?'

'Yes, of course. Why?'

'Does she clean the brass letter-box?'

'Oh, I'm with you, fingerprints. I'm afraid she does, first thing every morning. It's her pride and joy. It sparkles like a new pin, I'm afraid. Sorry.'

'Fair enough. I just thought I'd ask.'

Stark was smiling as he spoke to Wagstaff on the telephone. '. . . so that's the good news, sir, but the bad news is the obvious inference that there will be another murder.'

Wagstaff sounded thoughtful. 'Mmm yes. Well, there's no way we can do twenty-four-hour protection on all of them. The killer may not strike for ages yet. The world of crime hasn't stopped out of consideration for us, just because we've got a double murder running. It may prove detrimental if the killer sees there is protection. All he'll have to do is wait until we pull it off, and in the meantime our resources for trying to catch him will be cut drastically. The best way to ensure he doesn't strike again is to lock him up.'

'True, but if there's another murder, and we know there's a "hit list", for want of a better expression, we're deep in it.'

'Yes, you're right, of course. I'll have a word with Heap Big Chief and see what he comes up with. In the meantime, get police alarms put in all the houses.'

'Sure. It's worth mentioning to the boss that we can't do covert observations because we can't confine them to barracks, and to do covert surveillance on each target needs twenty blokes and ten vehicles each, if we don't want to scare the killer off, and as you say, we just haven't got the resources to do that indefinitely. I suppose we could have overt observations by uniformed officers, but again, how long for? And they can't live with them twenty-four hours a day and follow them around. I doubt whether all of them would agree to that, anyway,' Stark observed.

'Yes, David. Put alarms in for now, and I'll let you know if there's anything else to do.'

Stark was pensive. 'I've got a horrible feeling that our killer is on the warpath again!'

11

'A man who moralizes is usually a hypocrite,
and a woman who moralizes is invariably plain.'

Oscar Wilde

The walls of the CID office were covered with pieces of paper ranging from intelligence bulletins to spurious headlines like: ASHLEY SUBMITS EXPENSES CLAIM – CHANCELLOR RESIGNS! and STEVE ASTON ATE MY HAMSTER! Calendars depicting girls in various stages of undress were displayed at several vantage points, the more explicit being hidden behind cabinet doors. A heavy cloud of smoke poured from Stark's pipe as he chuffed away on it. Grant Donaldson rose briefly as Detective Superintendent Wagstaff came in. Wagstaff waved him to sit down.

'Morning team.'

'Morning sir,' came the replies.

Stark asked Grant to make them a drink, which he immediately did.

Wagstaff sat down and addressed them as a whole. 'I take it that we didn't have any success with the newspaper cuttings, since I wasn't contacted at home?'

Stark answered. 'No, sir. Whoever it is has merely pushed the letters through the letter-box with the appropriate amount of cash, but without leaving any details.'

'Wonderful. Have we submitted everything to the Forensic Science Lab?'

'Yes. The letters were typed, so we'll need the relevant typewriter to compare them with, which, of course, we haven't got. The murderer is obviously no fool. I'd like to think that there'll be fingerprints on the paper, but I'll be very surprised if there are. Still, we can but hope.'

Wagstaff smiled. 'Oh dear, never mind. It's a development,

and that's got to give us hope. I've been puzzling over why a killer would publish his involvement and his intent.'

'You and me both, sir. Who does he want to read the messages, if anybody?'

'I was hoping you might tell me, David. Anyone got any ideas?' There was much shaking of heads and muttered 'No sirs'.

Stark continued. 'We've got men doing observations on the *Evening Post* letter-box, and as far as I can see that's all we can do for now, apart from hope that Forensic turns something up.'

Wagstaff spoke. 'What about researching who of the gang has access to typewriters, and getting them seized?'

'Yes, we can do that, but when you consider that these people work in schools, hospitals and various business premises, there are endless sources of typewriters.'

'OK, leave that for now until we liaise with Forensic. They can give us pointers on what to look for, on samples taken from typewriters, so as to narrow down the seizures and to save us alerting the murderer, who could then dispose of the relevant one if we miss it.'

There was a lull in the conversation. Stark broke the silence. 'What we need is greater information on the suspects – on a more personal basis. Sex keeps coming up. Perhaps the answer lies there.'

Nobby chimed in. 'But how can you gain information from people who don't want you to hear it?'

A smile began to grow on Stark's face as he looked at Nobby. 'Today is James Deely's funeral, isn't it? So all the college cadre will be there, chatting with each other at the wake, won't they?'

Nobby began to smile too and they both pointed at each other, speaking in unison. *'Sammy Trench!'*

Stark spoke into the telephone. 'As I have said, Mrs Deely, I will be paying my respects as a representative of the police force. All I can do is thank you for your help, despite this being such a trying time for you.'

There was a muffled reply. Stark spoke again. 'So it's at the Green Gables public house at three o'clock. Thank you very much indeed, and if there is anything at all we can do, don't hesitate to ask. Goodbye.'

There was a knock on his office door. Stark beckoned Ashley to come in, followed by Sammy Trench.

'Thanks a lot, Ashley. We'll have a briefing shortly. Close the door behind you, mate, will you.'

Sammy Trench stood there in an ill-fitting, cheap, light-blue suit. He was very thin. He looked unkempt and nervous, flicking back a lock of thick dark hair from his bespectacled face.

Ashley went back to the CID office and joined in the laughter. All the lads had watched him show Sammy Trench into Stark's office. Jim spoke first. 'So that's the man who's going to solve our murders for us, is it?'

Ashley giggled. 'I've seen it all now. I knew things were desperate, but not that bad, surely? So much for Stark's ace informant!'

Even Grant appeared incredulous. 'Who the hell is he?'

Charlie Carter was smiling knowingly, but in tune with the banter. 'Give Stark some credit, lads.'

'Do you know who this guy is then, Charlie?' Ashley asked.

'Yes I do. But I won't steal the gaffer's thunder. He can tell you about him. All I'll say is that if he's used right, he'll be the best informant we could possibly use on this job!'

A few moments later, Stark entered the CID office with Sammy in tow. There was immediate silence, the atmosphere in the room tense with apprehension. Stark and Sammy sat down.

Stark was milking the moment: he was in no rush to make known his revelations.

'Gentlemen, this is Sammy Trench. To most people he appears relatively normal . . .'

Sammy laughed. 'Good morning, gentlemen. Hi, Charlie,' he said, his wry smile still evident. Charlie waved a hand in reply.

Stark continued: '. . . however, he's not. You see, Sammy here is deaf. He can't hear a word we're saying. But, and it's a big but, he's an expert lip-reader! Now, Sammy is a great friend of ours on the CID, and he's kindly agreed to help us out this afternoon at James Deely's funeral.'

Suddenly Ashley understood. 'I'm with you now. He's going to watch what the college gang are talking about.'

'Well done, Ashley, I knew you wouldn't let me down. Now there's no way on God's earth that they will talk openly with the police around, but they might if they think we're not. So, very early on I shall make my excuses and leave, having officially paid respects on behalf of us all. And I'll leave Sammy in a good position to "listen" to what the crowd is saying.'

Grant was intrigued. 'That's fine, sir, but surely Sammy won't remember the conversation word for word? How are we going to work that out?'

'Good point, Grant. Sammy will be in a perfect position in the pub, with an undercover detective from the Crime Squad with him. They will be positioned some distance away, and as the pub will be open to the public anyway, they won't look out of the ordinary.'

Ashley wagged a finger, his mind working overtime. 'Yes that's right, tape-record it.'

Stark smiled. Grant was confused. 'But how are we going to record it? We can't just have microphones in the pub. There would be too much background, and anyway, we don't know where they're going to stand or sit.'

Stark put his mind at ease. 'Sammy will be fitted with a throat microphone under his shirt and tie, close to the larynx. He will merely repeat the conversation of the college gang into the mike, which will record it for posterity, and more importantly, for our scrutiny.'

Ashley nodded. 'And the Crime Squad detective will just be a front to prevent people thinking that Sammy is a nutter talking to himself.'

'Correct, Ashley. My, you are on the ball today. You see, Sammy won't be overheard, as he only needs to speak quietly for the mike to receive the signal.'

'Brilliant! I love it.' Ashley gave his seal of approval.

Nobby and Steph had been giggling like schoolchildren all the way to Mrs Millichip's house. They were getting on better than they ever had, and Nobby was beginning to feel he might have found a point of weakness in Steph's unyielding claims to celibacy.

The Millichip house was in Newstead, a mining village with rows of terraced houses and an occasional corner shop giving a splash of colour to the drab, grey environment that lay in the awesome shadow of the towering pit headstocks, long since

151

redundant. Nobby hammered on the door. Steph wondered if he could do anything quietly; then a smile tickled her face. She quickly suppressed it as the wheezing and moaning of the approaching woman could be heard from outside.

Mrs Millichip was in her early sixties, and must have been at least eighteen stone. After a lifetime of smoking forty a day, her lungs strained to supply oxygen to her vast bulk. Despite her own untidiness, the house was clean and she made Steph and Nobby more than welcome.

'Come in lass, I'll put the kettle on,' she said to Steph. Although Nottinghamshire born and bred, the Yorkshire lilt that invaded many mining communities had encroached on her vocabulary. The living-room was compact. There was the obligatory television on full blast, an ironing-board with a pile of washing in the corner, two armchairs and a settee, well worn at the ends of the arms. The adjacent kitchen was small. Mrs Millichip busied herself with the kettle and teapot.

'I suppose you've come about Stuart.'

'Yes we have, love,' Nobby said. 'I'll chat when you've finished making the tea.'

Mrs Millichip came into the living-room. 'It's all right, it won't be long now.' She leaned against the wall, gasping for air.

Steph took over. 'Is there anything you can tell us about Stuart that might help us?'

'Of course there is, but I'm sure you know most of it already. You don't need me to tell you, lass!'

'I'm sorry, what?'

'Listen love, I call a spade a spade. I didn't relish the fact that Stuart was a . . . you know . . . a queer, but you can't hide it from a mother – there's very little you can. It's only mothers that hide it from themselves, if it doesn't suit their plan of happy families.'

'Did he know that you knew about it?' Steph asked.

'All I said to him was: Stuart, I know that you prefer men to women lad, but I shall stand by you as long as you don't desecrate this house.'

'And what did he say?'

'He didn't say a word. He just stared at the television and the subject hasn't been mentioned from that day to this.'

Nobby wondered if she knew Stuart had had Aids. Since he hadn't talked about his sex life to her since that occasion, it

152

seemed unlikely. Mrs Millichip staggered back into the kitchen, breathing heavily, and returned a short time later, bearing cups and saucers.

'I didn't know a lot about his friends, only one.'

'Who was that?' Steph asked.

'A lad called David. Shy, retiring boy, a teacher I'm told. He's a queer as well, I'm sure of it.'

'The most unlikely men can be homosexual Mrs Millichip,' Nobby said. 'Did Stuart tell you that this David was homosexual?'

'No, not in so many words.'

'What d'you mean?'

'Eyes give a lot away. They kept giving each other knowing looks, like a pair of teenage lovers at their parents' house for the first time.'

'Was Stuart having an affair with this David, then?' Nobby asked, slightly uncomfortable with his choice of words.

'You'd better ask David that. Let's be right, you can't ask my lad, can you?'

Steph spoke. 'No, we can't. You seem to be taking it very well, Mrs Millichip.'

'What's the option? Curl up into a little ball? Folks like us are no strangers to hard times, lass, and whatever life brings you, you have to stomach, it's as simple as that. I've two other sons who have been a big help.' She wagged a finger. 'Don't think I've not shed a tear, mind you, 'cos I have!'

'How often did he see David?' Nobby asked.

'Not too often. Once a week usually. Sundays. They'd go out into the country walking, usually Matlock, around there, you know.'

Steph asked if she could remember anything about Stuart's college days.

'A little. He never brought anybody home. Oh no, it would have been too embarrassing for him for his posh friends to see our poky little house. He used to mention a girl called Tracey – Tracey Oliver, that's it. That's why I was so surprised at his homosexuality. He really liked that girl.'

Nobby was to the point. 'Do you think he had sexual relations with women as well as men, then?'

'I honestly don't know. He appeared to fancy women, though.'

153

'What else can you remember about his college days?' Steph asked.

'I think he enjoyed hanging around with the crowd. They were a year older than him, but in fairness to Stuart he was mature for his age.'

'Is there anything at all you can remember from his college days that could have any relevance today?'

'No love, I can't. I can't believe any of that crowd could be involved, I really can't!'

From where they were parked, Jim McIntyre and Steve Aston could only just see the letter-box of the *Evening Post* offices. The two detectives were squatting in the back of an old box van parked some fifty yards away. To a passer-by the van looked empty. It was Jim's turn to peer out of the hole. They had agreed to do half-hour stints each. 'Why the hell can't Special Operations Unit do this? It's not for us to do, this isn't. We're supposed to be detectives!' Jim moaned.

'Stark has already told us that we may well have to speak to a number of people who use this letter-box, and as we know all about the intricacies of the murders, we're in a better position to assess whether they're already known to the enquiry, or are lying, or whatever.'

'Well SOU could have done the obs and notified us of the suspects, and then we could have stopped them.'

'What, and use four men instead of two!'

'All right, smart arse. You seem to forget I was pounding the beat while you were still in nappies.'

'OK. I'm just telling you what Stark said, that's all.'

'Stark this, Stark that – are you in love with the bloke or something?' Jim didn't have time to wait for an answer. 'Hold on a minute, someone's just put something in the box. Come on!' The two men jumped out of the van and approached the gentleman, Jim producing his identification. 'We're from the CID. Can you please tell us what you've just put in that letter-box?'

The gent was in his seventies and wore a black duffel coat. 'Yes officer, I can. It's an entry for the deaths column. My sister died last week.'

Steve was a little taken aback. 'Oh, I'm sorry to hear that. I'm

154

terribly sorry to put you out, and I'm afraid I can't really say why, but could I ask you just to come with us and have a word with this security man?'

'OK, then.'

'It'll literally take about thirty seconds, that's all.'

The three men walked back to the door to be out of sight. The security man, only a boy of around twenty, was in a blue uniform. He had been pleased with his new assignment, as very rarely did he have to work with the real police. He had been instructed to open all letters as they came through the letter-box, to verify the stories of the people stopped by the covert detectives. He had to wear surgical gloves for this, of course. He'd just finished opening the letter. He took it out and noted that there was some money enclosed. He read the message out loud: "Jean Bembrose. Died 3rd January. A loving and caring sister who will be sadly missed. Love Albert."

'I'm very sorry to put you out, sir,' Steve said to the man. 'Thanks very much for your help.'

'That's all right, young man. What's it all about, then?'

'I'm sorry, but I can't say for now. I'm sure all will be revealed to you through the press in due course, though.'

'Fair enough, lad.' The man turned and walked off down the street. As usual Jim had something to say.

'Nosy old fart, what's it got to do with him?'

'It's only natural, isn't it, if you've been stopped by the police, to wonder why out of dozens of people they've chosen you?'

'I'm surprised he didn't say we were only picking on him 'cos he was old.'

Steve laughed as they climbed back into the van. Jim let out a sigh; he was getting a bit pissed off, to say the least.

'This is bleeding stupid. I'm fed up of chasing fucking shadows!'

Nobby and Steph had stopped off at a pub for some lunch on the way back to the station. Nobby had ushered Steph into a quiet corner of the lounge. Inevitably he'd steered the conversation round to sex.

Nobby gave his version of events. 'Nobody's saying we should get involved. I've already told you that. It's quite simple really. I

155

think you're absolutely gorgeous and want to rip your knickers off with my teeth, and you're tempted to say yes, so what's stopping you?'

'Look, Nobby, it's not that I don't find you attractive, it's just that ... well ... you know.'

'No. I don't know. You tell me.' He stroked her hand.

'Well, you're my detective sergeant, my gaffer. It's an untenable situation.' Steph crossed her leg towards Nobby, the muscular contours of it hard and shapely. She welcomed Nobby's hand and stroked it in return.

'So who has to know about it?'

'Look Nobby, I'm thirty. All the eligible men are ugly and all the attractive ones are married. I'm fed up with secret assignations. Why can't I go to this particular pub, or to the pictures, without the fear of being seen by wives? And now more hiding in pub corners with you? I don't think so.'

Nobby agreed. 'All right. I'm not saying cut your boyfriends off or anything like that. I just can't see why if two people fancy each other like crazy they can't go to bed and have a good time. This is not a rehearsal, Steph, this is your life, and you get one shot at it, screw what everybody else thinks!'

Steph laughed. 'You always were a good interviewer, a good persuader.'

'You know it makes sense, Steph.' He smiled.

'Come on. Let's go.'

They paid, and as they were walking to the rear car park, Nobby took Steph's hand. At the car, they stopped and before either realized, they were kissing, Steph yielding to Nobby's rock-hard body. His strong arms held her. He caressed her. She felt the length of his penis growing, throbbing against her as their pelvises ground together. Nobby's hand stroked her tiny waist and eased up to a firm breast; the nipple was erect. Steph couldn't help herself: she, too, had to have a feel. She touched his penis. Oh my God, she thought. With all the will-power she could muster, she pulled away. 'For God's sake Nobby, not here!' she groaned.

Ashley was in the Incident Room leaning on the back two legs of his chair. Charlie Carter glanced up at him.

'I see you're under pressure then, Ashley?'

'Oh it's terrible. I'm going to ring up a bird.'

'Lucky you. I'd hate to think that work got in the way of your social life. Look at you, you look knackered. Another late night, was it?'

'Half-past three, and anyway this phone call is as much for the job as it is for me.'

'Oh yes. You're going to burn yourself out, you are.'

'Yes, I'm sure you're right, but what a way to go, though.'

'Make your phone call.' Charlie continued checking through all the cars used by the suspects. No Granadas, but any of them could have had access to one; it wasn't going to be that obvious. Ashley fished in his inside pocket for his diary and began thumbing through the pages. He eventually found Sharon's name. He would take a chance that she would be in nurses' quarters and not on duty. He tapped out the digits on the telephone.

'Hello.'

'Is that Sharon?'

'No. Hang on a minute, I'll get her for you.'

There was a momentary pause, during which Ashley could hear whispered, 'Who is it? What do you mean you don't know?'

'Hello?'

'Hi, it's Ashley Stevens.'

Her voice rose a pitch. 'Oh hi. Hey I was only talking about you this morning. How are you?'

'Fine, what about yourself?'

'Fine. When are we going out then? I hope that's why you called,' she said cheekily.

'Yes of course it is. What about on Wednesday?'

'Great, I'm on mornings then. About what time?'

'Let's say eight o'clock. I'll pick you up from the nurses' quarters. Number 23 isn't it?'

'That's right. Oh brilliant. I shall look forward to that.'

Ashley made small talk. 'So you aren't on duty at the moment then?'

'No. That's why I'm here talking to you.'

'All right, clever dick. What shift are you on?'

'I'm off today, would you believe?'

'I don't know, some people don't want work, do they?'

'That's right.'

'So you've not stitched anybody up today then?' Ashley asked.

'Funnily enough, I was just about to ask you the same question!' Sharon said, laughing.

Ashley laughed back. 'Well I can say, hand on heart, that, no, I haven't stitched anybody up today. God, you're cynical!'

'It isn't that, I just know policemen.'

'You'd have to be crazy to risk twenty grand a year, or, worse, prison, for crap like that?'

'I know, I'm only winding you up.'

'Eh, it's a shame you were with somebody the other night.' Ashley wanted to get the conversation back to Blitz's again.

'Yes I know. How do you know him?'

'Didn't he tell you?'

'No, he wouldn't say.'

'There's no big secret to it. I know him from our many trips to the hospital, that's all. He sometimes works in A and E, doesn't he?' Ashley lied.

'Yes, he does. Shame I was with him, really.'

'What do you mean, *really*? It was a shame, full stop.'

'Oh all right then.'

'I take it he's not still with you then, at your pad, I mean.'

'You're joking! He had a damn good try, but I don't know, I lost my appetite a bit, after I'd seen him standing next to you.'

'Charming! What's that supposed to mean?'

'No, I didn't mean it like that, it was meant as a compliment actually.'

'OK. Thanks a lot. Did you get rid of him easily enough then?'

'Oh God, what a pain! He turned out to be a bit of a jerk really. I shan't be going out with him again. For a doctor his vocabulary needs some attention.'

'I'm not with you.'

'Well, he doesn't seem to understand the word no for a start.'

'Oh right. Mind you, I didn't know you did for that matter!'

'Cheeky sod! It's different with you, though.'

'Listen, I'd better get going. I'll pick you up at eight on Wednesday then.'

'Yes, see you then. Thanks for ringing.'

'Bye.' Ashley put the receiver down. Charlie smiled over at him.

'Yet another female, Ashley?'

'I'm afraid so, Charlie. I saw her Wednesday night with that Jonathon Stacey, you know, the doctor.'

'Yes, so what?'

'Well, they were at Blitz's together, and it sounds as though he's as much of a pervert as I am!'

'That's obviously what attracted her to him then, if she's now going out with you!'

'Piss off, you daft old scroat!'

Jayne Warriner had worked in the Fingerprint Department at Sherwood Lodge police headquarters for almost five years, ever since she had been twenty-one. It was after working a couple of years in the department that she had begun to need spectacles: the fine scrutiny of hundreds of documents and fingerprint forms had undoubtedly been the cause. Her long black hair swung over her white coat as with great care she bent over the *Evening Post* personal column letters. She checked that the documents were dry. In front of her was a small, shallow tray, slightly bigger than a piece of A4 paper, which contained the liquid chemical ninhydrin to about two millimetres deep. Using fingerprint forceps, Jayne picked up the first document and placed it in the chemical, ensuring that it was completely submerged. Thirty seconds later the document was sufficiently impregnated, so she removed it from the tray and placed it in a humidifying cabinet for three minutes, careful that the temperature did not exceed 80° centigrade inside the cabinet itself. Once the three minutes were up, she took the document out and examined it. The amenal acids had now fully soaked in and the entire document was a pink colour. However, there were no fingerprints visible. It was to be the same story for each document.

12

'Never murder a man who is committing suicide.'

President Woodrow Wilson

The family of James Deely was barely visible as they stumbled from the churchyard towards the Green Gables public house across the road, grey silhouettes huddled together like a rugby scrum in the hazy mist of rain. Each one's private attempt at coping, at putting on a brave face, was wearing in this squalid, incessant drizzle. The weather matched the bleak graveside mood. Stark and Nobby were the last to turn away, the coffin already awash with rainwater mixed with the orange-brown clay that peeled away from the sides of the newly dug grave. Stark had been to several such funerals and he always felt a sense of alienation at these proceedings. He wasn't a family member and he wasn't a friend, yet everyone knew who he was, an intruder on the most private of emotions – grief. Stark spoke briefly with the uniformed officers at the church door who had recorded on pocket Memocords the names of all those attending. He dismissed them, thanking them for their assistance, before crossing the busy road into the Green Gables.

As the two detectives entered the pub, the noise level belied the attendance. There must have been about 150 people crammed inside, all speaking in hushed whispers. It wouldn't be long before the level would rise, perhaps with intermittent laughter from those least affected by the death of a young man in his prime. Stark was afraid that Sammy would not have a clear view, but a quick glance to the left revealed him apparently chatting away, facing the bar in an elevated position, with a full view of all those present, including, most importantly, the college cadre, who were milling in a group at the corner of the bar. Stark and Nobby kept themselves to themselves and had a pint of ale each

160

before bidding their farewells and giving their condolences to Mrs Deely. There was a definite wave of relief as the policemen left the bar, everyone seeming to grow more relaxed. The noise of the chatter heightened.

Meanwhile, Sammy was having to work hard. He spoke at an advanced rate of knots, each sentence beginning with the name of the speaker, and often with the person's movements tagged on before or after the perfunctory messages.

'Tracey, passing round sympathy card: "Come on, it'll be better from all of us. It doesn't matter if you've sent a separate one, it'll be from the gang. Come on, Jonathon."

'Jon: "Oh all right then." Taking card, writing in it. "That's a nice thought Tracey. Come on. Let's have a signature and personal message from you all."

'David: "I thought the service was quite touching."

'Jon: "It makes no difference mate, we all end up as dust. It's only words, isn't it? He's probably better off out of it all, poor sod."

'Caroline: "Oh Jonathon shut up, will you, his wife might hear you. I thought it was a nice service, too, David. Ignore him, he's got no soul."

'Jon: "Hark at Sister Mother Mary."

'Caroline kicking Jon's shin.

'Jon talking. Can't see what he's saying. Tracey nodding.

'David: "It's funny how life goes, isn't it? I mean, when we were at college, who would have dreamed that we would be standing at James's wake, with Stuart's yet to come." Hand to mouth; Caroline arm round shoulder. David: "I'm all right, I was thinking only last night about college. We had a great time, didn't we?"

'Roy: "You speak for yourself. Anyway, you only used to tag on. In fact, I don't know what you're doing here, because you and James were hardly the best of friends."

'David: "Oh and I suppose you and he were best buddies, were you? And what about Jonathon? He and James hated each other!"

'Jon: "Don't put words into my mouth, David, please."

'David: "I don't need to. There's plenty there already, without me adding to them!"

'Caroline: "Come on. Bloody hell, we're at a funeral. Let's not

161

drag the past up. We were just kids. A lot of water has passed under the bridge since then."

'David: "I'm just saying that I've as much right to be here as anybody. It was Jonathon who accused James of nicking the fifty quid from his jacket, not me."

'Roy speaking. Can't see what he's saying.

'Jon: "He did nick it, Roy. It was in the locker-room at college. I saw him walk away from it, and he knew I'd seen him."

'Tracey: "Just keep your voice down, will you! I still can't believe it's all happening. It all seems crazy to me."

'Roy: "Of course, you quite had the hots for James, didn't you?"

'Jon: "Tracey had the hots for everybody, let's face it."

'Tracey hitting Jon on shoulder; laughter. Tracey taking back sympathy card, looking in it. All appear to have signed it. Tracey: "I'll give it to Sarah later, when we go."

'Mark: "Yes, if we hadn't met at college – "

'Roy: "You wouldn't have met, that's very true, Mark, well done, mate. Your college education wasn't wasted, was it?"

'Mark: "Don't be such a smart arse all the time, Roy. Give yourself a day off, will you."

'Roy: "That's very good, Mark, on the spur of the moment, just like that."

'Jon: "I think that seems to be the only good thing about it all, Mark and Caroline getting married. For Christ's sake, look at us all, bickering like kids again, trying to score points off each other."

'David: "You're right, Jonathon. We should be thankful that we're all still here. Poor old Stuart can't be." Hand to mouth again.

'Jon speaking again but I can't see what he's saying. ". . . and bloody Stuart!"

'Tracey: "You really liked him, didn't you? I'm sorry, David. Come on, have another drink."

'Mark: "I'll get them." Moving up to the bar to get served.

'Jon, in Caroline's ear: "I'm going to fuck you so hard tomorrow." Both laugh.

'Caroline: "Not here Jon, for God's sake. Half-past two in the Mayflower, as usual." Apparently not heard by the others! Mark returning with drinks. Each of them taking a drink, Mark

162

returning tray to bar. Caroline holding Mark's hand, kissing his cheek. "You're the best hubby in the world. I love you, darling."

'Mark: "I love you too, babe."

'Jon: "Who's the murderer then? Anybody want to own up?"

'Roy: "I can't see it being any of us really. I mean, what motive is there?"

'Tracey: "None apparently, but nobody knows what private secrets and meetings we have, do they, Caroline?"

'Caroline: "No, they don't. Still, who could want to kill us, and who's to say that the killing has stopped?"

'Tracey: "Does anybody know anything about the post-mortem report? Have the police said anything?"

'Roy: "Don't get into that, you'll frighten us all to death."

'Tracey: "Has everybody had a police alarm fitted at home?"

'Jon: "Yes. Well I say yes, I know I have." Everybody nodding yes.

'Caroline: "I think the police are way off mark suggesting that it's one of us."

'Tracey: "I quite agree."

'Jon: "That makes a change, Tracey agreeing with Caroline. My, things are looking up."

'Tracey: "Don't be facetious, Jonathon, it doesn't suit you."

'David: "There must be some link, though, surely? Both James and Stuart in one week. That's strange, isn't it?"

'Roy saying something – can't make it out.

'Mark: "Strange yes, but not impossible. Stuart's death could quite easily have been an accident, with the driver panicking and driving off."

'Tracey: "Yes, it could be, but didn't the police say that the registration number was covered by a black cloth or something?"

'Jon: "Yes, that's right, they did mention something about that. I think the police could be right, it could be any one of us, and whoever it is, for Christ's sake fucking stop it while you're ahead!"

'Silence. Nobody speaking.

'Still nobody speaking.

'Tracey: "Perhaps we shouldn't talk about the killings, it just upsets everybody."

'Caroline: "Of course, Tracey, we are thoughtless, what with your little girl and everything."

'Tracey: "It's not that, Caroline. It's the thought that all our hopes and dreams for the future seem to have got lost along the way, to the point where somebody's committed murder."

'Jon: "You've done OK, Tracey. You've got a loving husband, a good job at the car sales. All of us have done OK, really."

'Caroline: "That's all well and good, Jon, but what sort of people have we become? Are we nice people to know? I don't think so. Sure, we've all got good jobs, but what about James? He had one too, and what good has that done him?"

'David: "Perhaps we're being too hard on ourselves. We are what we are and we can't change that. We just have to make the most of it."

'Mark: "And we know what you are, David!"

'Caroline: "Mark, that's not on. Leave him alone."

'Roy: "That's a typically ignorant comment and I insist you withdraw it."

'Jon: "Hello. Do I sense pistols at dawn? I think I'll be your second, Mark. I'm afraid I don't fancy your chances much, Roy. He works out in the gym, you know."

'Tracey: "Is there really any point in us remaining here? What are we achieving, other than showing each other what idiots we are?"

'Caroline: "I'm ready to go now – come on, Mark." Mark and Caroline going towards Sarah Deely. Both shaking hands. "Terribly sorry, we'll keep in touch." Winners now leaving.

'Jonathon and David approaching Sarah Deely, shaking hands. Jon: "If there's anything I can do, please give me a ring."

'David: "It's a sad loss." Both leave.

'Tracey and Roy shaking hands with Sarah. Roy: "I'm so sorry, Sarah, I still can't believe it. I'll be in touch." Roy kisses Sarah and leaves.

'Tracey: "There's nothing I can add, but all of us will miss him. Goodbye, Sarah." Tracey leaving the pub.'

Sammy sat smiling at Stark across his desk. 'So all in all everything went fairly well,' he said.

'Did you manage to get everything down?'

'Yes. Very occasionally I would miss the odd sentence, but that was about it. I was fortunate that they remained talking as a group and didn't split up.'

'Lovely. Well done, mate, that's a smashing job. Have you any views on the operation?'

'Not really. The tape should be self-explanatory. They all seem to dislike each other. I won't pass comment other than to say that if they did anything or moved anything, I did note it on tape, so don't assume they've done something if I haven't mentioned it.'

'Fine. That's great. Thanks a lot, Sammy. Now down to business: payment.'

'OK.'

'Two hundred and fifty quid.'

'Yes please. That will come in very handy, Mr Stark, thanks very much. When will you be listening to the tape, Mr Stark?'

'I was going to go through it quickly with you. Why?'

'That's OK then. Only Jonathon and Caroline have arranged to meet tomorrow afternoon at the Mayflower, for a bonking session by the looks of it.'

'Have they really? Well, that's a turn-up for the books before we start! The Mayflower is it? Perhaps we should have a reception committee waiting to pipe them aboard!'

Dave Stark sat at the dinner table with his family around him for the first time in over a week. His suit jacket was off and he had his tie loosened and his top button undone. His sleeves were rolled up, only two turns, the cuffs flared outwards. Carol sat opposite, wearing a baggy track suit, his sixteen-year-old daughter Laura at one end of the table and his fourteen-year-old son Christopher at the other. Laura gave the appearance of being slightly older than sixteen, particularly when she was made-up. Her hair was a mousy brown and hung over her shoulders with just a hint of a wave. Christopher had black hair with a fringe; he was still a boy. Just the clinking of cutlery on plates disturbed the silence.

'So, what have you all been doing this last week?' Dave asked.

Laura was openly aggressive. 'Well, you wouldn't know, would you, seeing as you've been missing without trace for days.'

'I haven't been missing without trace at all! I've been at work, earning money for my family so they have a roof over their heads and food to eat!'

Carol spoke. She didn't want the evening spoiled. 'That's

enough. You know your father would prefer to be at home if he could.'

Laura retaliated. 'No he wouldn't, he loves it at work. You know it and we know it. He just bloody sleeps here.'

Dave had heard enough. 'That's enough, Laura. There's only two people allowed to swear in this room, and you're not one of them. Now let's all try to get along, shall we, like a normal family.'

'Huh, a normal family, what's one of those? You're not a dad, you're a joke!' Laura said sardonically.

'Right, that's it, up to your room.'

'She's only just started her dinner, David,' Carol interrupted.

Laura beat him to the reply. 'It's OK, Mum. I'd sooner go upstairs than be at the same table as a stranger.'

David's heart sank; he didn't respond. Laura thumped her foot down on every stair as she flounced up to her bedroom. Her outburst was followed by the dull thud of music blaring from upstairs. Carol stared at Dave. 'Wonderful. Welcome home, Dave.'

'Eh, don't have a go at me. She was right out of order! How long has she been swearing like that?'

'She hasn't. That's the first time.'

'It's a bloody good job as well.'

Christopher chimed in. 'She's always swearing. You ought to hear her at school.'

'That's enough, Christopher. When we want your opinion, we'll ask for it, thank you.'

'Charming!'

The three continued their meal in silence, but then Christopher volunteered. 'Don't worry about Laura, Dad. She's going through a funny time – she thinks she's an adult.'

Dave smiled and gave Christopher a playful punch on the chin. 'Thank you, Christopher, I'm glad somebody understands. I'd love to see more of all of you, but I'm in a position where I can't, and there's no escaping from it. We have to pull together as a family the best we can.'

Christopher smiled. 'I know.'

The meal over, Christopher vanished to play on his computer. David and Carol smiled at each other. 'I'm sorry, love, it's not the sort of evening I'd envisaged. When I've sorted this job at work

166

out I'll have some leave. We'll all go away for the weekend,' he promised. Carol looked tired. 'Come on then, you can wash, I'll wipe.'

Later that evening, Dave knocked on Laura's door for the second time, in an attempt to be heard over the racket inside. The noise lessened and Laura opened the door. 'Can I come in?' Dave enquired.

'Have you got a warrant?' Laura smiled.

Dave sat on Laura's bed while she sat at her dressing-table, combing her long hair.

'Do you really think I want it to be like that?'

'I don't know, I don't even know you. You're my dad and I don't even know you.' She shrugged a reluctant laugh that was tinged with sadness.

'What do you suggest I do then, love?'

'I don't know. Can't you do another job?'

'How can I? All I know is being a policeman.'

'I didn't mean that, I meant another job in the police force.'

'Like what? If I went on a squad, I'd be here just as little, if not less. That leaves me one option: to go back into uniform. Working weird shifts, having spotty-faced young men underneath me, straight out of school almost. Locking up criminals would be a thing of the past; I'd just be a supervisor. Do you think that sounds like your old dad? Do you think I'd get any satisfaction from that?'

'But you'd see more of us, Dad.'

'When, though? You're out with your boyfriend most nights, or your friends. You're almost grown up. I do see you most weekends, don't I? It's only when there's a big job on – '

Laura turned to face him. 'Dad, there's always a big job on, you know that.'

'Do you really want me to stop what I'm doing?'

Laura paused. She shook her head.

'Come here.' He put his arm around her. 'I tell you what, do you fancy coming to the pictures, all four of us?'

'Yes, that'd be great – oh, I can't. I promised Terry I'd see him tonight.'

They both laughed. 'I know how it feels now.' Dave put his hand out towards Laura. 'Friends?' She shook his hand.

'Friends.'

*

167

Darrel and Pete were bored: it was one o'clock in the morning and it had been a quiet night. They were responsible for Uniform Two, or Panda Two, as it was known, the mobile response vehicle in the Bulwell area. They had been to a couple of domestics, a burglary and two fights at local hostelries, but for the last twenty minutes it had been dead. They were parked on Bulwell Market Place; Darrel had the driver's window down and was smoking.

'Hang on a minute, what's this coming across the Market Place?'

Pete couldn't see. 'Where? Oh, I can see her now. I've got you.'

They watched the leggy blonde clip-clop across the Market in her high-heeled shoes and a miniskirt which revealed the hint of stocking-top. The woman was obviously aware of the attention she was getting, since she exaggerated her wiggle and smiled over at the two uniformed officers.

'Goodnight!' Darrel shouted. The woman smiled and nodded, waving a hand displaying long fingernails.

'This is not good for a red-blooded male.' Darrel observed to his friend.

'She wouldn't let you anywhere near her. What's the matter with you?' Pete mocked.

'You saw how she was – a little bit of chat and I'm sure we'd get along fine. But no, I've got to look at your ugly mug all night.'

'Shut up and give us a kiss.' Pete pursed his lips.

'Piss off, you pervert.'

As their laughter diminished, Pete was the first to hear the unusual noise: two pips, then a pause, two more pips, then a pause, and so on, coming over their radio sets.

'That's an alarm sounding, listen.'

The pips were interrupted by the Control Room operator.

'Panzer two.' At night the radio operators liked to indulge in a bit of punning.

Darrel started the engine, whilst Pete replied in similar cavalier fashion. 'Mess your passage.'

'Police alarm sounding at 67 Wington Street, Bulwell, home address of Roy Prentice, potential target for murder.'

'Ten four, travelling.'

Darrel screeched the tyres as he pulled off the Market Place at great speed, flicking his cigarette on to the bricked square.

'Panda Two.'

Pete replied again, 'Go ahead.' The adrenalin had started pumping.

'Panda One is travelling from Hucknall to back you up.'

'Ten four, much obliged.'

Darrel was really thrashing the vehicle as they travelled along the almost deserted Main Street, the Control Room operator continuing his message: 'Sixty-seven Wington is a semi-detached house with front and rear access. Along Main Street to junction with Sandfield Road, turn left, second right and third left on to Wington. Over.'

'Ten four.'

Pete pointed at the red traffic lights ahead. 'Darrel, they're on red mate – *Darrel*!'

'Fuck the lights, there's somebody being murdered for all we know!' He turned the car sharply into the corner, ignoring the red light. 'There was a bit of green in there somewhere!'

Within moments they had arrived. They ran from the car, Pete's hand on his truncheon pocket. They saw the figure silhouetted against the light of the door as they approached. Pete withdrew his truncheon, ready to cave in the head of any maniacal murderer before he became his next victim.

'Good evening, or should I say good morning?' Roy Prentice's smiling countenance greeted them at the door. He was holding a stopwatch. 'I make it three minutes, seven seconds. Not bad, but I could still have been murdered in that time!'

Dave Stark lay in bed, reading. Carol had finished her chapters of Jackie Collins's latest best seller. She put the book on her bedside table, switched off her lamp and turned over, away from Dave.

'How long are you going to be, Dave?' she asked.

'Not long.'

'Come on, you'll be tired.'

'I'm tired already, to tell the truth, but I can't get to sleep unless I read for a bit, you know that. I keep thinking about the murders.'

'You've still no idea who's done them, then?' Carol's voice was slurred. Dave couldn't decipher whether she was interested or not. Usually she didn't bother to ask.

'Well, no. We had a bit of a break with Sammy Trench – he's the deaf bloke – I've told you about him before. It looks as though two of the college gang are having an affair, and then there's Tracey Sewell, who seemed to be asking a lot of questions, and Roy Prentice was quite protective towards David Seaton, but then again he's into gay rights and all that shit, so we'll have to analyse the tape again tomorrow. I mean, the tape isn't there to give us anything of any great evidential value, because a half decent barrister would simply make out that Sammy was mistaken or whatever, but it's a help just pointing us in the right direction for Caroline Winner and – ' Carol let out a snore.

Dave sighed. 'Is that right, Dave? Oh how interesting! How terribly, terribly interesting! Goodnight Carol,' he mocked. He turned off his lamp, closed his eyes and again let out a sigh.

13

'Whoever called it necking, was a poor judge of anatomy.'

Groucho Marx

The bedroom was dark, curtains drawn, red digits of the radio alarm clock the only light visible. As it clicked on to 7:00 the radio burst into life, the disc jockey merrily projecting amiable noises to the masses.

Nobby grunted and wearily opened one eye towards the commotion. He reached over and turned it off. It had been a long night. His body ached as he lay on his back, tanned and naked under the quilt. Nobby instinctively drew his legs together as his female company provided a moist sensation down below, licking and teasing before devouring. He squirmed with pleasure. His well-equipped manhood grew and pulsated in response to the glorious sensation. Her tongue tickled along his flat, hard stomach, which tensed to her touch.

Nobby threw the quilt back to reveal the wonderful body of Stephanie Dawson, erect nipples crowning impressive breasts. Her endless sexual appetite had made it a long night for the pair of them. The tongue continued its journey on to his chest and connected with his mouth. Their lips pressed harshly together, mouths open, tongues uniting. Steph slid on to Nobby, slowly and deliberately, her neck arching backwards. They both groaned. Steph shook her tousled hair. She gave him a knowing smile. 'Morning, Sarge!'

Stark arrived at the station just before eight-thirty. Nobby greeted him in the corridor.

'What's the matter with you, Nobby? Aren't you feeling well? You look as though you've just run a marathon!'

171

'No, I just had a hard night, that's all.'

'Oh aye. Hard being the operative word, no doubt!' Stark gave him a knowing look. 'Will you organize the troops today, Nobby? I want to listen to Sammy Trench's tape again. There's something niggling me about it.'

'OK boss. No problem. There's no joy on the *Evening Post* letter-box yet.'

Stark looked disdainfully at his detective sergeant. 'Yes, I know.'

Nobby disappeared into the CID office as Stark went into his. 'You look as if you've run a bleeding marathon. Had a good night, have we?' Nobby repeated to Steph.

'Excellent, but of course it's none of your business, Sarge!'

Nobby smiled. He felt the best way to behave was to be exactly the same as he had been the day before, masking the current situation between him and Steph with his usual debauched comments. He had long since tested the water with Steph. Some women officers hate the flirting. He knew Steph enjoyed it.

Meanwhile, Stark sipped at his mug of tea, kindly supplied by Grant Donaldson.

He placed the cassette into the player and pressed the button, fast-forwarding and rewinding to various parts of Sammy's commentary:

'Tracey, passing round sympathy card: "Come on, it'll be better from all of us."' *Fast-forward.* '"He and James hated each other!" Jon: "Don't put words into my mouth, David, please."' *Fast-forward.* '". . . nick it, Roy. It was in the locker-room at college. I saw him walk away from it, and he knew I'd seen him."' *Fast-forward.* '". . . it to Sarah later . . ."' *Fast-forward* 'Mark: "Yes, if we hadn't met at college – "' *Fast-forward.* '"Poor old Stuart can't be."' *Fast-forward.* '". . . fuck you so hard tomorrow."' *Rewind.* '". . . to get served." Jon, in Caroline's ear: "I'm going to fuck you so hard tomorrow." Both laugh. Caroline: "Not here Jon, for God's sake. Half-past two in the Mayflower, as usual."' *Fast-forward.* 'Mark: "I love you too, babe."' *Fast-forward.* '". . . killing has stopped?"' *Fast-forward.* '". . . about the post-mortem report? Have the police said anything?" Roy: "Don't get . . ."' *Fast-forward.* '". . . upsets everybody." Caroline: "Of course, Tracey, we are thoughtless, what with your little girl and everything." Tracey: "It's not that, Caroline."' *Fast-forward.*

'"Mark, that's not on. Leave him alone." Roy: "That's a typically ignorant comment..."' *Fast-forward*. '...Sarah Deely. Both shaking hands.' *Fast-forward*. 'Roy kisses Sarah and leaves. Tracey: "There's nothing I can add, but all of us will miss him. Goodbye, Sarah." Tracey leaving the pub.'

Stark tapped the tape recorder. A cloud of smoke billowed out from his pipe. He shook his head. 'Something isn't quite right, something's missing. What the bloody hell is it?' He rewound the tape, and pressed play again.

The Mayflower public house was one of the most fashionable places to be seen in. It was based on an American-style bar, with large lager glasses and cocktails with American tags to them. The bar itself was high, and the furniture was steel-rimmed. Part of the room was given over to the lunch-time clientele to consume their snacks: pancakes with various fillings, or hamburgers for the less fussy. The restaurant area was the most crowded, with yuppies in designer suits tapping their feet to the subtle music piped around the place.

Nobby and Charlie felt ill at ease in such a joint. Charlie was more at home in working-men's clubs and down-to-earth spit and sawdust pubs. They stood at the far end of the bar, with an unobstructed view of the glass entrance doors that led out on to the bustling city-centre streets. Charlie glanced at the clock: twenty-five-past two in England and twenty-five-past nine in Florida.

Nobby broke the silence, tearing his thoughts away from his night of lust. 'Well, they should be here any minute now.'

'What are you going to do then, Nobby? Take them back to the nick or what?'

'No, I think we'll invite them in for a drink and have a heart-to-heart chat with them. They're the ones who're being secretive about things; we'll put the ball in their court, but if they become aggressive or refuse to be open, perhaps we'll have to pay them a visit at home. I don't think that would go down particularly well with Mark Winner, do you?'

Charlie laughed. 'You're a hard man, Nobby.'

'Hang on a minute, there's Caroline. No sign of Jonathon Stacey, though,' Nobby observed. 'We'll wait for him to arrive before we make ourselves known. They should walk into us, so there's no great panic. Just keep your eye on them.'

Caroline was wearing a burgundy three-quarter-length overcoat, black stockings, and black gloves and handbag. Ten minutes became fifteen; there was still no sign of Jonathon. Caroline was becoming impatient. She glanced furtively at her watch several times. They'd always met outside before; he'd insisted that she shouldn't have to walk into a bar alone. She started to walk towards the door, concern etched into her features. Charlie and Nobby chased outside and shouted after her. *'Caroline!'*

The horror on her face illustrated the level of surprise their shouts had caused her. The two men walked over to her as she stood frozen to the spot.

Her heart was thumping as she tried to play it cool. 'Hello, fancy seeing you here.' She tried to smile.

'It's no coincidence, Caroline love,' Nobby said. 'We know why you're here.' Nobby's smile was a thin line. 'Let's talk about that inside, shall we?'

'Is somebody else with you?'

'You mean Jonathon?'

Caroline sighed. 'Perhaps we'd better go and have a drink. How the hell do you know about us? It's impossible!'

The three returned to the Mayflower. They sat at a table a discreet distance from the madding crowd. Charlie got the drinks.

Struggling to remain calm, Caroline asked, 'How the hell did you find out about us?'

Nobby did most of the talking. 'We can't tell you, Caroline. Suffice to say we know, and the important thing is that you're frank with us. If we feel that you aren't, we may have to get things out into the open, but otherwise there's no reason why we should tell anybody, is there, Charlie?'

Charlie shook his head.

'Please don't tell Mark. He'll go absolutely berserk,' she pleaded.

'Are you sure he doesn't know already?'

'Positive. I assure you, if he knew, I would know about it, and the Queens Medical Centre as well, I should think, because I'd be an in-patient!'

'Is he violent, then?'

'No, but he has such a temper and he's so strong – well, you've seen him – he's solid muscle.'

'Does anybody else know about the affair?'

'No. I certainly haven't told anybody about it, and I'm fairly sure Jon hasn't said anything. I wonder why he isn't here. Do you think he saw you?'

Nobby shook his head. 'No, I don't think so. Has he let you down before?'

'No, never.'

'Excuse my forthright attitude, Caroline, and don't be afraid to tell the truth, because as you can see, things always come out sooner or later, but are you having an affair with anybody else?'

She laughed. 'No. What do you take me for?'

'I don't take you for anything, love. There are millions of people having affairs; it's of no consequence to me. Are Jon or Mark having any other affairs?'

'I don't think Mark is. You never know, do you? But I doubt it very much. Jon has occasional flings though.'

'What about all those frustrated housewives Mark jumps about with at the leisure centre?' Charlie asked. 'Would he be tempted?'

'Maybe, but I doubt if they'd last long, because – perhaps I shouldn't say this – although Mark's very physical, he's certainly no sexual athlete. We don't do it a lot now. There's not much point – we've barely started before he's finished, if you know what I mean.' Caroline was blushing slightly, her honesty driven by fear of her assignations getting back to Mark.

'How and when did your affair with Jon start?' Nobby asked.

'About two years ago. It was at a point when our marriage, from a sexual side, was going through a bad time. I'm a very sexual person and I needed to do something about it. I had seen Jon in a pub once and we'd had a kiss and a cuddle. Jon was drunk. He lives life to the full, does Jon. He told me where he was working and one particularly bad day I gave him a call, and that was it. I think we ended up in the sack on that first date. It was wonderful, and well, that's it, really.'

'Are you and Jon in love?'

'That's a difficult thing to say. We're certainly in lust. I know Jon sees other women, but I can't complain while I stay with Mark, can I?'

'Does that bother you?'

'In one sense it does, but in another way it keeps the relationship alive, because I feel I'm competing and we keep making an effort with each other.'

'That's a very sensible attitude. Why haven't you left Mark?'

'I keep asking myself that question. Basically, I daren't tell him. I don't need the aggravation it would cause. And why should I? I'm happy as things are – why spoil a good thing?'

'Quite right. I wish there were more women like yourself.' Nobby smiled; so did Caroline.

'Listen,' Caroline said. 'I'm slightly concerned that Jon isn't here, especially in the light of recent events. The only thing I can think of is that he's seen you.'

Charlie was confident. 'I'd be very surprised if he had.'

'Is there any way I can try to contact him? He's never let me down in two years – I am rather concerned!'

Nobby glanced at Charlie. 'I think you'd better ring up Stark and put him in the picture. I think a visit to Jon's house might be appropriate, don't you?'

Charlie's face was serious. 'I think you could be right.'

Grant Donaldson was wearing a dark-blue suit, white shirt and Paisley tie. Ashley Stevens wore his grey woollen Italian double-breasted suit, a flashy silk tie, gold pin, gold watch and bracelet. He wore expensive black shoes with a buckle on the side of the instep.

Ashley carefully parked his Porsche in the road leading to Stacey's home address.

Grant spoke. 'I've got bad vibes about this, Ash.'

'Yes, I know what you mean. He's probably got another tart on the go. According to Charlie, he's been seeing quite a few of them.'

Grant stared up at the house. It looked as if nobody was in. The downstairs curtains were drawn, although the upstairs ones were open. The two marched up to the front door, boldly. Ash knocked. No reply. He hammered again. Not a sound. 'Let's have a look round the back.' As they walked round, Grant began to get butterflies in his stomach. All the curtains on this side, including those upstairs, were closed. 'You did check he wasn't at work at the hospital, didn't you?' Ashley asked.

'Of course I did.'

176

'He's not on nights, is he?'

'No. He was off yesterday and isn't due back until tomorrow at two o'clock.'

'He's out shagging. He can't have been attacked. He's got a police alarm, and none of them have been activated. He'll be seeing some tart somewhere.'

'Well, we can't just assume that, can we?' Grant answered.

'No.' Ashley used his car keys to clatter on the glass door. He stepped back and stared up at the bedrooms. He looked through the letter-box, seeing nothing other than the hallway and a couple of letters on the floor. He shouted through it.

'Jonathon, it's the police. Are you in?'

Deadly silence.

Grant put his hands in his pockets. 'I suppose he could be anywhere – he's a single bloke. Are there any other addresses we can check for him?'

'Only his mother's, and I rang her before we came out. She dropped out that she hasn't seen him for a week, but that's nothing unusual apparently. As you say, he could be bloody anywhere.'

Ashley glanced at his watch; almost four o'clock. He stared at the houses along the row. 'Come on, let's knock on a few doors.' They split up. Almost inevitably, the houses to either side were empty. Not a sign. Ashley finally got some success at the house next door but one. It was answered by a woman in her early thirties whose dark hair was tied back with a piece of cloth, no doubt to save her having to style it.

'Hello, love. I'm from the CID. We want to speak to Jonathon Stacey, next door but one, do you know him?'

'Yes, he should be in. I've not heard him go out this morning. Isn't he answering?' The woman fended off a small child as she spoke to Ashley.

'No, love, he isn't. That's why I've had to pester you, I'm afraid. I take it you didn't see him go out then?'

'No.' The woman stepped out of her house, allowing her boy to run out. 'Oi, come here!' She chased the lad on to the path and caught him before turning to look at Jonathon's house. 'His curtains are drawn. That's strange.'

Grant had joined them. 'Is it strange? I know a lot of single men don't bother too much with things like drawing the curtains.'

'Well Jonathon always does. I've never seen them like that before, but that's funny, the upstairs ones are open.'

'Do you know which room he would sleep in?' Ashley asked.

'Well, the front. That's where the main bedroom is, and there's only him in the house. Here, do you think he's all right? Because he was telling me that a couple of his mates had been murdered.' She put her hand to her mouth, underlining her growing consternation.

Ashley attempted to reassure her. 'I'm pretty sure he is OK, but d'you know of any other places he would be? Any girlfriends?'

'He's got plenty of those, but he laughs about the fact that he always brings them to his house, so that he doesn't have to get up and leave, and can "throw them out when he's had enough of them". He's a bit of lad, our Jonathon is, you know.'

Grant stared at Ashley. His butterflies hadn't gone away.

'Has anybody been to the house at all?'

'Not as far as I'm aware. I don't know.'

'Well, when did you last see him, love?'

'Last night, about six o'clock, as he was coming in.'

Ashley asked the obvious question: 'Which car does he drive?'

'A Ford Sierra. Bloody hell, it's there, look! Oh my God!' She pointed at the metallic-silver-coloured car across the road.

'I think we're going to have to force an entry. Just as a precaution, love. Can I ask you to stay in your house for the time being?'

'Shouldn't I come with you?'

Ashley was firm. 'No, I think it's better if you stay where you are now. We'll call you if we need you.'

Ashley walked over to his car and removed a truncheon from it. The two strolled sombrely towards the rear of the house. Grant broke the silence. 'Shouldn't we check with Stark before we go ahead?'

'No. He's given us a task to do. We don't have to keep asking him. He'd never be off the phone if everyone bothered him once there was a problem. The law says that we have a right to cause damage if it's to protect life or property, and for all we know, poor old Jonathon Stacey could be dying inside, so we've got to go in, bogger it.'

Ashley went to check if there was a key in the door, but it was a Yale lock. He told Grant to stand back as he smashed the rear kitchen window and knocked the loose pieces out before reaching through and opening it. The two men climbed inside. Ashley ran straight upstairs, while Grant tentatively opened the living-room door. He'd done this a few times. It was usually when elderly people hadn't been seen for a time, and milk and newspapers were building up. It isn't the sight of death that makes one apprehensive, it's the unknown. It's opening each door and not knowing what's going to be behind it. A decayed body? A suicide? A murder? It wasn't long before Grant knew exactly what was happening. He stepped into the living-room and stopped in his tracks. He froze, halted by the sight that greeted him. After a couple of seconds, he shouted upstairs.

'Ashley.'

'What?' came the reply.

'I think you'd better come in here.'

Ashley joined his friend at the living-room door. 'Oh shit!'

Jonathon Stacey was lying on the settee, his eyes fixed wide and staring, blind to the incredulous expressions on Ashley's and Grant's faces. After a moment Ashley spoke. 'Call up Stark on the radio. Then we'll check that the house is empty.'

14

'For three days after death hair and fingernails
continue to grow, but phone calls taper off.'

Johnny Carson

Stark was careful to wear gloves as he handled the ripped piece of
card with the scrawled message on it: *I'm so terribly sorry. Jonathon
Stacey.*

'Suicide sir?' Ashley asked.

'I don't know. It's all very convenient. I wish he'd been more
explicit in his note.'

He stared at Stacey. He was supine on the settee, fully dressed,
his shirt unbuttoned at the neck, both sleeves rolled up, tie
loosely hanging. His left arm dangled outwards, a pinprick of
blood apparent at the vein. A syringe lay behind him on the
settee. On the coffee-table was a cheap Biro and a glass of whisky.
Stark spoke aloud as thoughts entered his head. 'Preserve that
whisky for forensic tests.'

He picked up the pen from the table and requested a pad,
which Ashley promptly produced from his pocket. Stark wrote
out the same message on to the pad and scrutinized it, comparing
it with the scribbled note. He beckoned Ashley. 'Is it me, Ashley,
or is this Biro medium-tip, and the suicide note fine-tip?'

Ashley compared the two. 'I think you could be right, sir.
Obviously Forensic will tell us in seconds.'

'Seize every pen in the house.' He raised a cautionary hand to
the young detective. 'Not yet, Ashley! When Scenes of Crime
have finished.'

Stark looked around the room. 'Grant, are those Stacey's work
notes, at the side of that chair? Look.'

Grant put gloves on, gingerly picked up the notes and handed
them to Stark. Again he looked at the note and at Jonathon's

180

handwriting. They matched. 'It looks like it's his handwriting all right. Ashley, as well as pens, I want you to find whatever it is that this piece of card is ripped from.'

'OK sir.'

Stark shook his head. 'Is Wagstaff coming?'

'He's on his way, sir,' Grant said. 'He was at a meeting at Sherwood Lodge.'

'Who with?'

'The head of the CID, Detective Chief Superintendent Davies, sir.'

'Brilliant. So he knows already.'

'I think you'll find either he'll come or you'll be summoned to see him, sir, going on the conversation I could hear in the background.'

'I thought as much. This is going to cause so much shit, it's not true.'

Ashley was surprised. 'Why will it, sir? All it is is a suicide and an admission of guilt for two murders. I thought you'd be pleased. This suicide is the end of the line for the investigation, surely?'

'Is it bollocks, Ashley. It's another murder, man. It's bloody obvious it stinks. He's not committed suicide – look at the note. Signed, "Jonathon Stacey". How many suicides have you been to, Ashley?'

'Four or five. Why?'

'Well, I've been to dozens, and I've never yet seen a suicide note that's signed with the full name. We know who it's from! It's pretty bleeding obvious. So why this time? Why now, for the first time, do we get somebody signing their full name? I'll tell you why, Ash. Because it stinks, that's why, mate. It's a reasonable attempt to make us think it's suicide, that's all.'

'But how can you inject somebody in the perfect position without a struggle?'

'I don't know. Perhaps he thought it was a happy drug, or he was asleep, or drunk, or perhaps there's something in that glass of whisky that will tell us. It can be done – it can be done fairly bloody easily. Let's face it, it's not difficult to kill a man. It's not getting caught that's the hard bit.'

'I suppose you're right, and if you are, the shit has really hit the fan,' Ashley observed candidly.

181

'Yes, and guess where it's going to land.' Stark extended his thumb and stabbed it towards his chest.

Ashley laughed.

'Ashley, will you make a note that we must tell the pathologist to do a blood/liquor test at the PM.'

'OK.'

Stark went outside and examined all points of entry. There was evidence to support a forced entry, but only from the size twelves of Ashley Stevens and the smashed window. Ashley assured Stark that the house had been secure upon their arrival, otherwise they wouldn't have had to force entry. Stark insisted it be checked again.

Scenes of Crime weren't too long. Stark passed the time smoking his pipe outside, away from the scene, and briefing Wagstaff, who had arrived alone but with instructions for them both to see Detective Chief Superintendent Davies later on. Intermittently Stark instructed Scenes of Crime to do various things, or answered queries from them. 'Yes, take that.' 'No, leave it, I can't see the point.'

As soon as they had finished, Stark and Wagstaff went in to have a nosy around. Stark opened drawers and units upstairs and down. It was while he was in the kitchen that he made his discovery. He opened a cupboard door to discover a quite ornate whisky glass in amongst the wineglasses. He glanced at a circular table next to an armchair, where the decanter had stood prior to Scenes of Crime removing it. Around the perimeter were eight glasses all identical to the one in the cupboard and the one which had been on the coffee-table until also removed by Scenes of Crime.

'*Ashley! Stop Scenes of Crime quickly!*' he shouted.

Detective Sergeant Stuart Bradshaw, still in his white overalls, came in, smiling.

'Stuart, will you fingerprint me this glass, please?' Stark asked. 'The killer put this in here, I'm positive.'

Stuart unpacked his metal case of tricks and removed what looked like a very fine paintbrush and a pot of aluminium dust. He dusted the glass carefully.

'Sorry. Nothing. You can see for yourself.' Stark nodded, annoyed. 'Take it for Forensic, will you please, Stuart.'

Ashley poked his head through the kitchen door. 'The people who take you down under are here, sir.'

'Who?'

'The undertakers, sir.'

'OK, we've finished in here. Who is it?'

'Smiths, and they're handing out complimentary pens. Do you want one, sir?' Ashley proudly produced the inscribed plastic pen.

Stark laughed. 'No thanks. And for Christ's sake don't mix that up with the ones you've taken from here!'

'Don't worry. Scenes of Crime have got those.' He disappeared briefly before being followed back in by the three undertakers. The younger of the three winked at Stark as he entered, before inserting a piece of chewing-gum into his mouth. Then they expertly manhandled Jonathon into the bag and on to the trolley. As the young man zipped him up, he tapped Jonathon's nose. 'And no snoring!'

Stark sat at his desk, resting his head on his arm. His door was open and he was becoming increasingly infuriated at the conversation he could hear from the CID office. Jim McIntyre was pontificating again.

'Well, I still don't see what Stark's problem is, now he's got a bloke who's killed himself and confessed to the killings. The killings will stop now – we know that from the text of the *Evening Post* personal column messages. Two detected murders and a suicide sound a lot better to me than three undetected murders!'

'How can you say that?' Grant interjected. 'It's obvious even to me as the aide that there's been foul play. What are you suggesting – a cover-up?'

'I'm not suggesting that, I'm just asking where the actual hard evidence is that he hasn't killed himself?'

'We don't just deal with waterproof evidence. Look at the circumstantial evidence.'

'Hold on a minute. The courts don't deal with purely circumstantial evidence, so why should we?'

Grant stuck to his guns. 'OK then, look at it from the other angle. Where's the evidence that he did kill the other two? And if it is him, the *Evening Post* letters must be wrong, because there's no third killing!'

183

Stark smiled to himself; Grant was turning out to be a good lad.

'Look, I've been on this job a damn sight longer than you have, young Grant.'

'So what? So have Stark and Charlie here, for that matter. It still doesn't give you the monopoly on opinion and logical thought, does it?'

'Long words don't make you right, either.'

'What are you talking about, long words?'

'I'm just saying, you've got a lot to learn, son.'

'Yes, but not off you, Jim!' added Charlie.

Stark smiled, but his forehead furrowed into a frown. If only it was as Jim had said. Still, that's not what they pay us for; it's just tough shit, he thought. He knew that headquarters' top corridor would hit the roof, and they would be looking for someone on whom they could pin the badge of scapegoat. He fingered his lapel.

Detective Chief Superintendent Davies was only a couple of years older than Stark, though with a few more grey hairs. He was a clean-cut man, well groomed, and he wore tailored, if not a little old-fashioned, suits. Despite his rank his office was not over-large, crammed in between his 'worker bee' subordinates and the Force Intelligence Bureau at Sherwood Lodge. To the run-of-the-mill detectives he was God. They never saw the man, only his signature on various memos that filtered through the internal mail system.

This man *was* the CID. Any decisions made at the highest level, he was instrumental in, if not the instigator. He had the ear of the Chief Constable – 'which I keep in a drawer' was one of his regular jokes. John Davies had worked his way up the hard way, right through the ranks, all the time remaining on the CID, with every promotion other than sergeant – not an inauspicious feat in itself. Davies was very rank-conscious and was known for his overreaction to seemingly petty incidents apparently out of step with the norm. Stark could remember as a DC, Davies, then a detective chief inspector, ripping his head off and screaming at him for referring to a detective sergeant by his first name. 'He has been promoted by the Crown of this country and he will be referred to as Sergeant by the likes of you. Now get out until you have some common decency and an understanding of the rank structure of the police force.'

'Hold on a minute, sir . . .'

'Are you deaf as well as daft? I've told you, *get out*.'

Since then, Stark had disliked the man intensely. He considered his pettiness a weakness of character, and was averse to the way he used his rank rather than thrashing things out, man to man. Davies was not, however, a man to be crossed and Stark was not into professional suicide, so he kept his contempt to himself. Despite the austere approach which Stark found so distasteful, Davies was a cracking detective, undoubtedly the man for the job, an intelligent, streetwise copper who remembered the dodges and liberties that detectives occasionally took. Some officers' stunts he would let pass by; other officers would be wearing large pointed helmets shortly after their discovery.

Stark and Wagstaff stood outside Davies' office like two naughty schoolboys. The secretary informed them that he would see them now. That's very big of him, Stark thought to himself.

He tapped on the door.

'Enter!'

Keep calm; just keep your big mouth shut, Stark told himself.

The two walked in. Davies was scribbling at his desk and failed to acknowledge their presence. Stark coughed. Without looking up at them, Davies pointed a finger, indicating they should sit down, which they did. After what seemed like an age, Davies spoke; it was sharp and to the point. His piercing eyes flashed between Stark and Wagstaff.

'Mr Stark, you are Acting Detective Chief Inspector. Mr Wagstaff, you are a substantive Detective Superintendent. Why aren't you fulfilling these roles adequately?'

Stark glanced at Wagstaff incredulously. Wagstaff spoke. 'Well, we are – what . . . ?'

'I'm sorry, Mr Wagstaff, you perhaps didn't hear me correctly. I said, why aren't you fulfilling your obligations?'

Wagstaff was starting to sweat already. 'I take it you are referring to the murder investigation.'

'Yes. So?'

'You are obviously familiar with the case, sir. We have tried everything, and in recent days we have had a series of developments.'

185

'I take it by that you are making reference to the fact that another poor bastard has been murdered while you stand idly by?'

'I wouldn't say we are standing idly by – '

'Oh wouldn't you? Well, I'm not particularly interested in what you say. I'm interested in results, and I don't see any. You have failed, haven't you? You have failed me, you have let yourselves down, and more importantly, you have failed the public. I don't like failures, Mr Wagstaff, there is no place for them in my CID.'

Wagstaff was speechless. Davies directed his attention to Stark. 'You don't seem to be saying much, Mr Stark?'

'I've not been given the chance, sir.' Keep calm, don't lose your head, Stark told himself.

'The floor is yours. Don't let me stop you.'

'Well, our job is to see if there are any connections between the killings and a group of former college friends – '

'Oh for Christ's sake, Stark, of course there is a connection. A blind man could see that! But what the hell are you doing about it?'

'We are fairly certain that this last killing is not a suicide, which leaves the remaining college group as the suspects – '

'Well, with a bit of luck soon there'll only be one left and that will make things easier for you.'

'If you have read the reports, sir, you will know that the *Evening Post* personal column entries indicate that this will be the last killing.' Don't let him draw you, keep it cool, Stark thought.

'Don't even think of patronizing me, Stark, because you will be the loser.'

'I'm not with you, sir.' You pompous git.

'You're bloody right, you're not, and at this rate you won't be. Permanently. I don't like incompetents.'

'With respect, sir. I am not incompetent. We are open to suggestions from people who think they can do better.' That had torn it.

'Don't get fucking leery! You have three days to sort it. I want to read every single action you've done, and yes, smart arse, you may well find a few suggestions coming your way! So piss off out and do the job you are paid for!'

Wagstaff and Stark left. Stark was fuming. He knew he shouldn't have said what he did, but he had been his own man on

186

the police force for twenty-four years and he wasn't going to take that sort of shit, detective chief superintendent or not. Ah well, at least Laura would be happy if he got the boot.

Wagstaff was red in the face. 'I think you might just have gone a bit too far this time, David.'

'Stuff it. I'm not taking that crap. It was completely unjustified.' He had no intention of discussing the case. 'I'm forty years old, I don't need bollockings to motivate me. The man's power-pissed!'

Nobby had to shout down the telephone to Stark. He was struggling to be heard above the drone of the numerous trepans cutting off the tops of heads in the post-mortem theatre next door.

'We've just finished, Dave.'

'What's the crack then, Nobby?'

'Pretty much what we knew already. Syringe mark to left arm. It looks as though he died through an overdose of drugs.'

'What sort of drugs? I don't suppose we know yet, do we?'

'No. The stomach contents have gone straight to Toxicology for analysis. The pathologist has given me the nod, though.'

'Who was it? Disney-Hargreaves?'

'Yes. He reckons it could be a morphine overdose, off the record, like.'

'Morphine?'

'That's right. Not the most accessible of drugs.'

Stark pondered. 'Well he did work at a hospital. Would he have any lying about in the house?'

'I asked Disney-Hargreaves that. He says he most certainly shouldn't, but of course that doesn't mean he wouldn't have.'

'Still, the killer would have to have known that he had.'

'Assuming the killer didn't have his own supply.'

'Yes. We'll talk about it later. Anything else of relevance?'

'No, that's it.'

'Did he have Aids?'

'No, most definitely not.'

'Let's discuss it later, Nobby. Are you coming straight back?'

'Yes, I could do with a shower. I stink of death; it's on my clothes and everything.'

'Nip home and have a shower and change and I'll see you back at the station.'

'OK, mate. How did you get on with Davies?'

'Absolutely wonderful. Wouldn't hear a word said against the man.'

Nobby laughed. 'See you.'

Stephanie typed out the final warrant, as instructed by Stark. For an application to obtain a warrant, it was necessary to type out the warrant itself and an 'information', which had to be signed by the officer making the application. The warrant needed several copies: two for the magistrate's clerk, once it had been executed; one for the occupier of the house; and one for the Search Register Book at the station. Stark had told Stephanie to wait until it was out of court time, so that she could visit the magistrate's house for the application. Magistrates as a rule are most willing to issue warrants as long as it all sounds pretty reasonable. (A lot of the time, though, Stark felt they didn't fully understand what the hell was going on, and their grasp of Section 8.1 of the Police and Criminal Evidence Act of 1984 was sometimes quite bizarre.) Anyway, it was often less hassle to go to a magistrate's house and do it in one fell swoop. Stark felt that the application fulfilled the requirements of Section 8: a serious arrestable offence had been committed, and they had reasonable suspicion there was evidence at any one of the college gang's houses that could be of use to the investigation. A good firm application and some harsh facts about the killings should sway it.

Steph completed the 'persons or articles to look for' column:

Knife believed used in murder of Deely
Vehicle believed used in murder of Millichip
Morphine or container or syringes
Typewriter or evidence of letters to *Evening Post* personal column

She scratched at her head. After last night's session with Nobby, she was exhausted – she'd had little sleep. She couldn't think of anything else, so she merely added: 'Anything of evidential value regarding any of the murders'.

Steph glanced at the clock. She wanted to make sure the application could be done at the home address of the magistrate; it made life somewhat easier not to have the magistrate's clerk chipping in all the time. The magistrate she had been designated was a Geoffrey Minter, and the address was only a ten-minute drive away.

With the new roadworks on Hucknall Road, and a trilby-hatted driver insisting on driving at twenty-five miles an hour no matter what the circumstances, the ten-minute drive became twenty, but eventually Steph wove her way up the garden path, taking care not to step on the beautiful lawn or flower-beds. The house itself was quite large, a four-bedroomed structure with moss and ivy creeping up the walls, probably built in the 1930s. Steph found it eerie as darkness built up the shadows around the approach to the house. As she neared the door, a security light flicked on, illuminating almost the whole garden. It made Steph physically jump and she put her hand on her chest to emphasize the point. The door was answered by Mr Minter himself. He was in dinner-jacket and bow-tie and he removed his silver-framed spectacles to smile disarmingly at her as he let her in.

'Hello. I've been expecting you. Do come in . . .'

Steph could smell pipe tobacco on his breath as he spoke. She followed him into his study, which was large and had a whole wall crammed with books on various subjects. 'Do sit down.' Steph sat at the coffee-table, clutching the cardboard file that contained her papers.

'You look very smart, sir,' Steph offered. 'I hope I'm not interrupting anything?'

'No, not at all. I'm having a dinner party tonight, so I thought I'd get ready early, pending your arrival. No, I'm afraid I haven't dressed up for you alone . . . Not that I wouldn't have, if I'd known what a pretty detective was coming to see me.'

Steph's sensuality again scored her a few points.

Mr Minter continued: 'I'm afraid I don't entertain as much as I used to, since my wife died. I have to get a woman in now, and it's all a bit too much trouble, to be honest with you, just to sit around the table with a bunch of old fuddy-duddies and solve the problems of the world. Would you care for a drink?'

'No thank you.'

'What about a Martini? I know perhaps you shouldn't, but I won't tell if you won't.' He smiled.

'Really, no thank you.'

Mr Minter went to his desk drawer and got out a small leather pouch and a pipe. 'It's my only pleasure nowadays.' He sat down opposite her and lit the pipe with some aplomb. 'So what can I do for you, young lady?' he asked, smoke billowing out of his mouth.

Stephanie explained the situation to the magistrate, who nodded intermittently. He also swallowed a few times as well. It wasn't every day a magistrate came into contact with a murder investigation. Because of the gravity of the situation, he quickly agreed and signed on the dotted line. As he showed her out, he smiled warmly. 'Well, good luck with it all. Do let me know how you go on, won't you?'

'Yes of course. I hope you enjoy your dinner party. I shall think of you when I tuck into my cheese and onion sandwiches later on, sir.'

'I can always set another place.' The two laughed and bade their farewells.

Steph muttered to herself as she clip-clopped carefully down the path. 'A decent person, I knew there must be one somewhere!'

15

'I think of my wife, and I think of Lot,
And I think of the lucky break he got.'

William Cole

Steve Aston paced the white-walled corridors of the Forensic Science Laboratory in Birmingham. Various people passed by, eyeing him suspiciously. He peered through the glass window at the analysts inside, at the large microscopes and masses of documents scattered around. The lights in the room were dazzling, but necessary for the minute attention to detail paid by the examiners. It was this particular laboratory which dealt with handwriting analysis and typewriter comparison. When he had handed the messages sent to the *Evening Post* over to the receiver at the front desk, he had insisted that he wait for some sort of result. The analyst had only been in the sealed room above for an hour when she came out: a plain girl, with short black hair, misshapen teeth and glasses. Her dress was old-fashioned, a sort of woollen material with different shades of brown making an abstract pattern. She wore a wooden locket on a leather thong with a matching leather bracelet. All very ethnic. Steve thought they were quite attractive. He guessed that, like himself, she was a vegetarian. She took off her spectacles to speak.

'It's an Olympia portable typewriter. I can't seem to get any more details at the moment, other than it looks like it's an old machine. I'd have preferred to have had a look before the ninhydrin test had been performed.'

Steve smiled. 'That's OK, we don't expect miracles. A fingerprint would have been crucial to us, obviously. That's why we had it ninned first. Is there anything else you can tell us about it?'

'Not really. I could hazard a guess that it was typed fairly

191

quickly, but as I said to you, we need a typewriter to compare it with to say whether it was definitely that individual one.'

'That's OK. It gives us a start. Every little helps, you know.'

'Glad to be of service. By all means send us some typewriters to compare them with, and we'll let you know one way or the other very quickly.'

'Right. Thanks very much.' Steve walked back towards the reception area, escorted by the girl, whose name was Helen. 'Can I use a phone? I ought to let the lads back at the nick know about this.'

Helen smiled. 'Of course you can.'

Mark Winner answered the door to Detective Constables Ashley Stevens and Grant Donaldson. Instinctively, Ashley placed his foot in the door to prevent it being closed. He explained the situation. 'We have a warrant to search your house, Mark. Don't worry about it; you're not the only ones this is happening to. You see, somebody else has been killed.'

Mark was puzzled. 'Hold on a minute. You've had a look round the house before, so what's the point in doing it again?'

'Because, as I've said, there's been another killing.'

'What if I said no?'

'Well, I know you wouldn't say no, but if you did, then I'm here to tell you we're coming in anyway, mate. The warrant gives us the power to enter by force if necessary, so it's obviously better if we have your cooperation and prevent a scene.'

'In that case, you'd better come in, although it's not really convenient.'

'I'm afraid it never is, Mark.'

As they assembled in the hallway, Caroline came downstairs, obviously alarmed. 'He's dead, isn't he?'

There was no easy way for Ashley to tell her. 'I'm afraid so, love. Yes.'

Caroline collapsed on to the stairs, great sobs racking her body.

'What the bloody hell's going on? Who's dead? How does Caroline know?' Mark asked, anger in his voice.

'It's Jonathon Stacey. We think he's been murdered,' Ashley said.

'You *think* he's been murdered? Well has he or hasn't he?'

'Yes, he has.'

Caroline looked up, tears streaming down her face. 'How was he killed?' she howled.

'A drug overdose, Caroline,' Grant said in reply.

Mark was perplexed. 'What's the matter with you?' he asked. 'You weren't like this when the others were killed!'

'Just shut up, you ... you heartless sod.' She continued to weep wretchedly.

Mark tried to get some answers from Ashley. 'How does Caroline know about it?'

'I think you'd better ask her that one, Mark.'

'Caroline, I won't ask you again – what is going on? How do you know about it, and what the hell are you crying for?' His voice was getting louder.

Grant attempted to question him. 'There's no need to shout – it will be sorted out. Let's go into the living-room.'

Mark was becoming visibly angry: his eyes were wide, his breathing heavy. 'Don't you tell me what to do in my own fucking home, boy!'

Grant showed him some open palms. 'All right, calm down then.'

'I will not calm down until this cow gives me some fucking answers!'

Grant raised his eyes to the ceiling. Here we go, he thought.

Caroline continued to sob. She didn't look at Mark as she spoke. 'You know what the answers are, you just won't accept them!' She looked up and screamed the truth at her husband. *'Are you fucking daft? I've been seeing Jon! I love him, and now he's dead!'* She put her head back into the crook of her arm as she lay prostrate on the stairs.

Mark gritted his teeth, his anger welling inside him, all rational thought gone. He drew back his fist, aiming for Caroline's head. Grant caught the blow in mid-flight and pushed Mark by his throat into the living-room. Mark might be strong and aggressive with a woman, but he hadn't come across the likes of Grant Donaldson, who had been brought up with the fighting of the harsh streets of St Anne's, where the biggest maniac won, where there were no rules, and where every day was a fresh fight for survival. Grant, still with his hand around Mark's throat, explained the position to him as he held him against the wall. Ashley comforted Caroline on the stairs, keeping a watchful eye on the situation in the living-room. Grant's voice was loud, but calm and clear.

'Mark, we don't need to fall out, mate, because there'll be one loser and you ain't looking at him. *Comprenez*?' Mark nodded as choking noises issued from his throat. 'Now, I'm going to let you go in a couple of seconds. I sympathize with you, but the answer doesn't lie in violence, because all that will get you is a room without a view: namely a cell!'

Mark was getting increasingly red in the face. Grant gave him an extra squeeze for good luck before releasing him, and then adjusted his sleeves and straightened his cuff-links. Mark fell to his knees and held his throat, gasping for air. Eventually he obtained sufficient oxygen to speak. 'You can't come in here and assault me!'

Grant agreed. 'That's right. I suppose we should stand back and let you kick ten barrels of shit out of your wife, should we?'

Ashley brought Caroline into the living-room. She had calmed down a little and sat on an armchair, staring blankly at the carpet. There was a lull in the conversation. Ashley broke the awkward silence. 'Look, the pair of you have got a lot of sorting-out to do, so the sooner we've finished here, the sooner you can do some talking.'

Mark was resolute. 'There's no talking to do as far as I'm concerned. Caroline will be out of this house within seconds of you.'

Caroline failed to respond.

Grant explained the procedure to them. 'We will search the entire house and any outhouses and cars you have. We won't make a mess, and we shall put everything back from whence it came. Obviously the search includes you, so we shall have to ask you to empty your pockets.' The two complied grudgingly.

Ashley gave Mark the blue copy of the warrant, marked 'Invalid Copy', before beginning the search. Grant went upstairs, taking Caroline with him to cover any malicious allegations of theft or the like, while Ashley stayed downstairs. The two detectives searched every drawer, every cupboard, every crevice, every nook and cranny. It was over an hour and a half later that they left. Caroline had opted to stay in the house. As soon as the door closed behind them, the shouting inside started. Ashley

194

made a mental note for a patrol car to check on them in a short while, to make sure Caroline was all right.

'Well, that was a big fat waste of time,' said Grant.

Ashley, referring to Grant's throating of Mark, mocked the voice of Sylvester Stallone: 'You coulda bin a contender, Grant!'

Darkness shrouded the back garden of David Seaton's house, where the straggly dead grass and lack of plants displayed his lacklustre gardening ability. There was a group of children playing at the front of the house. They could only have been ten or eleven years old, but the four-letter words they so readily shouted at each other were indicative of the society they were forced to grow up in. The arrival of the suited strangers had caused some interest and they stood at the fence of Seaton's garden, craning their necks to see what was happening. Nobby swung the sledgehammer back with some relish, at which point David Seaton answered the door, causing Nobby to stagger backwards slightly, still holding the sledgehammer above his head. Seaton was aghast, and his mouth dropped open. 'What the – '

'Hello,' Nobby said cheerfully. 'We've been knocking for ages.'

'You were going to smash my door off with that, weren't you?'

'That was the general idea, yes,' Nobby said smiling, the sledgehammer now resting at his side.

'What the hell for?'

'We have a warrant here to search your house, and without an answer we enter by force. We've been knocking about five minutes.'

'I thought it was the local kids messing around again. They're forever hassling me.'

'Anyway, it's sorted now. Let's come in and start.'

Seaton, surprisingly out of character, became aggressive, his heartbeat almost visibly raised. 'You're not coming in here, I'm afraid.'

Nobby glanced at Jim. 'Ah. Oh dear. You see, David, the problem is we've got the full weight of the law behind us . . .' He gave David his copy of the warrant. '. . . and unfortunately, whether you want us to come in or not, come in is exactly what we are going to do, my duck.'

'Well, I'm terribly sorry and all that, but it's just not fucking

195

convenient at the moment for the likes of your lot to come tramping through. You're welcome to come back tomorrow.'

Nobby and Jim laughed. 'Oh, that's it then. If it's not convenient, give us a call when it is and we'll drop by.'

Seaton sighed. 'OK, thank you.' He started to close the door.

Nobby stepped inside, pushing the protesting Seaton along with him almost as if he wasn't there. 'Get out the fucking way, you prat.'

Seaton wasn't going to give in. What had been a minor irritant to Nobby suddenly took on a different slant when Seaton ran into the kitchen, produced a carving knife and yelled at the two.

'*Get out! I am sick and tired of being bullied and you can't do this. You just can't! So just piss off!*'

Jim took a step behind Nobby. This man has something to hide, Nobby was thinking. He pointed a finger at Seaton. 'Put that bloody thing down. What's the matter with you? You've got nothing to worry about, have you?'

Seaton stammered his reply, the need to answer a question taking the edge off his aggression. 'I've got nothing to hide. I am simply fed up with everything. Stuart is dead. I've got nobody. And you march in here . . .' Tears were welling in his eyes as he spoke.

'Put it down. Let's have a chat.' Nobby spoke reasonably and calmly, an air of sympathy evident in his suggestion. He held out a hand for Seaton to give him the knife.

Seaton threw the knife across the room, well away from the officers. He burst into tears and sat on the arm of a settee, his head in his hands as he sobbed. Nobby placed a comforting arm on his shoulder and glanced at Jim, who stifled a grin at the unlikely scene. 'It's all right, David. I know you're upset. Calm down. There's nothing to worry about,' Nobby said reassuringly. He patted Seaton's back but, suddenly aware of what he was doing, quickly withdrew his hand.

Jim began to search the house, Seaton following him around. When Nobby started to search also, Seaton flitted between the two, protesting, insistent that there was nothing to find, that it was an outrage. Nobby threw off a sheet covering something on a table. It was a portable Olympia typewriter. Nobby looked over at Seaton, who returned the stare. Jim opened a door 'What's in here?'

Seaton froze. 'Nothing. It's just the airing cupboard. Come on, I'm sorry I was aggressive with you. Let me make you a cup of tea!'

Jim turned away from the cupboard. 'That's very kind of you, thank you. Two sugars, David, please.'

David went into the kitchen, Jim following him, conscious of the array of sharp instruments in there should David suddenly decide to throw a wobbler again. Nobby moved over to the airing cupboard. He took out his mini-torch and shone it behind the copper cylinder. He could see a box jammed behind the pipes, and with some effort removed it. The contents were a revelation. Nobby removed several homosexual magazines, depicting men in stages of full buggery and oral sex. He took out a scrapbook and opened it. Inside were cuttings of the coverage of both the murders and more importantly, the personal column letters to 'Baby darling'. Nobby gulped. 'Bloody hell,' he muttered. Also in the box of goodies were letters that Stuart Millichip had sent him, outlining explicit sexual favours they had performed together, in return for giving Stuart money to fuel his drug habit.

Seaton's heart sank as he entered the room with the teas, Jim in tow, and saw Nobby rifling the box. Nobby looked up at him. 'Now I see why you didn't want us to search the place.'

Seaton put the mugs down. 'It's not what it looks like, honestly. I was having an affair with Stuart, fair enough. Surely that's not a crime?'

Nobby was sceptical. 'Not if it's in private, David, but what about these?' He displayed the scrapbook with the newspaper articles about the murders and the cuttings of the personal column letters.

'I have an interest in the cases, don't I?'

'But what about the personal column letters? How do you know about those?'

'It was obvious they were connected, for heaven's sake!'

'So why didn't you tell us about them?'

Seaton was rattled. 'Well, you obviously knew about them, didn't you?'

'Yes, but you didn't know that, did you?'

'Look. This is crazy. I'm sorry I didn't tell you about them, OK?'

'I think we'd better have a chat back at the station, David.'

'No, please. Why there? We're OK here, aren't we?'

'I'm afraid not, mate. You'd better come with us, eh?'

Seaton stepped backwards. 'Am I under arrest?'

'I haven't decided yet. Let's go to the nick and sort it out.'

'I've got news for you. I'm not coming!' Seaton's chest was heaving with fear, and he felt sick.

Nobby weighed up the situation. He had evidence that Seaton had the newspaper clippings, knew of the personal column letters, was paying for homosexual favours off one of the victims and had an Olympia typewriter, the same as that used by the writer of the personal column letters. Seaton had been most aggressive at their arrival, producing a knife in desperation. Should he arrest him, or leave and give him the opportunity to flee the coop? Nobby had to think on his feet.

'You leave me no option, David. I am arresting you on suspicion of murder.' He cautioned him of his right of silence. Jim took hold of Seaton and bustled him out of the house, handcuffing him at the same time. Nobby took possession of the incriminating box. Other officers would have to return and complete the search. Seaton was silent. He was in a state of shock. He had been a fool.

Stark has listened to the tape for the umpteenth time. Realization dawned slowly, but it came. He could hardly tap out Sarah Deely's telephone number; he was shaking with excitement, praying that she would be in and would respond to the ringing. Mercifully, within moments Stark heard the somewhat despondent voice of Sarah. His enthusiasm grew as he drew his conversation with Mrs Deely to a close. '. . . so you definitely didn't get it, then?'

'No. I was surprised. I only looked at them an hour ago and when there wasn't one from them I was a little bit disappointed to say the least.'

'You're sure you haven't misplaced it at all?'

'Positive.'

'Thank you very much, Sarah. I'll leave you in peace now. Thanks again.' He put down the telephone and pressed rewind on Sammy Trench's tape. Once more, he played the end bit. He nodded to himself. It was finally all coming together. 'You bastard. It was staring me in the face all the time.' He now knew who it was. All he had to do was confirm why. He had his suspicions and the next call would tell him. Excitement had raised his heartbeat. He thumbed through his diary and found the number of the Central Register of Births, Marriages and Deaths. He was smiling as he tapped out the digits; he had it sussed. After being put through to the third person, he had a result.

'So what does it say as cause of death?'

'Pneumonia, facilitated by acquired immune deficiency syndrome.'

'I knew it! Thank you very much.' He slammed the phone down and leaned back in his chair. It had turned out to be Stuart Millichip who had had the disease, but the killer couldn't have known that, only that it was one of the three.

'Screw you, Detective Chief Superintendent frigging Davies!'

16

'I don't believe in an afterlife, although I
am bringing a change of underwear.'

Woody Allen

It wasn't a busy time in the custody suite at Nottingham Police
Station; in fact there was only a juvenile in the Detention Room at
the time that David Seaton arrived. There were three female cells
and twelve male cells to choose from. The uniformed sergeant –
the 'Custody Officer' – was in his early thirties, with bright ginger
hair. He stood behind an elevated desk, an array of clipboards
visible behind him for the safe keeping of all documents relating
to all prisoners in each individual cell. To his right was a Perspex
board with categories for each prisoner: name, custody number,
time arrived at station, time detention would be reviewed by a
senior officer, officer dealing with that prisoner, and any
remarks.

The officer scribbled on to the custody sheet all details of David
Seaton. He instructed him to take off his belt, take out his shoe-
laces and empty his pockets. Jim McIntyre donned disposable
gloves and frisked him carefully to ensure there were no offending articles secreted anywhere. Jim finished what Seaton felt to be
the degradation and then completed Seaton's ignominy by writing in large red letters in the remarks box of the Perspex 'runners
and riders' board, CAUTION SUSPECTED AIDS!

Seaton was handed a piece of paper outlining his rights: To
have someone informed of his detention; to consult a solicitor or
legal representative; to read the Codes of Practice.

Seaton quickly gave his intimation. 'I want the lot!'

Nobby had been itching to get to a phone since they had
brought Seaton in. He used the telephone in the privacy of the

200

adjacent sergeant's office. After what seemed a long time, Stark answered.

'DI Stark.'

Nobby was so excited he garbled down the blue scoop. 'Hello boss, it's Nobby. I've arrested David Seaton! Before you say anything, I didn't have any choice, he refused to come. But guess what? We've found a whole box of goodies hidden behind some pipes in an airing cupboard. There were gay porno mags, love letters from Stuart Millichip indicating that Seaton was paying for sex off him, but, more importantly, there were newspaper clippings about the murders and cuttings of the personal column letters to the *Evening Post!* As you know, we haven't released that to the public, and the *pièce de résistance* was a portable Olympia typewriter under a sheet on a table. I wasn't going to nick him, but he threw a right wobbler, picked up a knife and all sorts, so I couldn't very well leave him there. I had to nick him. What do you reckon? It looks as though we've finally got a result!'

'Bloody hell, Nobby. Take a bloody breath will you? That's very well done, mate, but I've got a little visit of my own to make.'

'What! But this is our man. This is the killer. What d'you mean you've got a little visit to make? Surely we've got to concentrate on Seaton?'

'You concentrate on him, but I'm confident I know who the killer is, and I'm afraid it isn't Seaton.'

'You're joking.'

'Sorry, mate. Have a chat with him about his relationship with Millichip and about the various stuff you've seized. He's obviously not right and when we can verify it isn't him or that he wasn't working with my killer, he can go. See you later.' The line clicked off. Nobby still held the handset to his ear, mouth open, disbelief spreading across his features.

Gary Sewell peeped through the net curtains at the stern-faced visitors. They saw his concerned face at the corner of the window and he reluctantly let them in. DI Stark and Stephanie Dawson removed their coats and remained in the hall, despite Gary's invitation to go into the living-room.

'Is Tracey in?' Stark queried.

Gary appeared to have a lead weight around his neck, but he

still tried to be chirpy for appearance's sake. 'No. No, she's been out most of the day, Mr Stark. Can I be of help?'

Stark handed Gary the warrant and scrutinized his reaction to it. He decided to overemphasize the significance of it. 'I think you're aware that the magistrates don't give these out willy-nilly, Gary . . .' Stark prevented his reply by a raised palm. '. . . Let me finish, duck. All I will say is that you're not in trouble for keeping the secret to yourself, but it has to stop now, hasn't it?'

Gary paused momentarily, his eyes widened, and he swallowed deeply, his mouth dry with anguish. 'Yes,' he said.

'Now, are you sure Tracey isn't in the house?'

'Yes, sure. She's not here, honestly. God knows where she is.'

Stark nodded to Steph, who briefly checked all the rooms and possible hiding-places before the search proper, which would take place after they had had a little chat with Gary. Stark stared out of the living-room window, hands in pockets, silhouetted against the low-level winter sun shining into the room. He didn't speak for a while. After a time Steph came into the room with a sympathetic smile on her face. He quietly sat down. Stark turned and faced Gary, who bit into his nails, sitting cross-legged on the soft chair. Softly softly catchee monkey. 'I suppose it's all a bit of a relief to you?'

Gary bowed his head. 'Yes, I suppose in one sense it is.'

Stark continued his tentative verbals, conscious that the slightest mistake or variation in tone could disturb Gary and switch him into a defensive mood instead of the currently fatalistic one. 'How long have you known?'

'I think almost from the first one, since James. Well, let's say, I had an idea.'

'Did you discuss it with Tracey, Gary?'

'Not at first. I mean how do you accuse your own wife of murder? Eventually I dropped hints, told her that the killer would be caught soon unless he stopped, things like that.'

Steph stood up and spoke briefly and quietly to Stark and to Gary. 'I'll make a start with the search now and leave you in peace.' Again she gave a smile tinged with empathy.

While Steph went upstairs to begin her search, Stark continued his 'chat'.

'Did she come home bloodstained from the killing of James Deely?'

'No.'

'Didn't you see the stained clothing at all?'

'No.'

'Has she lost clothing since then?'

'Oh yes, it's her all right. All I'm saying is that I personally haven't seen the clothing. She has a pair of jeans, a beige-coloured top and a thick black woolly jumper missing.'

'She was obviously out of the house at the time of the Deely killing. Was she out of the house for both the others?'

'Yes, she was.'

Stark shook his head as he sat down on the settee. 'Why didn't you tell us about it, Gary? We could have prevented the murder of Jonathon Stacey at least!'

'The last couple of years have been hell for us, Mr Stark. It hit Tracey particularly hard – obviously, it's driven her to murder! But to physically tell you about it and send her to prison for however long she's got, seemed pointless to me.'

'But you could have prevented a murder. That's hardly pointless, is it?'

Gary shook his head. 'I know, but . . . in any case it's too late now. What's the point in saying what should have happened? It hasn't, and that's it.'

Stark restrained himself. 'Is she mentally ill?'

'I'd say she has had a breakdown. I wouldn't make any excuses for her, don't get me wrong. But what has happened, Sally I mean, has taken its effect on all of the family.'

'Now, I know she's done the killings and I know why, as do you, but can you tell us anything, or produce anything tangible, that points to her having been involved in the murders?'

'Other than her being out at the time, and that she has the only possible motive that connects the three, no, I haven't. As I think I said to you, she hasn't admitted it to me, and I would imagine that as she's no fool, any clothing or the like will have been disposed of.'

Steph appeared in the doorway. 'I'm afraid that's not strictly true, Gary.' She looked at Stark and made reference to their earlier conversation at the police station when Stark had told her what he thought must have happened. 'Did you bring that bit of card?'

Stark produced the piece of card that was supposedly Jonathon Stacey's 'suicide' note. It was sealed in a see-through plastic bag. Steph melodramatically produced a 'With Deepest Sympathy' card from behind her back. 'Look what I've rescued from the wheelie bin!' Part of the card was soggy and dirty, but it was more or less intact.

It was Tracey's failure to give the sympathy card to Sarah Deely at the wake, as highlighted by Sammy Trench's commentary, that had eventually alerted Stark to the possibility of Tracey being the killer. A few telephone calls fitted the other pieces in the jigsaw comparatively quickly. Steph was beaming, her need for discretion diminishing. She took hold of the piece of card that Stark held out to her and placed it against the sympathy card. Despite the sealed bag, it was apparent that it fitted perfectly, though this would of course be verified by Forensic at a later time. Stark remained composed. 'I suppose you could say that's the final piece of the jigsaw, Gary.'

He nodded, tears welling in his eyes. The nightmare was drawing to a close. Stark was not surprised by Gary's selfish question: he had seen it before.

'Will I be prosecuted?'

'No, I don't think so, but you will be called to give evidence against your wife, though.' He could be asked, but not forced.

Gary nodded.

Stark radioed for others to come and continue the search. His beliefs had been vindicated. It was time Tracey Sewell saw the inside of a cell, and he wanted to be the man to put her there.

He gave a final comment to Gary as the search team arrived.

'What a mess. Why?'

'Because of Sally. She could never forgive that. It just changed her completely. It sent her to hell and back.'

The manager of Sceptre: New and Used Motor Vehicles was in the process of closing when approached by the two men. Derek Matherson was most helpful. Smartly dressed and in his late thirties, he was a big man, with blond hair slighly thinning on top. He invited Stark and Stephanie into his office adjoining the showroom. They turned down his offer of tea. Stark was after answers, not refreshment. 'So you say she isn't at work today?'

'No, she hasn't been in for a couple of days now. I've rung her at home, but either there's no reply, or her husband fobs me off with excuses. To be honest with you, only this afternoon we were discussing her future here. She was given three days to give notice of her absence and the reason for it, otherwise she had to go. We are very sympathetic to people's domestic problems, but we thought she had got over Sally.'

'You obviously know about Sally then?'

'Oh yes indeed. A cot death is such a tragedy, isn't it?'

Stark agreed, without a hint of a lie.

'You've no idea where she may be? You see we have to talk to her most urgently.'

'Oh dear, she's not in any trouble, is she?'

'No, nothing like that. We just need to speak to her about something, nothing too serious, just important to us, that's all.' Stark was a good liar; he was well practised.

Matherson seemed relieved. 'Oh good, thank heavens for that. Um, in answer to your question, no, I don't know where she is. Sorry, but as I say, I haven't seen her for days.'

'Does she have a company car?' Steph asked nonchalantly.

'Yes. Well, I say yes. She just used any of those in the compound.'

Stark's mind fleetingly pictured the death scene of Stuart Millichip. He stood up. 'OK, Mr Matherson. Thanks for your time. We'll say goodbye.' They shook hands and left.

Steph looked despondent as they walked slowly back to their car. 'I hope she's not done a runner.'

'I doubt it very much. I'll tell you what, Steph, just humour me. You drive and I'll direct you where to go. It's only a hunch, but it's worth a try.'

'Turn left here.'

Stephanie gave Stark a puzzled look. 'The graveyard?'

'Just do as I say, Steph. Bear with me.'

The local graveyard was a huge complex, with a mini road system of its own. The main 'ring road' had ornate street lamps generously spaced out along the way, some dedicated to loved ones long since gone to the hereafter. Numerous tributary paths fanned out from the main thoroughfare, branching out to the thousands of graves, shadowy in the light given off by the headlamps of the detectives' car.

Stark instructed Steph to drive slowly around the main drive, while he stared out into the diminishing light of the cemetery. Occasionally he would focus on individuals, mainly elderly people, in the murky glow. A mist had descended, adding an eerie silence to the tension they both felt.

'There, look!'

Steph jumped at Stark's unexpected shout. She braked sharply, causing the car to stall. She craned her neck to look further down the drive, to the left, where she saw the huddled figure of Tracey Sewell sitting, about fifty yards away, on a small perimeter wall.

Tracey had her arms folded and was rocking gently backwards and forwards, a large shopping bag by her side. Her damp hair straggled over her face, which appeared strained, grimacing with anxiety. Her coat was open over a thin T-shirt and miniskirt that barely covered her midriff. She did not appear to notice their arrival.

Stark opened the car door, as did Steph. He touched her arm. 'Wait here, there's no need for us both to go.'

'Are you sure?'

'Yes. Reverse the car. Keep us in view, but I'll do this alone.'

'OK, you're the boss.'

Stark quietly got out of the vehicle and Steph reluctantly obeyed his instructions. She took the added precaution of requesting a backup vehicle to remain in a nearby street, away from the cemetery. Tracey might be a woman but she had managed to kill three men with ingenuity and guile. Steph did not want there to be a fourth.

Stark walked slowly towards the crouched figure. He felt calm, yet excited. He pulled the collar of his overcoat up to shield him from the chilling air sweeping across the desolate surroundings. As Stark grew close, Tracey stopped rocking, but she did not look up to acknowledge his presence. He sat down on the wall next to her, at a safe distance. He didn't want her to feel threatened. He didn't speak. He peered at the gravestone opposite them, where he could just make out the inscription in the gloom.

Sally Anne Sewell, born 25th January 1989
Taken from us 4th August 1991
Beloved daughter of Tracey and Gary
Too young to know, too young to die

After a short time, Stark said 'Hi' softly.

Tracey didn't answer.

'How long have you been here? You must be freezing.'

Tracey remained silent. Stark could hear the distant hum of the CID car engine.

'This grave is beautiful, Tracey. I'm sorry, love.' They sat a while longer, neither speaking, Tracey intermittently sniffing and wiping her nose with a handkerchief.

She spoke in a whisper, too quietly for him to hear.

'I'm sorry, Tracey?'

'I said, I wondered how long it would take you.'

'You must have known this day would come.'

'Oh yes, I knew all right. It doesn't make things easier, though, does it?'

'No.' There was more silence. Stark blew into his hands to relieve the encroaching numbness.

'You should have brought some gloves. You obviously aren't practised in sitting by graves.'

'No, you're right, I'm not.' There was a pause. Stark spoke softly. 'I think I know why, Tracey, but all three of them?'

He listened patiently as Tracey opened up. He said little as slowly she explained just why it had all happened.

'We were so happy, Gary and I. For once we had something, you know? Something money couldn't buy, something, somebody that was mine, that had been created out of love. When I discovered I was pregnant, my whole life had meaning. There was a reason for me being here, it all fitted in. God, I was happy. We did all those crazy stupid things couples do. Gary did the nursery. I bought clothes – neutral colours. I didn't care what sex it was, but I knew, secretly I knew it was a girl.' She clenched her fists. *I should have known what would happen. I should have fucking known!'* Her voice tailed off. She whispered, 'Sorry Sally'. She seemed distant, disturbed. She was speaking to Stark, but she addressed her words to the grave.

207

Stark warned her. 'You don't have to tell me this. I can tell a court what you are saying, love.'

'I'll tell the court. Don't worry about your precious evidence. Just give me a bit longer here . . . please.'

'Sure.'

'As soon as I heard that first cry, I knew it was a girl. Sally Anne Sewell. I had the name in my head for months. It wasn't easy. God knows it wasn't what I'd envisaged. God.' She laughed sardonically. *'God? That's a frigging laugh!'* She closed her eyes tightly. 'Sorry . . .' She let out a sigh. 'I should have guessed when she had her first illness – a cold. Every kid has them, yes? So we coped and things got better, they did, things actually got better. But we were plagued by her little illnesses. I told that stupid doctor at the hospital, I told him, each illness it took longer for her to get better. You know what he did?'

Stark shook his head.

'He laughed. "They all go through it," he said. The prat. I had to insist that I see the Registrar. He examined her, looked down her throat, all the stupid things they do. His face changed when he saw the inflammation at the back of her mouth and her gums, yellow and swollen. Foul, it was. I had to wait in a side-room for nearly two hours. Then he came poncing back in. Had I considered an Aids test, and one for Sally, too? Well, I just went berserk, man, I tell you. I shouted. I screamed at the mere suggestion. What did he think I was? A whore? A druggy? He just stood there. He never said a word, never retaliated. Just stood there with his puny little arms folded. They brought a nurse in with tea, all very cosy. There were whisperings, and then he came smarming over in his white coat. He asked me everything, and I mean everything! Personal things, you know. About me and Gary. It was obvious I wasn't a druggy and I had only had sex with three people before I got married . . .'

Stark spoke with concern. 'James Deely, Stuart Millichip and Jonathon Stacey.'

'Gary was the obvious choice. He'd been with a few women before me, but when all the tests came through, he was negative and I was HIV positive! I had given my poor little baby, my baby darling, I had given her Aids!' Tracey covered her head in her hands and sobbed. She groaned and wailed, her heart breaking. Then she jumped up, startling him.

'Don't touch me!' She had a weird smile that wasn't a smile. She put her face close to Stark's. 'You see, I'm infected, I'm unclean! A leper!'

'OK, sit down, love. I'm sorry.'

Tracey sat down again.

'Sally had got full-blown Aids, the poor little sod. What did she know about anything? She was innocent. But that was it, you see. It wasn't *me* that had given it to her.' She shook her head, her teeth gritted. 'It was them, one of the *bastards*! I made a decision there and then. There was no drama. It was a calm, calculated decision. I didn't cry again. I was determined to get him. I didn't know which one it was, so it would have to be all of them. Then I would be sure. You see, I swore to my baby that I would get revenge for putting her through such hell! I know what you're thinking. I'm as much to blame. Why let them do it without a condom? I'd hardly heard of bloody Aids! None of us knew about the heterosexual side of the disease when we were at college. I was on the pill. What problem was there?'

'I wasn't thinking that, Tracey,' Stark assured her.

Tracey stared at him with blank eyes. 'Hour after hour, I stayed with her, by her bed at hospital. I told her all about it, what I was going to do. I worked it all out there . . . It was late at night – I remember it as if it was yesterday – some drunken whore came into the ward to see her baby. She was swearing and fighting with the nurses. I noticed that the red light above the drugs cabinet was on. That meant the cupboard was open – you learn these things over the days and nights in a hospital. The nurse who had opened it was rolling around the floor with the whore and a male nurse, trying to stop her pulling the drip feeds away from her baby. I got up. Bold as brass, I was. I calmly walked up to the cupboard and took three vials of morphine out. I never looked back, I just took them and went and sat down again. After everything had calmed down I nipped outside and hid the morphine in the fuses compartment of my car. They didn't even know I'd gone out. I was just a piece of the furniture by then. It was the next day that the police came. They didn't have a clue. They spoke to me and contacted others who'd been there, but what could they do?'

Stark was worried that Tracey might become reluctant to repeat her revelation, once she'd got it off her chest. 'Come on, Tracey. Let's go back to the warmth.'

'Not yet. I haven't finished ... Jonathon Stacey. A big-shot, important doctor killed by his own drugs. What a fool he was.' She laughed. 'He thought he was going to get his leg over again, dirty git! Towards the end, you know, Sally could only just manage a smile, nothing else, just a smile when her mummy stroked her hand. If it was anybody else – nothing! But if it was me, she smiled, bless her. She was part of me, she had grown inside of me!'

Tracey paused momentarily, tears welling up. 'Sally died at 11.56 p.m. on 4th August 1991. I knew she was going. I was helpless. I just cuddled her as she ebbed away. I kissed her little cold nose and hugged my little baby. I died that night, too. I became numb. I didn't want to live. What did I want to live for? But why should *they*? Why should they live, when they'd killed my innocent little child? You tell me, come on, tell me!'

Stark was solemn. 'I can't. I can't begin to imagine it, love. It must be hell on earth.'

'Yes, hell. You're right. And that's where they've gone. Hell! Never to see my Sally, because you're in heaven, darling, aren't you?' She stared at the grave, a tear trickling down her face. 'All that love I had for her, all the love there was in the world turned to hate. Have you ever hated anybody?'

'Not like that, Tracey, no.'

'Well, believe me, it's as powerful as love.'

'Surely your family knew about Sally?' Stark asked, puzzled.

'Of course. They didn't know what she died of, though. How could we tell them that? We said it was pneumonia. They were heartbroken, obviously.'

'Excuse my ignorance, Tracey, but how come Gary hasn't got it?'

'Good fortune. You aren't forced to catch it the first time or the hundredth time, unless you're unlucky like me, of course. I know I've got it, but I could, if I wanted, last another few years yet. You never know, they might create a cure. It's too late for baby darling. I don't want to live anyway. I've been true to my word. That's all that matters.'

'But to kill three people ...'

Tracey laughed. 'Killing? That's easy! You just control your

210

aggression and brother, I had enough of that, believe you me. When I killed James it was as if it was someone else, you know? As if I was watching somebody else do it. I felt quite calm beforehand, crouching in the back – he never bothered to lock his car at night, so it was a doddle. Strange . . . Stuart was even easier. I just used one of the compound cars from work. They're always getting vandalized, so when I'd finished I returned it, washed it down and bumped it backwards and forwards into the other cars. In fact I think it was you or one of the other policemen who was there when they rang me at home to tell me about the "bloody kids again"!'

'Very clever,' Stark observed.

Tracey stood up again. *'Clever! Clever? What's clever about death and murder, eh? What the fuck do you know? Clever my arse!'*

'OK, OK, I'm sorry. Sit down. That was silly of me.'

She sat down. 'You're damn right it was.' She became quiet. Stark thought he had blown it.

'What about Jonathon Stacey?'

'Fool. I thought it might be Jonathon who had Aids.'

Stark shook his head. 'No.'

'Who was it then? Stuart?'

'Yes, it was Stuart.'

'Drugs I suppose.'

'He was a practising homosexual as well.'

'Dirty sod. I'm glad he's dead, I hope he festers in hell! Sorry . . . You asked about Jonathon. That went like a dream. The way things were going, I thought he wouldn't trust me, but no, not our Jonathon, the chance of a quick jump was just too tempting. He gets pissed very easily does Jonathon, and after a few whiskies it was fairly easy to drop some morphine in his drink – just enough to overpower him. I wanted him to see me kill him, feel the syringe go in and know that there was sod-all he could do about it. And that's just what did happen. It was very simple really. A bit like Jonathon.' She laughed bitterly.

'What made you try to fake a suicide?'

'The sympathy card. Have you found it? It's in the bin at home, outside.'

'We've got it, thanks.'

'Oh, right. Well I got him to sign the card and when I saw what he put, well, it was perfect. So I hung on to it, for future use.'

211

'That's what put me on to you initially. Before then I wouldn't have dreamt it was you.'

'Ah well, as I say, so be it. How did you know about the card? Did one of the others tell you?'

'No. I had a couple of men watching you in the pub at James's funeral.'

'Very good. I'm impressed, Mr Stark. I knew I'd get caught – stuff it, I don't care now. I couldn't give her the card when I had a better use for it.'

'What about the messages in the *Evening Post*?'

'That was our little secret. How else do you communicate with someone who's . . . who's passed away?'

'I don't know. Was anybody else involved at all?'

'Just me, the one person I can trust. Nobody knows about it, well . . . possibly Gary now, I don't know.'

'Only, my mate has arrested David Seaton for the murders.'

Tracey laughed. 'No, he hasn't got anything to do with it. What will happen to him? He won't be in any trouble, will he?'

'No. As soon as I get back to the station we'll release him without charge.'

'Good. He's a bit of a poor specimen, isn't he?'

'Why did you bother disguising the last murder if you're HIV positive? Surely if you're going to die anyway . . .'

'I didn't purposely go out to be caught, certainly not until I'd killed them all, and all right, I'm HIV positive, but it doesn't mean I want to be quarantined in a cell for years, does it . . .' She fell silent again.

'I feel sorry for Gary,' she continued. 'He's suffered too, you know. Perhaps he's stronger than me, perhaps it's because of what's happened, I don't know any more. You know, I thought I'd feel better, but I don't. I'm glad I got the bastard that gave it me, though.'

'Surely you regret killing James and Jonathon?'

'Not really. What choice did I have? I couldn't ask them outright, could I? They were just a necessary evil!'

Stark stood up. 'Come on then, Tracey. Let's get going, love.'

'No. Not yet. I need time to say goodbye. Just one more minute, please.'

Stark remembered the advice he had received from his first days at training school all those years ago: 'Always show

212

compassion'. He walked away some paces and sat down on the perimeter wall again. 'No more than a minute,' he called.

Grant Donaldson opened the small brown envelope marked 'Staff In Confidence'. He read the typed contents. '. . . that you were rude and discourteous to the complainant and were negligent in your duty in that you failed to protect him from imminent danger to his life.' Grant shook his head. 'Roy Prentice!'

Ashley peered over his shoulder. 'You've got no worries on that score, mate. Forget it!'

'That's easy for you to say. I was with Steve Aston, you know, not you. I've never relished the prospect of going into a witness-box after him, never mind a complaints tribunal!'

'It won't come to that. Charlie was saying he had a similar complaint a few years ago that was proved. He just got a Divisional bollocking.'

'Yes, but if I get one of those, that could mean my place on the CID goes begging.'

'No it won't. Jesus, how many more times? Give it us here.'

Ashley took the notice from Grant. He screwed it up and threw it into the bin. 'Put it where it belongs, in the fucking bin!'

Steph could see Stark standing a few feet away from Tracey as she pawed the headstone. 'Come on, boss. Bloody hell, what are you pissing about at?'

Stark was merely an observer as Tracey knelt in front of the grave.

'Goodbye, baby darling,' she said, kissing the marble stone. She reached into her shopping bag. Stark saw a flash of steel. What on earth . . . ? He stood rooted to the spot. She looked over at Stark, her face contorted. Her mouth opened to form an horrendous scream. Stark stared incredulously as her hand plunged a carving knife through her opened coat and ripped it across her belly. He leaped towards her to see a great cluster of intestines belch out. She collapsed on to the grave, letting out another awful scream, the knife clattering to the ground.

'Fucking hell,' Stark sobbed as he bent over her and tried to cram her insides back, the warmth of the sloppy mess and blood covering his freezing hands before the futility of it all entered his consciousness. Steph was with him in seconds. Stark turned towards her, his hands red. He was in a state of shock. He stammered, 'Call an ambulance, Steph! Fucking hell!'

Steph screamed into her radio, but it was too late. The two detectives stared at the gory mess lying on the grave, Tracey's insides still pumping forth in a spasm of death.

Steph went to wipe Stark's hands with her handkerchief. Then his numbed mind switched quickly back to reality. *'Stay away! She was an Aids carrier!'*

Steph didn't need telling twice.

Once Stark had cleansed himself of the gore and arranged a change of clothes, he felt better. He stared down at the young woman's face, now on the slab in the Queens Medical Centre mortuary. He shook his head. 'Crazy. The whole thing's a mess. There are no winners to be had here, Steph. That's for sure.'

'No. I don't know about you, boss, but I could murder a drink.' She smiled.

'Don't ever mention that word to me again, Steph.'

'What's that?'

'Murder.'

'Don't bother about it. It'll be somebody else tomorrow. The world keeps turning, you know.'

'You always were a bit of a philosopher, Steph.'

'Fancy the last hour then, sir, before we have to sort this mess out?'

'You what? You bet your life I do. Where have the lads gone?'

'The Nag's Head.'

'What are we waiting for then? Let's piss off. I owe the lads a drink for their hard work.'

As the two set off, Stark saw Tracey Sewell's bag amongst the pile of blood-soaked clothing. He carefully picked out a piece of paper that stood out, attracting him like a beacon. He unfolded it carefully and read the typed message:

> Baby darling, I have ceased.
> You may now rest in peace.

Stark shook his head. He felt sad. He watched Steph's shapely figure disappear out of the door, then walked back to the corpse of Tracey Sewell. He touched her hand. He sighed, his eyes closed. Steph poked her head round the door. 'Come on, sir. It'll be closing time soon!'

Steph's comment jarred him back to reality. He squeezed the dead girl's cold hand and placed it carefully beside her. 'Coming, Steph.'

Steph was abrupt. 'Wash your hands then, sir, for God's sake!'

Stark approached Stephanie with his hands outstretched. She backed away.

'Come here. Let me give you a kiss!'

'Get off, sir. You shouldn't mess about with things like that.'

Stark chased Steph out of the block. He stopped and walked back towards the mortuary loading bay. He was smiling. Things were getting back to normal already.